Edgar Allan Poe on Mars

The Further Memoirs
of
Gullivar Jones

also by Jean-Marc & Randy Lofficier

from Black Coat Press:
Arsène Lupin vs. Sherlock Holmes:
The Hollow Needle
The Blonde Phantom
(*adapted from Maurice Leblanc*)
Despair
(*screenplay adapted from Marc Agapit*)
Doc Ardan: City of Gold and Lepers
(*adapted from Guy d'Armen*)
Doctor Omega
(*adapted from Arnould Galopin*)
The Phantom of the Opera
(*adapted from Gaston Leroux*)
Robonocchio
Royal Flush
Shadowmen: Heroes and Villains of French Pulp Fiction
(*non-fiction*)
Shadowmen 2: Heroes and Villains of French Comics
(*non-fiction*)
Tales of the Shadowmen: The Modern Babylon
Tales of the Shadowmen: Gentlemen of the Night
Tales of the Shadowmen: Danse Macabre
(*editors*)

available from iUniverse:
The Doctor Who Programme Guide
The Nth Doctor
Into the Twilight Zone

Edgar Allan Poe on Mars

The Further Memoirs
of
Gullivar Jones

by

Jean-Marc & Randy Lofficier

A Black Coat Press Book

Acknowledgements: We are indebted to David McDonnell for proofreading the typescript.

This book is dedicated to Roy Thomas and Roger Corman.

Gullivar Jones created by Edwin L. Arnold.

Visit our website at www.blackcoatpress.com

ISBN 978-1-934543-09-2. First Printing. December 2007. Published by Black Coat Press, an imprint of Hollywood Comics.com, LLC, P.O. Box 17270, Encino, CA 91416. All rights reserved. The stories and characters depicted in this novel are entirely fictional. Printed in the United States of America.

Prologue
The Golden Age of Mars

From The Memoirs of Gullivar Jones:

These tales happened during the Golden Age of
Mars, millions of years ago. If they are not true, then it is
the Elders of Seth who told them to me who lied, not I.

It was during the Golden Age that the spiral of life
began on the fourth planet of the Solar System. From the
end of all things that were before came a new beginning.
Dawn at last broke through the darkness of the everlasting night that had endured.

It was during the Golden Age that a world of volcanic mud arose from the viscous, boiling waters of that
which came to be named the Sarkean Sea. Water and
land slowly separated, at first intermingling in vast
marshes that eventually became the birthing place of the
various Martian races.

The cosmic storms abated and living creatures began to move freely across the surface of the new kingdoms. The Elders of Seth remember the Time of the
Great Fear, during which the Golden Race's then-pitiful
armies were forced to flee from the demons, zigzagging
across the Dark Territories, bravely struggling to escape
the Horrors.

Most of the southern regions were safe. Yet, there
were places were Old Chaos still reigned. There, the

storms above and the fires below combined to shake the ground and mold what stood upon it into strange new shapes. There, the age-old battle between fire and water, Heaven and Earth, remained undecided. There, the Horrors still lurked in the crevices of the unsettled landmass. It was a visceral reminder of what the world had been like, before.

Wisely, the Elders of Seth forbade these lands to their people, so they went unmentioned among the Golden Folk, unnamed, even unmarked upon their maps. The very direction of the Great North, beyond even the mighty Nihan Mountains, became both accursed and sacred, because there be monsters, and worse.

There dwelt the Macrocephales and their enemies the Southrons and, under the great, icy waters of the Polar Seas, the hostile tribes of the reptilian Setissi.

In the Far South, beyond the Desert of Tears, it was said that powerful faults could still tear mountains apart and release entities that destroyed cities, burned forests and gobbled life as water quenches the flame. But mighty earth would surge again, or perhaps the sky would fall, and the chasms would close reluctantly, groaning and heaving, trapping within them the horrors that ought never to have been released.

It was the Golden Age of Mars.

It was a time of immeasurable change. Seas of living eggs had spawned endless new forms of life. Vaporous mountains had dissolved into puffs of fetid gas. Yet, great covers of ichor-filled clouds still blanketed valleys, and sprawling carpets of ferocious grubs encroached upon the plains of the equator. Rains of black soot and toad-like things were reported in the East.

To the West, beyond the furthest reaches of the Sarkean Sea, the great god Rhiannon held sway over the people of Caer Dhu, who still worshipped the Serpent.

It was the Golden Age of Mars.

It was also a time when the Sun began to drain the marshes that lay east of Zekar. A time when the ravenous beasts of the Scalding Plains died or disappeared, leaving behind a bleached desert littered with the giant bones of long-forgotten creatures. It was a time when order was hammered out of burning chaos.

Little by little, the Golden Race spread across the land, across the snowy peaks of Yamur and the fertile plains of Dorgé. They reconquered what they had once been forced to abandon. They fought the winged folk, the great reptiles, the sons of Phra, the swarm of the Noltoi and the creatures of the depths, driving the things from below back into the chasms. They chased the ethereals from the skies back to their astral cities in the Heavens above, back to the two moons, which they called Nooma and Eelesh.

The Demons fled before the power of the Golden Race and found refuge in the Old Places, or died, unmourned and unnoticed.

The Elders of Seth told me stories of the Old Times: the Time of the Dark Rain, which had followed the Time of the Great Fire, long after the almost-forgotten Time of the Red Dust. From the skies fell a ceaseless black rain that covered the proud spires of the Golden Race with filth, shattered their citadels and filled their hearts with fear.

Only the Nine, who now called themselves Enchanters, remembered the Time of the Great Fear, and none truly understood what had been before. As if the destruction was not complete, the Demon Lords sent great fires and even more terrible disasters. The survivors of the Golden Race fled their ruined cities and famine and new plagues claimed even more lives.

These deadly trials continued for decade upon decade, until the face of Mars was once again changed beyond recognition. Gone were the delicate spires of the cities, the music, the laughter, the days of peace and contentment. Now the Golden Folk knew only madness. Only amongst the Elders of Seth were there still left a few arcane scraps of the old knowledge, but some among them were jealous and greedy men, who would not help their starving people. So wars were fought again, battles of great sorcery between mighty Enchanters.

Then came the Great Migration, as the Golden Race scattered throughout the wild and hostile lands to the East, West, North and South. Separated now by thousands of leagues, the tribes took up new ways of life, new laws and customs. Some clung to half-remembered ideals of justice, others became like beasts.

Over thousands of generations, the sons and daughters of the Golden Race changed. The harsh environment demanded adaptation. The ancient art of shape-shifting was revived. Some remained human. Others mated with the winged folk, or the sons of Phra, or the spider-like Noltoi or the snake people of Caer Dhu and took on the traits of their adopted races. And all forgot the greatness of their Ancestors.

All except the Elders of Seth.

It was the Golden Age of Mars.

If these tales are not true, then it is the Elders of Seth who told them to me who lied, not I.

Gullivar Jones' Homecoming

The village was ancient. Once, it had borne a name, but that had long since been forgotten. For its inhabitants, it was known simply as Nûr–*home*.

It had existed for thousands of years under the rays of the Sun, protected by the shadows of the Nihan peaks, lying on the eastern reaches of the Desert of Tears. Its adobe houses nestled in the cracks of the rock, hiding its people from even the rare traffic of the caravan trail that traveled along the Nihan northward towards Edora and south to the land of the Malachites. Only its mighty aeyries, home to flocks of eagles, proud, jagged needles of rock jutting against the sky, betrayed its presence to the observant traveler.

Although the season of mists was barely over, and summer was still many moons distant, that morning burned hot as the stones of the baker's oven. Nature remained silent in the heat, not betraying itself by wind or buzzing insect or beating of wings.

Yet man was not silent.

The evil cacophony of murder shimmered hotter than the Sun.

The village was dying.

Troops of azure-clad soldiers ran through its streets like an invading army of ants, spilling blood in their wake. Smoke rose from houses put to the torch; the crackling of the flames mingled with the wails of women and the dying cries of men. The acrid stench of blood permeated ancient streets, which had previously only been washed by the rarest of winter rains. Carnage fed upon itself and grew like some great, bloated beast.

The village's defenders fought bravely, but in vain against an overwhelming force.

Bodies sprawled, left to become fodder for flies, worms and the grim, black muru birds. The invaders moved deeper into the village, an unstoppable force, exacting a terrible price on whoever stood in their way.

In the center of the village stood a building larger than the others, made of carved greystones that had been painfully extracted from the Nihan and hauled down their narrow trails. It was not an ostentatious building, as temples in the big cities often are; through the patina of its ancient stones, it bore witness to centuries of humble devotion. The slow passage of time had worn its once elaborate carvings into gently rounded shapes, yet still recognizable images of eagles could be seen in their smoothness.

Heaving and puffing, the brutish invaders launched themselves with a wooden battering ram at bronze doors not meant to ward off such hostility. The sound of the shattering of the metal gates echoed throughout the village like a gong of doom, and for an all too brief moment, managed to drown out the cries of the dying and the obscenely victorious shouts of the blue-clad warriors.

They rushed into the temple, dealing deadly blows to those few acolytes who tried in vain to bar their way. Inside, all was cool and dark, but not the oppressive darkness of the tomb, rather the friendly hearth-like atmosphere of the last hours of a summer's night.

Having secured the great hall, the invaders roughly pushed and dragged the bodies of the acolytes aside to make room for he who followed them: their master.

The Unholy One walked tall and silent, dressed in an ornately decorated azure cloak, through the paved streets of the village. His chalk-white face looked ancient, yet ageless. Strange energies seemed to lurk behind his pitch-black eyes. Even the bravest of soldiers averted their gaze at their master's passing; none but the eyes of the dead dared stare at him.

Behind him walked a squadron of elite, blue-garbed warriors, led by a gaunt, silent, zombie-like wraith, clothed in scarlet tatters, and whose skull-like face was hidden deep inside a cowl.

The One in Blue arrived before the desecrated temple. He took account of its bronze gates torn from their hinges and surveyed the carnage. With grim pleasure he beheld the blood of the dead as it slowly seeped, drenching the courtyard, and the smoking ruins of what had once been a thriving marketplace.

"It is indeed the Hour of Darkness," he said with satisfaction, before brazenly stepping into the temple.

At the sound of his steps, the soldiers stood to attention, letting their fearsome leader and his followers pass by.

The One in Blue quickly made his way to the inner sanctum of the temple. There, in front of him, stood a golden-skinned woman, with green eyes and long, jet-black tresses, dressed in ancient ceremonial robes and holding a staff. Her name was Princess Heru. She was the last of the Kings and Queens of the Golden Race, who could trace their line to the Time of the Great Fear and before.

Behind her, huddling in terror, were a group of wise men and women, also dressed in ceremonial attire, and their vestals, young women dressed in white.

"Rodrik-Usher," spat Heru. "Rodrik-Usher of Seth. Rodrik-Usher the Damned."

Rodrik-Usher roughly pushed the Princess aside, as he would brush away a fly. The woman fell to the ground and was quickly attended by a vestal. Behind Heru were three well-worn stone steps that led to a small altar. On the altar was a tabernacle. In the cities of the south, such a place would have been enshrined in gold and alabaster. Here, only wood and the lovingly carved greystone from the Nihan housed the villagers' holiest treasure.

Rodrik-Usher climbed the steps and opened the tabernacle. Inside was a glowing shard of blue crystal, held delicately by a golden bird claw.

"The Blue Shard!" he whispered in a low, angry voice that did not need to be raised to be heard throughout the room. He looked at it with envy and naked greed. "At long last. Stolen from me by that fat pig, Montressor, and his wench, Ligeia. Here. In this miserable village forsaken by all."

"May the Keepers curse you forever, Rodrik-Usher!" said Heru.

Rodrik-Usher laughed, an evil, self-assured laugh, his ageless face cracking wide in an expression of malignant mirth.

"I am beyond curses, Princess," he said. "Especially those issued by one as weak as you."

The One in Blue stretched his hands forward to grab the Shard from the tabernacle. But as they touched the stone, there was a burst of sharp, blue fire and it exploded, shattering into microscopic fragments that evaporated like snowflakes in the sunlight.

The evil Enchanter screamed in anguished pain. His face became contorted with suffering, fury and impotent rage. He raised his hands, which were now black, charred and smoking. The smell of burning flesh filled the hall.

"Montressor!" Rodrik-Usher shouted. "He's the only one capable of doing this!"

The sorcerer then turned to the scarlet, wraith-like figure that had been standing motionless and silent at the altar's feet.

"Andrevar! My Red Death! Go seek him out! He must be hiding somewhere in this thrice-accursed village. Find him and kill him!"

The creature that Rodrik-Usher had called Andrevar, and who had himself once been a mighty Enchanter of Seth, but was now known among men only as the Red Death, nodded silently, and left, striding from the temple trailing a cloud of fear.

Outside, the blue-garbed soldiers gave wide berth to the Red Death as they saw him emerge from the holy place. They feared Rodrik-Usher, but were terrified of the Red Death. The grim figure stood for a moment, amidst the dead bodies, sniffing the air like a hound searching for the odor of its prey in its currents.

The Red Death strode purposefully through the blood-soaked streets, moving unerringly towards an unremarkable adobe house.

Inside a man and a young woman waited. The man was short and portly. His face was rubicund and jolly, and would have resembled that of a contented baby were it not for the air of intense concentration it bore. He was dressed in blue and yellow robes that had once glowed in the sunlight, but were now dull and used. Virtually all adepts of the ancient arts would have immediately recognized him as Montressor, the notorious Enchanter of Seth, whose prowess was legendary from the Manses of Denay to the shores of the Sarkean Sea.

The young woman was his pupil. Her name was Ligeia, and she, too, was an Enchanter of Seth. She was slender and beautiful, with flowing black hair and sparkling violet eyes, and was also dressed in a blue garment.

Montressor and Ligeia had just finished performing a magic ritual in front of a small tripod brazier. The Enchanter wiped his brow, then rubbed his hands in glee, and added with a mischievous look: "Well, well. That should teach Rodrik-Usher not to put his hands where they don't belong. I'm so glad we thought of boobytrapping the Shard."

But his satisfaction was short-lived as, suddenly, the Red Death kicked down the door of the house and rushed in.

A man of Montressor's experience was not easily taken by surprise. The Enchanter turned around and made a magical gesture. A rainbow hued, flaring burst of light sprung from thin air and stopped the wraith dead in his tracks.

Montressor took advantage of those few seconds to grab Ligeia by the hand.

"Come, my dear. We have overstayed our welcome."

Dragging her with him, he ran through a backdoor hidden by a curtain.

Their flight did not go unnoticed

The Red Death had recovered swiftly from Montressor's bit of magical trickery and lunged after them. He was soon in close pursuit.

As the fugitives ran through the village streets, soldiers recognized them and joined the hunt.

Despite the Enchanter's portly nature, neither Montressor nor Ligeia slowed their pace and thus, they managed to stay ahead of their pursuers, nimbly evading them in the maze-like network of cobbled streets that comprised the upper part of the village. Had there been living observers, they would soon have realized that this was not mere flight, but that instead the runners moved with a sense of purpose, in a particular direction, towards a precise goal...

Indeed, they eventually reached what at first glance appeared to be an exitless alley, squeezed between the steep and windowless walls of three mundane houses. The only noticeable exceptions to this featureless cul-de-sac were two intricately carved totems on the stone wall that closed off the alley.

Montressor made several magical passes in the air, his hands moving easily in rhythm with the humming of a spell song.

Suddenly, a portal of light appeared between the two carvings. The Enchanter addressed Ligeia.

"This is the Gate of Lu-Pov, our last hope. This leads to the Other World. Through space *and* time. You realize what this means, my dear?"

"Everything that was precious to me has already been destroyed by Rodrik-Usher, Montressor. I welcome this. So be it," responded the young woman, grimly.

Ligeia stepped decisively through the shimmering portal of light and vanished.

At that same moment, the Red Death, leading a mob of bloodthirsty soldiers, entered the cul-de-sac. The wraith was barely in time to see Ligeia, already almost entirely through the Gate, and Montressor, waving an ironic farewell with his hand, stepping through in her wake.

"Tell Rodrik-Usher good-bye, Andrevar," he said to the Red Death. "At least, he won't have to worry about biting his fingernails for a while!"

Then, Montressor, too, disappeared into the Gate, which vanished, restoring the stone wall to its initial, blank form.

The wraith stood there, silently, no longer able to obey his Master's commands. The soldiers milled about helplessly, unsure as to what course of action they should take.

Suddenly, the crowd of armed men split to let Rodrik-Usher through, followed by more blue-clad soldiers, dragging and pushing the hapless Princess Heru and the other elders and vestals from the temple.

Unhurriedly, Rodrik-Usher examined the two totems, paying special attention to the carvings. He traced them with his charred, blackened fingers, causing bits of carbonized flesh to fall off, revealing the bleached bone beneath, and seemed not the least bit surprised by what he saw.

"I would have preferred to destroy Montressor myself, but it is good to have him gone in whatever fashion it takes," he said at last. "I will make sure that he can never return..."

Then, he turned towards the soldiers, and indicated the elders and the women.

"Kill them. Eradicate them all. I want this village drowned in blood."

As Rodrik-Usher walked away without looking back, the horrid sounds of hacking blades and gut-wrenching screams filled the alley, until silence once again returned.

As the Sun set over Nûr, the azure-clad soldiers began to leave in a single file, walking towards the Desert of Tears. Only the dead, and the screeching, scavenging birds, remained as ghastly witnesses to the carnage they had left in their wake.

Gullivar Jones had flown along the caravan trail on his magic carpet. During his stops, he had earned his meals by playing music and telling stories to the merchants, as they traveled south, their wagons loaded with precious skins, rare herbs and other goods that would fetch much gold in the land of the Malachites, beyond the great Desert of Tears. The tales they most enjoyed were about the Blue Star, Earth, the world upon which he had been born–or *would be born*, someday far in the future.

Eventually, Gullivar had bidden farewell to the caravan leader, resisting the old man's entreaties and promises of a bonus for more stories of the Wild West and the great Buffalo Hunter whose name was "Bill." He had flown off towards the foot of the mountains, before the great stretch of desert beyond.

He had found his way along a series of narrow canyons, carefully flying his carpet between the sharp cliffs and rocky spires that made this part of the Nihan Mountains nearly inaccessible. It had been many months since he had flown through these gorges, yet he had never forgotten the way.

Gullivar Jones was going home. Or at least, to the only home that now truly mattered for him.

He flew onward and upward towards the village of Nûr, reflecting on the failure of his mission, despite the many obstacles he had overcome during his wanderings. As he approached the village, his eyes noticed the circling black muru birds in the skies above.

Gullivar's heart leapt to his throat, but resisting the urge to rush forward, the Earthman immediately flew lower and landed behind a cliff. He dismounted and cautiously made his way to the village through a rocky shortcut.

Then, he beheld the horror.

Gullivar slowly walked through the corpse-littered streets, his face becoming increasingly grim as he realized the absence of survivors. Still, he progressed cautiously in case the attackers had left men behind. It seemed that there was no one left alive in the entire village.

His steps took him to the alley where Heru's body lay among those of her companions, in a pool of blood. Miraculously, faint breath still emanated from the woman's lips.

Gently cradling the body in his arms, Gullivar dropped some essence of germande that he had brought with him into the dying Princess' mouth. Returned to dim consciousness, Heru opened her eyes, recognized the Earthman who was also her lover, and whispered one name–that of Rodrik-Usher the Damned.

The small effort had taken her last breath, and she died in Gullivar's arms, staring up into his face.

The warrior stood and released a long, bestial scream that plaintively spoke of his grief, pain and fury.

With Many Cares & Toils Oppres'd...

Letter from Edgar Allan Poe to John Allan, March 19, 1827:

Richmond, Monday

Sir,

After my treatment on yesterday and what passed between us this morning, I can hardly think you will be surprised at the contents of this letter. My determination is at length taken to leave your house and endeavor to find some place in this wide world, where I will be treated not as you have treated me. This is not a hurried determination, but one on which I have long considered– and having so considered my resolution is unalterable. You may perhaps think that I have flown off in a passion, & that I am already wishing to return; but not so. I will give you the reasons which have actuated me, and then judge–

Since I have been able to think on any subject, my thoughts have aspired, and they have been taught by you to aspire, to eminence in public life; this cannot be attained without a good education, such a one I cannot obtain at a Primary school. A collegiate education therefore was what I most ardently desired, and I had been led to expect that it would at some future time be granted, but in a moment of caprice you have blasted my hopes because forsooth I disagreed with you in an opinion, which opinion I was forced to express. Again, I have heard you say (when you little thought I was listening and therefore must have said it in earnest) that you had no affection for me—

You have moreover ordered me to quit your house, and are continually upbraiding me with eating the bread of Idleness, when you yourself were the only person to remedy the evil by placing me to some business. You take delight in exposing me before those whom you think likely to advance my interest in this world.

These grievances I could not submit to; and I am gone. I request that you will send me my trunk containing my clothes & books—and if you still have the least affection for me, as the last call I shall make on your bounty, to prevent the fulfillment of the prediction you this morning expressed, send me as much money as will defray the expenses of my passage to some of the Northern cities & then support me for one month, by which time I shall be enabled to place myself in some situation where I may not only obtain a livelihood, but lay by a sum which one day or another will support me at the University.

Send my trunk to the Court House Tavern; send me I entreat you some money immediately, as I am in the greatest necessity. If you fail to comply with my request, I tremble for the consequence.

Yours &c

Edgar A. Poe

Letter from Edgar Allan Poe to John Allan, March 20, 1827:

Richmond Monday

Sir,
Be so good as to send me my trunk with my clothes. I wrote to you on yesterday explaining my reasons for leaving. I suppose by my not receiving either my trunk, or an answer to my letter, that you did not receive it. I am in the greatest necessity, not having tasted food since yesterday morning. I have nowhere to sleep at night, but roam about the streets. I am nearly exhausted. I beseech you as you wish not your prediction concerning me to be fulfilled to send me without delay my trunk containing my clothes, and to lend if you will not give me as much money as will defray the expense of my passage to Boston and a little to support me there until I shall be enabled to engage in some business. I sail on Saturday. A letter will be received by me at the Court House Tavern, where be so good as to send my trunk.

I am Yours &c.

Edgar A. Poe

P.S.: I have not one cent in the world to provide any food.

Baltimore was to many people like a lighted candle to the moth, reflected Poe. Year after year, they were attracted to it in swarms; filled with the vague idea that they could get along as well here as anywhere, since, as many put it, something was *bound to turn up*. Most were, like him, young men unsettled in life, fresh from good homes, with sincere hopes of getting a start in the city and making something of themselves.

Alas, few of them had money to waste while accomplishing this, and thus they naturally gravitated to the egalitarian heart of the city, the cheap lodging-houses that provided the only rooms they could afford.

As the 18-year-old walked through the back alleys, he passed a horde of dirty children playing in the gutter; the worn, grey, greasy walls muffled their shouts, almost as if the street itself was apologizing for their small moment of joy. Few happy noises made this neighborhood sing. Morning and evening, it echoed with the groans of endless toil and the rumbling of the passing carts. Only a year earlier, a colony of blind beggars had found harbor within its dark burrows, tenants of a peg-legged landlord, whom every child in the neighborhood knew, even if he had no idea that John Quincy Adams was President of the United States.

Despite the bleakness of his surroundings, something to which he was quite accustomed, Poe was in good spirits. He was a handsome, lanky young man of strong constitution, brimming with energy. His ample forehead, dark hair, burning dark eyes and proud bearing made him a distinctive, unusual figure in the bowels of the city. His cheerful manner was due to having heard of a new literary opportunity a few weeks earlier from his brother Henry. He hoped that it might, if only temporarily, resolve the matter of his gambling debts.

After the death of their parents, Henry, or as he had been christened, William Henry Leonard, had had the luck, or so it seemed to Poe, to have been allowed to remain with their grandparents. He, however, had been adopted by the reprehensible John Francis Allan, who had done his best to keep the two boys separated, including writing his brother a letter three years earlier in which he threatened to disclose a scandal about their mother.

But Allan had failed, and Poe had met his brother in Richmond during the summer of 1825 and had even introduced him to his darling Elmira. Their common dislike of Mr. Allan had only served to draw the brothers closer together.

Since the death of their grandfather nine years prior, Henry had been living with the Clemm family. Then, soon after Poe's visit, Henry had embarked on the *U.S.S. Macedonian* (his uniform had greatly impressed Elmira, Poe recalled), and had visited South America.

He had just returned to Baltimore and, eager to publish accounts of his journeys, had made contact with a newly launched weekly magazine, rather ambitiously called *The North American*, not to be confused with the more prestigious *North American Review* in Boston. Not only had its editor been willing to print his articles, but he had actually offered Henry a modest, but nevertheless genuine, advance. According to Henry, he had also expressed interest in a story entitled *The Pirate*, inspired by Poe's brief affair with Elmira, and on which the two brothers had collaborated.

Encouraged by this response, Poe had quickly gathered as much material as he had, mostly poems, and presented them as best as he could. He had also enlisted the help of a kindly neighbor to clean and press his rumpled suit and shirt in an effort to impress the *North American* editor. At last he had set off carrying a black leather portfolio filled with his ink-covered pages beneath his arm.

Spring had been early that year. It was another blandly beautiful day. The air was neither too hot nor too cold, even in breezy downtown, and Poe felt as if the wind itself was carrying him on his way, so light was his mood.

When the aspiring writer at last arrived at the offices of *The North American*, his buoyancy faded and he suddenly felt as if his nerves were on fire. What would he do if he were to be rejected?

Best not think that now, he told himself. And, swallowing hard, he pushed open the heavy wooden door of the entryway.

The North American was located on the fifth floor of the building. Even though the day was not hot, by the time Poe had climbed what he soon perceived as a never-ending staircase, he was covered in sweat. This did nothing to improve his mood as he tapped on the door to the editor's office.

A jovial voice bade him enter, and after a brief hesitation, he walked through the door.

The office was astonishingly chaotic; papers were stacked on every surface, practically hiding the dark, heavy furniture. From the desk, a disembodied voice welcomed Poe. It took the young man a second or two to find its source behind the piles of manuscripts that hid its owner.

"Are you Alexander Montressor?" he asked the short, portly man with the jolly, rubicund face that looked incongruously as if it should belong to a contented baby rather than an adult man; especially one in a position that Poe held in such high regard as "editor."

"I am indeed, young sir!" answered Montressor. "I'm so delighted you have come to see me, Mr. Poe."

"But... How did you know my name?" asked the young writer, astonished.

"Er... Oh, that's easy enough. You look quite like your brother, Henry. He told me that he thought you might call on me shortly."

Poe was not entirely convinced by this explanation, but in the event decided to take it at face value.

"Sit down, young sir," continued Montressor.

The writer looked around him in confusion. There did not appear to be a single surface upon which he could carry out the request, unless he started moving the stacks of papers; something that appeared to be a Herculean task.

Montressor, undaunted, simply grabbed a pile and threw them to the floor, uncovering what appeared to be a velvet-covered chair, which, judging by its condition, had suffered beneath the weight of many an aspiring writer. Then, he indicated the uncluttered space to his visitor with a wave of his hand.

Poe took him up on the invitation and sat, putting his portfolio on his knees.

"I've come to see you, sir," he began as he opened it, "to ask if you would be interested in some of my other work."

"Let's see what you have there," said the portly editor as he started to peruse the bits and pieces that Poe had assembled.

As he read, the young author felt suddenly uncomfortable, as if he was being watched. He looked up to see a large raven staring at him through the slightly dirty window, and gave a shiver of apprehension.

"Hmm... hmm... yes, indeed... quite interesting," Montressor mumbled half to himself as he read. After several minutes, he looked up at the expectant visitor, and read:

> "*In visions of the dark night*
> *I have dream'd of joy departed—*
> *But a waking dream of life and light*
> *Hath left me broken-hearted.*

"I like it, young sir. It's a bit conventional, but I can see you have potential. Why, when I was your age, I was writing about clouds and daffodils.

"In any case, there's not enough here to fill even a small volume; I need more."

Poe could not believe his ears; this was the moment he felt he'd been awaiting his entire life.

"You mean you're interested in it?"

"Isn't that what I said? If you can give me more, I'd be happy to publish a collection of your work."

"Yes, of course, I'd be happy to... Only..." he hesitated with embarrassment before continuing, "I'm a bit short of funds at the moment and I wonder if you would be able to pay me a small advance. I'm not sure, you see, that I'll be able to pay for my rooms if I don't earn some money soon."

Montressor placed his hands on the desk before him, steepling his fingers and tapping them together as he thought.

"An advance, hmm? Yes, I see how you could imagine... but I don't know... This is a new publication, our investors are, understandably, concerned about throwing good money after bad... No advertising to speak of, you see..." Suddenly, he brightened, as an idea seemed to spring into his head.

"How would you like to live rent free while you complete your work, young sir? I have a big house that is all but empty except for my ward, Ligeia, and me. To be honest, we just rattle around inside it most of the time. You could have your own room and we'd even provide your meals. Ligeia is quite a splendid cook and is often frustrated that the only one who tastes her efforts are the two of us."

Poe sat in astonished silence at this generous and unexpected offer. Montressor seemed not to notice and continued:

"Yes, yes, the more I think about it, the more I like this idea. You will have the freedom from mundane worries you need to be able to create, and Ligeia will have someone else to fuss over besides myself. It's settled then, you must come to us tonight."

"Sir, are you sure about this? I barely know what to think, as it is far more than I could have ever hoped. I find myself almost speechless with gratitude."

"Nonsense, young sir! This will suit us all perfectly. I know that you will enjoy Ligeia's company as well, in those moments when you are not hard at work providing new material for our project.

"By the way; have you thought of a title?"

"I was thinking of the title of the work you cited, sir, *A Dream*…"

"No, no, that will never do! It's, well, it does nothing to draw the attention of the reader. Let me look through these for a moment… Yes, this will do nicely: *Tamerlane*. It's intriguing, gripping. Yes, yes, that shall be the title.

"Now, shall I send a cab around to help you bring your belongings to us?"

"Sadly, sir, I have few enough of those. I can easily bring them along on foot."

Montressor quickly wrote down an address on a rumpled bit of paper, which he handed to Poe.

"Then, hasten home and be at our door in plenty of time for supper. I shall go and tell Ligeia to prepare a room for you. Oh, she will be most delighted, I assure you!"

So saying, the rotund editor struggled to his feet, which were surprisingly small for a man of his size, and made his way through the clutter to the door, ushering his young visitor before him.

"We shall have a fine time, young sir. A fine time indeed."

As the door shut behind him, Poe felt as if he should pinch himself to be sure that he was awake. Montressor's offer had lifted the burden of impending homelessness from his shoulders.

If he had been buoyant on the walk to the offices of *The North American*, he practically floated on the return to his lodgings. It took him mere moments to gather up his meager effects and once again set out onto the streets of Baltimore.

On a tree outside, a raven shook out its feathers, bobbed its head several times, then flew off into the windswept sky.

Rodrik-Usher

Once upon a time…

The city-state of Mazan was located deep in the heart of the Baltan Peaks. Like most of the Tiny Kingdoms, it had suffered mightily through the War of the Wing-Men, and was further torn apart by the coming of the Black Wardens of Qiml, during what later came to be called the Time of Ashes.

It was a truly horrible time, when neighbor turned against neighbor, and roving bands of looters and marauders seized upon any pretext to steal and murder with impunity. The folk of the Lower Estates, near the river Tahim, could rely upon the armies of Edora to enforce order, even at the cost of the odd mistaken hanging. But for those who lived in the bleak mountains of the Baltan, there was no such succor to be found.

The only ones to derive any dark glee from this state of chaos and anarchy were the Baltan Lords, who saw in it a unique opportunity to avenge old wounds, settle ancient accounts, steal more land from a hated neighbor and generally behave like the bloodthirsty robbers they were. Little did they care for theological arguments, no fear had they of the armies of the South, or even the powers of Seth. War bred its own justification, and discord provided fertile ground to find new wrongs, real or invented, to redress.

From behind the massive stonewalls of their mountain fortresses, the Baltan Lords struck at their neighbors, caring little for religion or politics, motivated only by a thirst for blood and rapine. Truly, it was a mournful era, the last dying breath of the Dark Times before the peaceful influences of Dorgé to the North, and Edora to the South, combined to finally bring peace to the Tiny Kingdoms.

Many names were written in blood in the dark annals of history: Bro Heris, the bloody Count of Ibhad, Duke Rajen of Tuliphan, the mad Bussi the Munificent of Danjhar and the unspeakable Vard of Bulkar, who made the river Ifliz run red with the blood of his victims. To this shameful enumeration would have to be added Baron Usher of Mazan, perhaps the most evil of them all: a thin, unnaturally pale man whose lanky face was circled by a small, short-cropped black beard and bore a perpetual expression of malice.

Mazan was a town located deep inside the Baltan Peaks, buried beneath the snow for most of the year, scorched by the summer sun for the rest. It was surrounded by dark, impenetrable forests, in which some of the older horrors of times long gone were said to yet live.

None who knew Baron Usher dared defy him, for the list of his crimes and depredations was endless and would take far too many scrolls to retell. His vassals, indeed all the residents of Mazan, trembled in fear at the mere mention of his name. There were many who chose exile when it became known that they had incurred his displeasure.

Among his many actions were his brazen attacks upon the merchant caravans of Dorgé during their crossings of the Baltan Peaks in defiance of the ancient compacts. The corpses of innocent merchants were often found hanging on trees, their flesh devoured by the rapian birds. As a result of this foul banditry, the merchants had taken to avoiding Mazan, and the local fairs and markets suffered greatly, but the Baron cared little.

Having run out of strangers to murder, Usher showed no hesitation in turning on his own people. Peasants were hung, quartered or publicly eviscerated for the most minor peccadilloes. Burning irons were used to blind those who had dared cast a disapproving look in the Baron's direction. Tongues were ripped out of the mouths of those who had dared whisper behind his back. The rapians found much food in the barony from the seemingly unending stream of corpses that were thrown from the highest tower of the Baron's castle into the yawning chasms below.

Worse yet, when Usher went hunting, he had developed a taste for selecting the wife or daughter of a peasant, or even of a local merchant or tradesman, and using her as his prey. His barely clothed victim was condemned to run through the hills and the valleys, the thick forests and the icy streams, until out of breath. When, inevitably, she was captured, she was mercilessly slaughtered and gutted by the Baron, and fed to his pet muru, an evil black bird that sat on his shoulder.

No man, no matter how powerful or high his rank, was safe from Baron Usher.

One day, the Baron fell in love with, or rather lusted after, for in truth his heart knew not love, the beautiful Maline, the blonde-tressed daughter of Baron Dornoday of Ibhad. His demand for the lady's hand having been

31

rebuffed in horror, Usher's heart was filled with hatred and a dark desire for revenge. Thus it was that no one from Mazan was truly surprised when it was later reported that Baron Dornoday had been found dead, hanged by his feet, gutted, in the forest of Gormac that bordered the two kingdoms. And of his daughter, who had vanished at the same time, no word was heard. No human eyes, save perhaps those of Usher himself, ever saw Maline alive again.

Still, a year or so later, with great pomp, the Baron presented a son to his assembled vassals. His name, they were told, would be Rodrik. But of the child's mother, there was no trace, no acknowledgment, and the fate of Maline remained a mystery.

Much time passed, and if age was expected to have a slowing effect on Baron Usher's rage, people were soon disillusioned, for his crimes continued as before. His son, Rodrik, grew into a tall, lanky adolescent, having inherited his father's ghastly complexion but, seemingly, none of his propensity to erupt into blood-curdling screams of hatred. Yet, for all his manners, there were those who believed Rodrik to perhaps be just as dangerous as his sire. The servants at Castle Usher–those who had learned to survive the Baron's moods–called him the "sly one" and were not duped by his civil demeanor.

Then, one day, after a particularly horrible incident that involved the desecration of a mountain shrine, Baron Usher vanished.

A regent was appointed by the council, for Rodrik was not yet of the age to rule. The regent was Hayrult of Tuliphan, a stout good man, and the people of Mazan began to feel joy. Hayrult ordered a search of the mountains and of the forest, but no clues were found as to the Baron's whereabouts. Some said that he had been ambushed by one of his many victims, killed and buried in an unmarked grave. Others blamed the local spirits, whose shrine Usher had desecrated.

Soon after, a rumor spread throughout the land. Shepherds whispered tales of a new, fantastic beast that had made its appearance and that preyed on their herds with unrivaled ferocity. Many travelers also reported having seen the beast. Lonely mountaineers were attacked and more than a few died, leaving only bloodied remains to be identified. Witnesses reported that the beast was not unlike a huge wolf, but walked upright, on two feet like a man. Its burning red eyes shot sparks of fire and smoke came from its huge jaws. Its uncanny speed enabled the beast to strike at distant locations mere hours apart. Although some of these accounts were undoubtedly exaggerated by fear, there was certainly truth to be found amongst them as well.

Soon, the beast no longer contented itself to prey on herds of cattle and isolated travelers, but began roving ever closer to isolated homes and feasting on those who foolishly strayed in the night. Bowing to public pressure, Hayrult offered rich rewards and launched expeditions into the peaks and forests to track down and kill the beast. Yet, somehow, it always managed to elude its pursuers. Each time the hunters had returned home, its depredations began anew.

Eventually, the frightened peasants came to believe that the beast was none other than the reincarnated Baron Usher, who had returned as a merkul, an accursed creature of the night.

At that time, Hayrult had a young, bright and handsome blond scribe named Leng in his service. Leng was the youngest son of Duke Khalviz of Rizu. He was smart and physically nimble, yet knew his prospects at home were limited because of his seven older brothers. He had thus sought his fortune elsewhere, as was the tradition. Plotting the locations of the beast's crimes on a local map, Leng noticed that they all seemed to occur within the radius of a single central point, the clearing of Rona, which appeared to be the beast's favorite haunt.

Leng took a squadron of armed men to the clearing to investigate further, and while he could see nothing out of the ordinary, he nevertheless felt uncomfortable standing in its center. His men felt the same. It was as if some palpable, miasmic evil was reaching through their skins and lightly stroking their very nerves.

Leng decided to call on the services of Andrevar, the renowned Enchanter of Seth, who had taken temporary residence in the coast town of Eridol. Andrevar had a well-deserved reputation for unpredictability and eccentricity, even by the standards of Seth. His curiosity piqued, Andrevar agreed to come to the city's aid.

Upon his arrival, the blue-robed Elder was immediately taken to the clearing of Rona. There, he performed the Spell of Enlightenment and was immediately plunged into a deep trance from which no man dared awaken him.

After an hour or more had passed, Andrevar awakened from his trance, and silently, performed yet another spell. Before the startled eyes of Hayrult, Leng and their entourage, the ground began to heave, the earth opened wide, and a mangled skeleton pulled itself out of the dirt. The spectators shrunk back in horror, watching the undead thing that stood there, staring at them with vacant eyes. Andrevar made another gesture, and the bones, which had been held together by his mysterious powers, collapsed in a macabre heap onto the ground.

"That," said the Enchanter of Seth, "was the Lady Maline of Ibhad, gruesomely murdered by Baron Usher."

"So that is what happened to her," said Hayrult. "Many had guessed but no one knew–save for the Baron."

"The Baron–and one other," said Andrevar, his hooded eyes coming to rest upon one of the members of the crowd.

Suddenly, the people began to move as one body, as if they were puppets on strings manipulated by a will stronger than their own. They recoiled from the thin, lanky figure of a pale young man, whose face now bore an expression of malicious glee.

"Rodrik learned what his father had done to his mother," Andrevar continued in a toneless voice. "This youth is uniquely gifted in the ancient arts. Such a crime could hardly remain hidden from the eyes of one such as he. And when he found out…"

"My dear father paid the price," finished Rodrik.

"But no more," said Andrevar, looking at the young man with grim determination in his hooded eyes.

Whatever wordless communication was silently exchanged between the brazen young man and the aged Enchanter of Seth remained forever unknown to those who witnessed that day. They saw only that, after a few instants, Rodrik bowed his head to the older man and meekly said, "As per your desire, I will make it so, Sire."

The young man snapped his fingers and, in the distance, a powerful agonizing wail was heard. No one doubted that it was the wail of the merkul, the wail of Baron Usher, transmogrified into an unnamable thing by his own son.

"Good-bye, father, and may the Horrors feast upon your soul," said Rodrik softly. He snapped his fingers again, and the wail stopped as abruptly as the flow of water to a dammed spring.

All believed that the beast of Mazan was gone forever.

That day, Rodrik, now Rodrik Usher, left with Andrevar for Seth, the city of the Enchanters, in the Mounts Arcane, past the Desert of Tears, far, far to the south.

And by public acclaim, young Leng was made the new Baron of Mazan.

Of a Wild Lake with Black Rock Bound

Strangely, it was less easy to find Montressor's house than Poe had imagined. Several times, he was forced to stop passers-by to show them the grubby piece of paper and get directions. Each set of directions sent him on a different path, and therefore, it took him an hour longer than he had planned to finally arrive at the mansion.

At last, he stood in front of the place he sought. It was an imposing structure, set at the end of a long, tree-lined drive. There was something disturbing about the place, although what it was, the young man was at pains to understand. Somehow, its proportions seemed off, almost as if part of the house stood on another plane of reality from the rest.

It looked far older than it could possibly be, given the age of Baltimore. The stones showed the discoloration of centuries, and a lacework of fungi ate away at the mortar. Yet, despite this, it was far from dilapidated nor unkempt; the building itself seemed sturdier than its masonry and looked as if it could stand thus for many more centuries to come

Finally, the young writer shrugged and walked down the drive to the magnificent oak doors. Poe grabbed a knocker representing a beast he had never seen, but before he could use it, the door opened wide.

For a second, the writer forgot to breathe. He was sure he would faint as he stared at the beautiful creature that stood framed in the doorway.

Clearly, this was Ligeia, Alexander Montressor's ward. She was tall for a woman of her time, standing barely two inches less than Poe's five feet ten inches. Her figure was lithe and willowy, her eyes were violet and startling in their clarity, her skin was porcelain smooth and her hair the shining blue-black of a raven's wing. Poe was instantly smitten.

Ligeia, however, appeared totally unaware of the effect she had had on the young man. She smiled at him warmly and said, "You must be Mr. Poe. Uncle Alexander told me to expect you. We've gotten a room ready for you. Please, do come in."

At last, Poe regained his composure and was able to stutter out, "Thank you," as he crossed the threshold into his temporary new home.

The writer was astonished at what he saw once he was inside the house. In sharp contrast to the gloomy exterior, there was a sense of light, brightness and color everywhere he looked. After having seen Montressor's office, he could only assume that the gentle young woman in front of him was responsible for all of it.

"Why, you're... it's beautiful," he exclaimed.

"Thank you," answered Ligeia, laughing. "I thought the old place needed some cheering up. I don't really like dark houses, do you? They tend to sap the energy of the soul."

Poe could only nod as he tried to take in the somehow otherworldly decoration; bright swatches of fabric covered the walls and a large chandelier seemed to provide more light than seemed possible from its dozens of candles. The floor was of a golden stone that looked as if it glowed of its own accord, adding an extra layer of warm, welcoming light to the hallway.

Ligeia put her hand lightly on the young author's arm, sending an electric shiver through his entire being.

"Come with me, Mr. Poe, and I'll help you to get settled in your chamber."

The overwhelmed Poe followed her dumbly. As they walked through the labyrinthine house, his hostess pointed out the various rooms.

"This is the dining room; we have dinner at eight, but there's no need to dress formally... You'll probably want to spend some time in here; it's Uncle's library. He has some rather unique volumes. We usually meet here before dinner to discuss the events of the day..."

As they were about to start up the staircase, Poe noticed they were passing a doorway with elaborate, bizarre carvings on the molding. The door was closed and bolted.

"What's in there?" asked the writer, his curiosity piqued by the strangeness of the thing.

"Oh, that's the cellar; no need to worry yourself about it. You're better off not going down there on your own.

"Here is your room," said Ligeia, stopping in front of a very mundane looking door, halfway down the corridor of the first floor. "I hope you'll be comfortable; I've tried to make sure you'll have everything that you need." So saying, she opened the door.

The room the young woman had made ready was a huge improvement on the small attic chamber Poe had barely been able to afford in downtown Baltimore. It was, in fact, a suite with a large, separate sleeping area that contained a bed that looked soft and inviting, as well as a huge armoire that would hold ten times the amount of clothing than what the budding writer owned.

But the room that caused him awe and gratitude was the sitting room/study. It had clearly been set up with great thought for his needs and comfort. A large, oak writing desk was set with its back to a large, bay window, so that as much light as possible could aid him to see during the daytime hours. An oil lamp sat on the desk so that he could more comfortably work once it became dark, even though there were new candles in the holders on the walls.

The desk chair looked as if it would be comfortable for hours, as he sat there writing. A fireplace burned brightly on one wall, making the whole room cozy and comfortable

"This is wonderful," Poe said, turning to his hostess. "I feel as though I could sit here and work forever."

"I hope it won't take you that long to finish your book!" she said, smiling.

"Now, let me leave you to set up your belongings. There is hot water on the washstand, so that you can refresh yourself if you wish. Remember, dinner is at eight."

She turned and walked out of the room, shutting the door gently behind her.

It only took the writer a few minutes to put away his belongings, which looked almost lost in the vast armoire. Then, he took out his pen and inkwell and sat down at the inviting desk to begin work.

He was so intent on what he was doing that he only noticed that night had fallen when he could no longer make out his own words on the paper in front of him. Rather than lighting the oil lamp and continuing, he decided instead to take a candle and go explore the library that Ligeia had shown him on his arrival.

The writer took a candle and set out to retrace the route he had taken to his room. It was far more complicated than he had remembered, and several times, he found himself walking along corridors that he didn't recall having seen earlier in the day. He felt a light frisson of fear, again getting the sense that he was in a place that was not quite of this world.

At one point, he found himself standing in front of the locked cellar door, strangely drawn to it as if something from within were calling to him. He was reaching his hand towards the handle when a sound behind him caused him to start. He turned to look, but there was nothing there but shadows.

Shaking his head to clear it, Poe walked to what he was sure was the library and went inside. This time, he was correct. He set his candle on a low table and started to look at the volumes on the shelves with all the joy and excitement of a child in a shopful of sweets.

He had never seen a library quite like this one before. Besides all the books one would normally expect to see on the vast shelves, were countless volumes written in languages totally foreign to the young author. Sometimes, when he caught sight of them in his peripheral vision, he even had the odd feeling that he could almost understand what was written on their bright covers. But, when he turned his head to look at them directly, they were just as mysterious as before.

Poe felt as if he could happily spend the rest of his life simply living in that amazing room.

A loud laugh of delight awoke him from his meditative contemplation of a large volume of unusual poetry.

"How delightful to find you here, young Mr. Poe!" said a beaming Montressor as he entered the room. "I see you've found my favorite place in the whole house. It's quite a wonder, is it not?"

"Indeed, sir, it is. I believe it would take me more than two lifetimes to make my way from the first volume to the last, and that is without being able to read those in tongues which I do not recognize."

"Ah, yes. There are several unusual works to be found here. Perhaps one day I will tell you how I acquired them. But, that is a story for another time.

"Tell me, are you pleased with your accommodation? Has Ligeia provided you with everything that you need? How is the work coming along?"

The writer found it hard to even follow the rapid-fire succession of questions, let alone answer them coherently.

Luckily for Poe, at that minute, Ligeia walked into the library.

"Uncle!" she said, chiding him, "You are overwhelming our guest. He can't possibly answer all your questions when you ask them like that. At least, let him breathe between his answers."

The writer was both grateful and charmed by her intervention. He realized again that he was quite smitten with her.

"Forgive me, sir," he said. "I've had the most overwhelming day since I first met you. Your niece has treated me with great kindness since my arrival, and I have been able to make a great start on my work.

"Your house is magnificent, and I find that I am almost without words to express my gratitude for your hospitality and generosity. I really have no idea what I would have become if it weren't for you."

"Think nothing of it, young sir. We are delighted to have you. I know that Ligeia must be bored having only her old uncle to talk with at dinner. You will provide her with a most welcome distraction."

"Don't be silly, Uncle," laughed Ligeia. "You are quite the entertaining companion. But, I am happy to have Mr. Poe here. I hope he doesn't find us too strange for his liking, however."

Before the writer could reassure his hostess, she spoke again.

"Gentlemen, I came to tell you that our dinner is ready and to ask you both to be so kind as to join me in the dining room."

To Poe's delight, she placed her hand lightly on his arm so that he could escort her. His day was beginning to feel as if it was all a dream.

Dinner turned out to be as exotic as everything else the young writer had come across so far during his amazing day.

"You are a wondrous cook, Miss Ligeia," he said. "I've never tasted anything like this combination of spices before. Is it something of your own invention?"

Ligeia smiled at the compliment.

"Mr. Poe, you are a flatterer. I'm lucky to have some old family recipes that I'm able to carry out reasonably well. I'm so glad that you like it."

As the meal progressed, the trio's conversation waged far and wide. Poe was convinced that he had never before spent such an agreeable time in his entire life. But, at last, as all things must, the evening wound down.

"This old man feels a need for his bed, youngsters," said Montressor. "But you should feel free to stay up as long as you like."

"Thank you, sir," responded the author, "but this has been a long day indeed, and I fear my presence has been tiring for Miss Ligeia as well. I will follow your example and go to my chamber.

"I don't know that I have ever felt this happy and contented in all my life, and for that I will be eternally grateful to the both of you."

The three finished saying their good-nights, then each headed to their rooms.

Poe had no idea how long he had been asleep when he felt as if there were a presence in his room and started awake.

"Who is there?" he whispered. But no one replied.

Feeling a sudden shiver down his spine, he quickly lit a candle next to his bed so that he could look around his room. He could find no sign of anyone else there, however.

Before he could fall back asleep, he thought he heard a faint noise in the corridor outside his room. He knew he would be unable to sleep again if he did not look to see what was causing it.

He hurriedly got up and put on his dressing gown, then cautiously opened the door and peered out into the darkness.

But it was not totally dark! He could make out the faint glow of a candle far down the corridor, heading towards the stairs. Not knowing why, he felt compelled to follow it to see who was about at this clearly late hour.

Trying to be as quiet as possible, he eased out into the corridor holding his own candle, and followed the now dimming light ahead.

Before he knew it, he was at the mysterious door that had drawn him so strongly earlier in the day. He felt a current of air and realized that it was open just a crack.

Without a second's hesitation, he took hold of the handle and pulled the door wide, then walked through to the other side.

As he started down the steps, a sudden gust of wind seemed to come from nowhere and the door slammed shut. Frightened, the author turned back and tried the handle. It wouldn't budge; he was locked in.

I don't suppose I have any choice but to go down, he told himself. *After all, if the light I was following was carried this way, I won't be alone and the other person may have the key to the door.*

Resigned, he continued down the stairs.

As with everything else he had come across in the strange house, the stairs seemed to be not quite what he had first imagined. They were damp, slippery, and covered in places with mold and rotted moss. They went down a very, very long way. Poe began to wonder if he would ever reach the bottom.

At last, though, he came to flat, stone ground. He was starting to panic, as his candle was burning low and he worried that he would soon be stuck in total darkness. As he tried to figure out his best course of action, he saw the flickering of the light he had originally followed. He almost trembled with relief and walked towards it as quickly as he could.

It seemed to Poe that the distance he traveled to reach the light was, again, far longer than it should have been, given the size of the house. But he put it out of his mind, hoping only to find someone who could help him escape the locked basement. For a cellar, it was remarkably empty. There were no wine barrels, no crates, no tools of any kind; just the damp stone, sweating its mildewed ooze. And it seemed to go on forever. After several minutes, the writer saw a figure holding a lantern ahead of him.

As he approached, he realized that it was Ligeia.

"Hello!" he called. "Miss Ligeia! It's me, Mr. Poe!"

"Ah, I wondered how long it would take you to get here," she said.

"You were expecting me?"

"Well, let's just say I was hoping you would come. It will be much easier this way."

What does she mean by that? wondered Poe. *What will be easier?*

The author looked around and realized that, rather than being in the cellar, he and the young woman were actually standing in some sort of tunnel.

"You were hoping I would come here?" he asked. "What manner of place is this?"

"Dear Mr. Poe, that is going to be a long story, and I believe we need to move on before I can begin to tell it."

Ligeia took his hand and led him through the darkness.

"To move on? I don't understand," said Poe, puzzled to suddenly feel a fresh breeze on his face. "Are we going outside? Are we in a tunnel?"

The writer suddenly noticed two intricately-carved stone monoliths, each about ten feet high, standing on either side of the dark, rocky walls of the tunnel. He felt slightly sick as they walked past them, experiencing the kind of frisson that is commonly associated with the idea of *someone walking on your grave*.

"Where are we?" he asked Ligeia again.

But the young woman did not answer. She kept walking briskly, dragging him with her hand. To his amazement, Poe discovered that they now stood on totally different ground, in what seemed to be an entirely different world.

Instead of the damp cellar with its moss-encrusted walls, they now found themselves in a barren, rocky landscape littered with huge boulders. These were made of stone so black that they stood out eerily against the surrounding darkness. Poe shivered–the stones reminded him of marbles, as if giant children had played some kind of incomprehensible game on this plain, and left their toys behind when they ran off. There was also a small lake, its waters as dark as the stones and utterly still. But the most amazing sight of all was the presence of two moons in the sky.

"I don't understand," said Poe. "Where are we? I feel sick... Miss Ligeia, do you have any idea where we might be?"

"The sickness will quickly pass, Mr. Poe," said the young woman. "It's an effect of going through a Gate. As to our present location, we are on the world you know as Mars–but not Mars as it exists in your time, the dead husk of a once-thriving world, but the red planet as it was aeons ago, long before life of any kind emerged on Earth."

"That is impossible. Mars is a million miles from Earth. How could we have crossed that impossible gulf? Even Professor Lowe's hot air balloons cannot travel..."

Ligeia smiled. "We did not travel by air, Mr. Poe, nor did we journey through what your men of science call the *aether*. We took... Well, I suppose, you might think of it as a *shortcut*. Come along; I'll show you."

Ligeia took the baffled young writer back to the two stone posts.

"These are Gates, gateways set up by the Keepers, a god-like race about which we know very little, except for the artifacts they left behind. For those who have divined their workings, they are like doors between worlds, enabling you to go from one star to another, just as easily as you crossed from the library into the dining-room last night..."

Poe touched the totems, examined them and ran his fingers over the alien carvings. The rocky surroundings were overpoweringly real, and the tunnel that, only a few minutes ago, had led to Montressor's damp cellar seemed to have totally and completely vanished. For as far as the eye could see, there was nothing but a bleak, boulder-strewn landscape, stretching into the horizon, beneath the two indifferent moons.

"This is impossible," said Poe for the second time.

He walked cautiously through the stone posts, putting his head forward, as if through a screen, fully expecting to disappear and find he was back inside the cellar. But nothing of the sort happened. A few steps took him around the totem and back to where he had started.

He was still on Mars.

The young man banged his fists against the monolith in a vain attempt to bend it to his will, as if it were an obdurate horse refusing to move.

"I'm afraid most of them only work in one direction," said Ligeia. "You cannot return to Earth this way, Mr. Poe. In fact, even if you knew how to open this particular Gate from this direction, it would only take you to another far-off world. Trust me, you wouldn't want to go there."

"So I cannot go back? Ever?" said Poe.

"No, I didn't say that."

They returned in silence to the shores of the lake, eventually reaching a spot where gigantic rocks formed a natural shelter against the wind. There, in the relative tranquility of the surroundings, Ligeia spent some time searching, until she finally found what she was looking for: a bundle of blankets tied together. Inside were various items of food, some firewood and various tools, including two bowls, a pair of knives and a compass.

"My Uncle Montressor—who isn't really my uncle, but my teacher and mentor—still has friends here. They were told of our coming and asked to leave us supplies here. We should have enough for the journey ahead of us."

"So, the two of you are not from Earth? You are—Martians?" said the writer, almost choking on the words.

"So are you, Mr. Poe," replied Ligeia, laughing. "Don't look so amazed. All life on Earth came from this world first. You are just as much a Martian as I am." She smiled a secret smile, which Poe found irritating, then continued: "But to answer your question more meaningfully, yes, both Montressor and I came from this world. We are fugitives, exiles, if you will. We were forced to flee because of an evil madman, a sorcerer named Rodrik-Usher..."

"I see."

"I'm not sure you do, not yet, at any rate. But you will eventually. Montressor cannot yet return to Mars, so he is forced to remain behind, for the moment at least. The Gates won't work for him. Rodrik-Usher saw to that. One of the goals of our journey is, in fact, to make it possible for him to come back. I am not under the same *interdict* as Montressor, however, and I hope my

49

own return will have gone unnoticed by our enemies. Our undertaking here may well seal this world's fate—and yours, by way of consequence, since its future will also be decided here and now. Your assistance will be most precious, Mr. Poe."

The writer smiled. "I would certainly never refuse to assist you, Miss Ligeia, but why me? Surely, for one such as Mr. Montressor, whom from your description I take to have great powers, it would have been child's play to hire men far better equipped than I for this sort of thing."

"Do not think that, Mr. Poe. It had to be you." Sensing the question budding on the writer's lip, she raised her index finger and quickly added, "But I cannot tell you why. Not yet. Please, just be aware that you have a part to play in this. You are a most extraordinary individual."

"Thank you, Miss Ligeia."

"Now it's getting late and neither of us have had a full night sleep; the road ahead of us in the morning will be long. I suggest we spend the night here and tomorrow, I'll cook you a memorable breakfast," she put a somewhat false note of cheer in her voice.

Poe, sensing the young woman's concerns beneath her brave facade, went along with her pretense. "Good idea, Miss Ligeia. I shall look forward to it with delight."

He wrapped a blanket tightly around himself and before he could dwell on any of the astonishing developments of his day, fell quickly asleep.

In the morning, Ligeia unpacked some food from the supplies she had found the night before while Poe set up a small fire against the shelter of the rocks.

Had they felt the desire to explore their surroundings, or had they merely been able to see above and behind the rocks, they would have frozen in dread at the sight of small, glowing yellow eyes, shining softly in the darkness, or at the sound of a whispered flurry of nonhuman, sibilant grunts. But they had no reason to mistrust their new environment, so it simply had not occurred to them to look.

They started to cook. Poe looked at the food that Ligeia had placed near the fire.

"What are those?" he asked, pointing at two sausages that were startlingly yellow in color.

"They are a delicacy from Dorgé..."

Ligeia did not have time to complete her sentence. Suddenly, a band of hideous gnomes jumped from the top of the rocks. They bore a somewhat reptilian look, and spoke in screechy, guttural voices. They were dressed in raggedy, makeshift skins, and were all armed with spiked clubs.

For a few seconds, Poe just stood there, transfixed in disbelief. He had clearly never seen anything like this in his life, and nothing in his daily experience had prepared him for an encounter with a pack of hostile creatures, which, to him, seemed to have stepped straight out of a painting by Hyeronymus Bosch.

Unable to take it all in, he simply stood there sputtering wordlessly until Ligeia nudged him with her elbow. "Let's not panic, Mr. Poe. They are what we call Mountain Gnomes, although they are rarely seen this far to the west. They may be harmless. I shall try to communicate with them."

"I wonder whether that will have much effect, Miss Ligeia," said the writer. "Look at their clubs..."

Ligeia took a step forward and raised her hand in salute, as Poe had seen Native Americans do. "We travel in peace," she said. "We are sorry if we have trespassed upon your lands. We shall soon be gone, however, with your permission," she added, diplomatically.

But the Leader of the Gnomes, whose name was Basso, ignored the young woman's peaceful advance and swung his club at her, missing her by mere inches, and shouting something that sounded like a mixture of grunts and groans.

Poe jumped back and grabbed the first weapon he found, which was, unfortunately only a modest fork. Valiantly he started waving it around.

"Miss Ligeia–grab something–anything. We must defend ourselves."

"I'm afraid, Mr. Poe, that a fork is probably not the most threatening thing these creatures have ever seen."

Still, not willing to simply give up, Ligeia grabbed the hot pan that she had prepared for the two yellow sausages and, wrapping her two hands around the handle, carefully took a few, slow steps backwards.

Meanwhile, against all expectations, Poe's rather ineffectual jabbing at the Gnomes with his fork appeared to have slowed the creatures down to an extent. He had succeeded in stabbing one of them with his instrument after it had gotten too close, and it had yelped in pain.

"We are in luck, Mr. Poe," said Ligeia, brightening up considerably. "Our dinnerware appears to be made of solid silver. It is very painful, even deadly, to Mountain Gnomes..."

It was clear that the Gnomes had not expected their prey to fight back.

"But even so, we cannot hope to hold them at bay forever," said Poe.

The two continued to move back cautiously, never losing sight of their adversaries, which watched them with their small beady eyes squinted in concentration.

"I will cast a Spell of Protection," said Ligeia. "Step closer to me."

But while trying to carry out the young woman's instructions, the writer stumbled over a bowl and lost his balance. He swore loudly, regretting it instantly, worried that would make a poor impression on his companion. To make matters worse, it acted as a kind of signal to the Gnomes, who rushed in to attack, shouting war cries in their garbled tongue.

Ligeia had the reflex of throwing her scalding pan at the onrushing attackers, forcing them to scatter to avoid it. This gave the two humans the extra few seconds they needed to get close to each other.

Ligeia lifted her right hand towards the sky and called out a few words in a language that sounded like Latin, but was not.

Immediately, a glowing, silver bubble took form around them. From inside it, they could still see the silhouettes of the Gnomes outside. The creatures had recovered from the attack and began hammering at the bubble with their clubs to no avail.

Poe and Ligeia took a moment to catch their breath while blood pounded in their ears and sweat made small shining trails on their dusty faces.

"They don't appear to have been overly interested in communication," wheezed the writer.

"Mountain Gnomes do not usually have a reputation for such hostility; I wonder what has made them behave thus?"

Outside, the Gnomes had completely surrounded the bubble and poked it, smelled it and banged on it with hands and weapons. One of them even tried to bite into it, which only resulted in his spitting a few rotten teeth out in disgust for his pains. Basso finally pointed at the sphere and shouted an order. Obediently, the rest of the tribe moved to one side of the bubble and started to push it.

The sphere began to roll forward like a ball

"They're going to roll us home like a wine barrel," said Poe, losing his balance and slipping. "Can you do something, Miss Ligeia?"

Just as the writer turned his head to look at his companion, Ligeia gave a piercing scream. The Gnomes' maneuver had managed to cause her to lose her concentration, and the cohesion of her spell had been affected.

Poe discovered with horror that one of the Gnomes had somehow forced his upper body into the sphere. The creature grinned at them with terrifying malice, while holding a knife at Ligeia's throat with one hand and gripping her hair tightly with the other.

The Gnome shouted something that brooked no argument. The words may not have made any sense to Poe, but their meaning was clear.

The bubble vanished.

They had lost.

They were prisoners of the Mountain Gnomes.

Montressor

Once upon a time…

A cruel fever wracked the body of Montressor, the famous Enchanter of Seth, who had recently taken up residence at the Court of Suman, the powerful merchant city of the Kingdom of Lanchais, by the river Vaur, on the edge of the Sarkean Sea.

For an Enchanter, Montressor was a short and surprisingly portly man. His face was rubicund and jolly, and would have resembled that of a contented baby, were it not for the air of impish malice that it often wore. He was dressed in the shimmering blue and yellow robes that befitted his rank, which sparkled and seemed to throw off small flakes of brightly-colored matter when he walked.

That evening, feeling as if his very blood was on fire, Montressor decided to take a walk along the river Vaur, hoping that the cooling breezes would bring him some measure of relief.

He left Suman by the northern gate and walked along the great river, near its estuary. Like the thin blades of a knife, a few rays of sunlight pierced the low clouds and struck the reddish waters, seeming to shred it into millions of small, golden claws. The Vaur rolled and thundered, its mighty waves stiffened by a fierce wind. The noise was such that the waters sounded like a horde of lizards crossing the plains. The place was so grim and lonely that Montressor was struck with an overwhelming feeling of fear and anger at the beautiful, mighty river.

On impulse, he raised his hand and, slowly, performed the Spell of Banishment. Then, as he readied himself to leave, he noticed a sudden bubbling of the river. There, in front of him, the frothing wave split asunder to form a flat, round pool, an oasis of calm in the midst of the fiery waters.

A woman stepped from the pool, and onto the river's bank. Her beautiful hair was long, curly and blonde, but her face contained an expression of almost unbearable sadness. In her arms, she held a bunch of rags.

"I lost my baby daughter's shirt in the river. If I don't find it, she will drown," she said to Montressor, referring to a common, local superstition.

"Your child will not drown," the Enchanter answered. "Do not believe in such ill omens. Instead, pray to the gods for their help. But, please, tell me, why do you come from the river?"

"I came to the river tonight to wash the clothes of my family, but I lost my soap and had to go into the water to retrieve it. Then, I tripped on a stone and fell into the water. The undertow twisted me around for a good minute. I thought I'd drown. I still feel dizzy."

Montressor looked carefully at the young woman; her hair blew softly in the wind, free of moisture; her dress floated gently in the breeze and did not stick to her body; there was not the least trace of a single drop of water on her.

For a second, the Enchanter thought that his fever was causing him to hallucinate, so, spotting a passerby, he hailed him to join them. But as soon as the man saw the young woman, he turned pale, his body became taut, and his eyes filled with fear.

"Is it you?" he said. "Can it be you? Tennar? Likni's wife?"

"Of course, it is me," she said. "Do I look ill? How can you ask me that? We saw each other not later than noon today."

"Save me, mighty Montressor," said the man, falling to his knees. "This woman must have been sent by Phra-kan, or else she is a demon who has taken the shape of Tennar, who fell into the Vaur and drowned with her daughter seven years ago while she was doing her washing. The undertow carried her body away and she was never found. Likni, her husband, became half-mad with grief, and would have died if my wife and I hadn't fed him. But he hasn't smiled for seven years, and his eyes are heavy with sorrow."

"I am indeed Tennar, the wife of Likni," said the woman. "But I didn't drown, and neither did my daughter. I fell into the Vaur this very night, and I have only been in its waters for a few minutes, the time needed to breast-feed Phra-kan's spawn. I don't understand what you're talking about. I must see my family."

She seemed calm, yet sad and troubled. An incomprehensible power held thrall over her. They took her into Suman, and if she noticed any changes, such as a clinging vine now covering an entire house instead of just a wall, she did not say a word.

When they reached her house, she went inside. A man was standing there, alone by the fire crystal. His arms hung loosely, and his eyes were empty. It was Likni, her husband. When he saw her enter, he shook violently, then two tears slid down his face.

"Tennar! At last, you've come home," he said. "They all said you'd died, but I knew you'd come back. It has been a very long time, but all will now be well."

The two kissed tenderly.

"He'll be fine now that she's back," the neighbor said.

"I want to see my daughter," said Tennar after she finished embracing her husband. "Where is the flower of my life? Where is my little Ligeia?"

Likni lowered his head to avoid meeting Tennar's eyes. The charitable neighbor again tried telling the woman that it had been seven years since she and her daughter had disappeared beneath the Vaur's blood-red waters. With eyes sad and shining, Tennar looked at him, yet no comprehension illuminated her face.

"I don't understand what you say," she said. "I hear noise, but no words. I want my daughter. I want my Ligeia."

The neighbor began to be frightened by Tennar's behavior and turned towards Montressor. The Enchanter realized that the woman was still not free of whatever curse had affected her. But he knew there was nothing else he could do that night, so he left.

When Montressor returned the following day, he hoped that he would find the family at peace, but his hopes were dashed when he saw Likni, alone, by the fire crystal. The man told him that Tennar had gone to the Vaur to do her laundry.

Sensing that the time had come for his intervention, Montressor hurried to the river. It didn't take him long to locate Tennar, who was sitting by the water's edge with a basket of laundry, looking at the red river like a bird watches a snake. Then, with a sad, melancholic smile on her face, she began to do her laundry

Suddenly, she threw her soap into the water. The bar floated there, gently, as if daring her to follow. Almost as if in a trance, she stepped into the water.

But Montressor was quicker. Rushing into the water, he grabbed her before she was fully immersed. Tennar then shook her head, as if she had just awakened from a dream.

"That was yesterday. This is today," the Enchanter said, gently. "Yesterday, you and your daughter went into the Vaur. Today, you alone came out of the Vaur. What happened?"

Tennar finally answered, hesitantly at first, then faster and faster. "It was as I told you. I was washing my laundry, with my daughter Ligeia by my side. The red waters reflected the setting Sun and made me feel drowsy. The noise made by my beating the clothes filled my head like the sound of a spell song. Ligeia was playing along the water's edge, pushing a bar of soap as if it were a toy boat. Suddenly, the soap seemed to slip from her little hand and floated away into the water. I stepped in to catch it, but it eluded me. It began to dance in front of me. It seemed to turn into a bar of gold. I felt a strong urge to grab the bar. I tried again, but each time, it escaped my hand. Ligeia tried to help me; she, too, went into the water after the soap.

"It seemed to wait for us, but each time one of us approached, it floated a little further away, until I realized I was in water up to my chest. Then, I slipped on a round pebble, and dropped the shirt I had been washing: my daughter's best shirt. I tried to grab it, but I was too late. I saw it float an instant, then sink like a stone. I knew it was an omen of death. It meant my Ligeia would drown. I tried grabbing her, but slipped again. So, there and then, I cursed the gods!"

At this confession, Montressor sighed heavily and made the Sign of Forgiveness, but did not interrupt her.

"Then, the undertow grabbed us and twisted us all around," Tennar continued. "A thundering noise filled my head. I saw my life and my death in front of me. But suddenly, I felt myself grabbed by something. I was like a small fish in the talons of the hawk. I could not resist.

"When I awoke, I was in a cave, perhaps at the bottom of the river, I do not know. Ligeia and I were lying on a bed of fine sand. Through the cave's opening, I could see the reddish light of the Vaur. It made me feel very sad, like when you think of all the spring days of your youth that have fled. At the other end of the cave was a corridor filled with a bright, golden light. I took my baby daughter in my arms, and I walked along it until I arrived at an immense plain, covered with trees and golden flowers, and a lake of diamonds. In the center was a beautiful castle made of crystal and aqua-marine."

Here, Tennar marked a pause. She looked as if she was dreaming; her eyes were filled with nostalgia.

"I entered the castle," she continued. "Phra-kan himself awaited me. His hair was long, flowing and red, his skin was white and translucent, like in the tales you told the Court. He looked at me with fish-like eyes, and not a muscle of his beautiful, inhuman face moved, as if it was made of bone. Yet, I wasn't afraid.

" 'Daughter of the Golden Race,' he said, 'If not for me, you and your child would be like carcasses floating in the waters; after a week, your bloated bodies would be dragged up by the fishermen's nets. But if you do as I ask, you will not be unhappy here.' I remained silent, waiting. 'My own child almost died tonight,' he continued, 'and so great is my pain that I feel compelled to wreak havoc once more on the world of men. Yet, he can live again if a Daughter of the Golden Race feeds him once, for only one night. Will you do it?'

"I nodded. Phra-kan then went to a wall, where a fountain seemed to spill drops of glittering, liquid diamonds into a gold cup. He made Ligeia and I drink from it. It tasted delicious, but cold and sharp like fresh mountain snow. Then, he gave me his child..."

At these words, Tennar shivered like a person suddenly immersed in a cold lake.

"He was naked and inhuman like his father, and pale as if sculpted of soft ice. I saw a diffuse light throughout his body. As I gave him my breast, he made small, squishy sounds, like beetles in the summer grass. Soon, he began to acquire the color of the autumn mist, then that of the silver clouds we see in the skies in the month of Jondar, then that of the purest marble from the Baltan Peaks.

"But at the same time, it felt as if my own life was being drained from me. Yet, Phra-kan held me in his gaze, and I could not stop feeding his child.

"Meanwhile, on the wall, the diamond drops were falling, one by one, into the cup, which once again became almost full. My little Ligeia played in the sand, trying to catch small silvery things that darted along the ground. She would occasionally dip her hand into the cup and lick her fingers. I thirsted for those crystal drops, but I could not move, held in thrall by the gaze of Phra-kan. I began to feel weaker and weaker.

"Suddenly, Ligeia caused the cup to spill; it was as if a spell had been lifted. Phra-kan's eyes left me, distracted by the sound of the cup falling. The inhuman child I had been feeding shook and twisted in my arms like an eel, and finally jumped to the ground. He turned into a silvery thing and swam away.

"His father looked at my daughter, then at me. I will never forget the expression in his inhuman eyes. But he merely laughed, and abandoned me to chase after his son. I was then able to grab Ligeia, leave the castle, retrace my steps to the river and come home."

"Child," said Montressor, "you've been the toy of a powerful demon who got hold of you when you cursed the gods. And you might have perished down there if, by some divine inspiration, I hadn't blessed the river tonight. The curse that held you lasted seven years: it took seven years for that fountain to fill the cup, and you fed that demon's spawn for seven years. But now, you are free. However, Phra-kan does not let go of his victims easily, and he has managed to keep your daughter. You came out of the Vaur not with her, but with only her shirt."

Hearing the truth in these words for the first time, Tennar burst into tears. "O mighty Enchanter, is there anything you can do to rescue my daughter?" she cried.

"Thank the merciful gods for forgiving you," said Montressor. Then, raising both his arms, he performed the full Ritual of Repentance. Upon its completion, the water again began to boil, and an eight year-old girl stepped from the water. For the first time, Tennar began to smile

"This is Ligeia, your true child," said the Enchanter. "Take her home. Love her."

Tennar opened her arms and the girl ran into them. They hugged, they kissed, they laughed. Then, they ran home to Likni and from that day onward, happiness reigned in their home.

The next day, Montressor stopped by the river Vaur to again perform the Ritual of Banishment. It was the last ceremony he performed before he left Suman.

As he walked away from the city, he did not have to turn to know that the preternaturally aware eyes of an eight-year-old girl who had drunk from the cup of Phrakan were following him.

In due course, he would return to Suman to fetch his new pupil.

That was good, because that was what the gods desired.

Kind Solace in a Dying Hour

Poe and Ligeia both felt themselves sink into despair at the sight of the Gnomes' mountain citadel, clearly the hoped for effect.

The tall peak was massive and hollow, carved with the hugely hideous faces of all the Gnome Kings that had once ruled that miserable kingdom. Windows and stairs had been dug into the rock, and a malevolent, orange light shone from the glowing openings. The entrance at the bottom of the peak was reached by crossing an immense drawbridge.

The two humans saw all this in reverse, as they were tied upside down to poles, rather like trussed-up chickens. They were being carried towards the entrance. The Gnomes were singing a barbaric tune as they moved along at a rapid pace.

Once inside the mountain, the prisoners were shuttled through a maze of torch-lit corridors; in the distance they could hear the sound of faintly-menacing chants being sung deep within the bowels of the peak.

Poe twisted his head to better see their surroundings.

"Put us down, you scoundrels! Where are you taking us? By Jove, answer me!"

"It's useless, Mr. Poe," said Ligeia. "They don't understand a word of what you're saying."

But to their surprise, one of the Gnomes answered in English–a gravely, broken English, but nevertheless understandable.

"You no make demands. Stop struggling. No good, no good. Hark!"

Poe was dumbfounded. "You speak English? Where are we? What the blazes is going on?"

"What *English*? Hear music? Songs of sacrifice. Holy ritual. Torture, mutilation. Singers become as one, in joy of victim's pain. Hark!"

"There must be some mistake," begged Poe. "We haven't done anything to you."

But all the Gnomes yelled "Hark! Hark!" and continued to march forward. Nothing said by Poe or Ligeia was able to tear another word from the one who had spoken English.

Eventually, the small cortege arrived at what looked like a dungeon. The two prisoners were untied from the poles and unceremoniously dumped inside a dark, dank cell. The door clanged shut, leaving them alone in the gloom.

"I do hope that your sorcery can get us out of this predicament, Miss Ligeia," said Poe in a voice that he fought to keep from trembling.

"I am afraid my magic will not work inside here, Mr. Poe," replied the young woman. "There is just too much evil surrounding us for it to be properly effective."

"I'm sure you're selling yourself short," said Poe, although he felt his companion's hopelessness. "We'll find a way out of here..."

Suddenly, a rattling noise from the far end of the cell caught Poe's attention. He and Ligeia cautiously stepped towards it through the darkness. The floor was covered in wet straw and littered with objects that might have been bones, but the writer felt it was wiser to not examine them too closely.

When they arrived at the far wall, they saw a fierce, athletic man with a starkly chiseled face, his arms and legs bound with ropes, dangling upside down from a gruesome torture device, above a pool of pitch black liquid. He appeared to be in bad shape, possibly close to death. His semi-naked body was covered with the grisly evidence of recent torture. Blood dripped from his wounds into the pool with clockwork-like regularity.

Poe shuddered when he saw the dark, menacing shapes of small carnivorous fish, splashing to the surface in greedy delight whenever the blood hit the water.

"Is he dead?" whispered the writer when he had recovered enough from the extraordinary spectacle to speak.

"I... I don't know," said Ligeia.

A wheezing sound from the hanging warrior answered their question.

"My God! He is alive," cried Poe. He turned towards the man. "Can you understand me?" He motioned to his companion. "Maybe we can get him down..."

But the warrior, his eyes still closed, said in what sounded strangely like Southern-accented English, "Please. I wish only to be left to die an honorable death."

"You wish to die?" said Ligeia. "Why?"

There was a long pause. Finally, the man answered reluctantly, every word dragging out of his mouth as if they defied the warrior's desire to keep them locked inside.

"I failed in my mission. Because of me, my adopted people are all dead. Death is all that I deserve."

Poe looked at Ligeia, raising his eyebrows in a mute sign of surprise. "We will leave you alone if that is what you truly want; but first, could you at least tell us where we are and how we can get out of here?"

The warrior remained silent, lost in his grim meditation.

Poe made a last try and grew more insistent, "We're strangers here, like yourself, it seems. We're from a place called Baltimore and..."

Suddenly, the man's eyes snapped open. He looked at the writer with curiosity.

"Baltimore?" he said.

"Yes," said Ligeia. "We come from the Other World; I am Ligeia, an Enchanter of Seth, and this is Mr. Edgar Allan Poe, born of that world. We were on a mission for the Enchanter Montressor when we were captured and transported here by the Mountain Gnomes..."

"Montressor. The Other World," the man muttered almost inaudibly. Then, he stated, "You are the Otherworlders I was charged to meet."

Poe was still trying to figure out the proper answer to this when the stranger uttered a screeching war cry, which reverberated throughout the cell. Before they could react, the man had swung his upper body, caught the torture device in his mouth, and begun to manipulate it. After few seconds, it clanged open, plunging the warrior into the black pool.

The waters immediately erupted with the horrifying sound of snapping jaws and the fierce splashing of the carnivorous fish. Ominous, dark-colored bubbles broke the surface.

"Why, the man is clearly mad!" said Poe, eyes wide in astonishment.

"We must do something," said Ligeia.

"Yes, but what? I cannot possibly jump in there after him. It would mean certain death."

They stood uncertainly at the edge of the black pool. After the first few seconds of feral violence, the waters had quieted and, except for the occasional, foul-smelling bubble, remained generally undisturbed.

Suddenly, the warrior leapt from the pool with a huge splash that drenched the writer and his companion with the stagnant water. He nimbly landed on his feet in front of the amazed captives. Gone were the ropes that had bound him, chewed away by the deadly fish. If it were possible, he looked in even worse physical shape than he had before. Numerous bleeding wounds inflicted by the voracious inhabitants of the pool marred his body. A nasty-looking fish was still gripping his shoulder in its teeth, but the man just ripped it off casually and threw it to the ground, another bit of flesh going with it. Poe could not help but flinch at the sight.

The stranger's body may have been in shreds, but his eyes burned with a passionate flame that made anyone looking into them dismiss the warrior's physical condition as a minor, irrelevant and, at worst, temporary, inconvenience. They were the eyes of a man with a re-newed sense of purpose, a man of pride, a man who had plumbed the depths of despair and had managed to come out triumphant if not unscathed.

"Are you well? You seemed so–helpless before," asked Ligeia.

"I was never helpless," answered the warrior stoically.

Then, he walked to the cell's door in slow, meas-ured steps. There, he stopped, taking a long look at the door, feeling it with the palms of his hands, applying the minutest of pressures. He took a step back, closed his eyes for a second, took a deep breath, and with a prodi-gious kick, sent the door flying into the corridor.

The awed Poe, who looked at the broken door in wonder, and Ligeia, followed the warrior as he ran out of the cell. The writer had often read the expression "cat-like," but he had never truly understood it until that minute. The stranger's movements reminded him of the pacing of a mountain lion he had once seen in a cage at Baltimore harbor, where the great beast awaited shipment to England.

On the other side of the door, a Gnome sentinel lay unconscious on the floor. The force of the door as it had exploded from its hinges had obviously knocked him out. The warrior picked up his sword, and then the three of them started running through the stony corridors, seeking the exit.

Suddenly, somewhere from within the vast depths of the mountain, the unmistakable sound of a gong was heard. It reverberated ominously through the tunnels.

"Blast!" said Poe. "That sounds like an alarm."

This proved to be an accurate, if simplistic, prediction. In the next few minutes, a horde of hostile Gnomes, their weapons drawn and their beady eyes alight with a vicious gleam, ambushed the escapees.

At the sight of their attackers, Poe instinctively shrank back against the wall while Ligeia whispered spells through clenched teeth, without success. Surrender seemed their only option. But the stranger stepped forward to face their foes, an almost manic look in his eyes. He began twirling and juggling his sword in a masterful display of skill. The blade moved so fast that the eye could barely follow it. As if animated with its own life, it jumped from one hand to the other, leaving a trail of cold silver light behind. One moment, it was one place, the next, it was somewhere else.

The Gnomes had stopped in their tracks and were silently looking at the prodigious display with a mixture of awe and contempt, radiating hatred in powerful, almost tangible waves. The looks on their faces left no room for doubt: they knew and feared this man.

At the end of yet one more spectacular sword maneuver, the warrior grabbed the blade from mid-air and held it up, silently, poised in a dramatic gesture. The Gnomes huddled a bit closer together. The bravest of them took a timid step forward, uncertainty showing in his face.

Suddenly, the warrior made a powerful, bellowing laugh, which caused Poe and Ligeia to jump and the daring Gnome to immediately take several steps back. The laughter stopped as suddenly as it had started. And the man, slowly and deliberately, slashed himself several times across the chest, adding fresh new cuts to his already ravaged torso. While he did this, he stared the Gnomes in the eyes and roared in defiance, something that could only be construed as a challenge; a challenge to the death.

He then took a measured step forward.

"Who will be the first to die?"

This proved too much for the Gnomes' frayed nerves. As one, they turned and scattered, howling in panic.

The warrior rushed after them in fevered pursuit, brandishing the sword high, still screaming incomprehensible challenges in the Gnomes' garbled tongue. Poe and Ligeia had no choice but to follow, trying hard not to lose him in the rocky maze.

Huffing and puffing, they soon lost sight of him, although they could hear a commotion ahead, and see rapidly moving shadows in the flickering, sooty light of the torches hanging on the walls. Turning a corner, Poe and Ligeia came to a sudden stop, at last beholding the source of the fracas. The stranger now stood almost knee-deep amidst several hacked-up Gnome bodies, while savagely fighting with three, fierce opponents who looked determined not to share the fate of their late companions.

The blows fell and were parried in a dazzling succession of clangs and sparks. Powerful sword thrusts were avoided with clever feints. The Gnomes occasionally uttered short guttural screams when they felt the sting of the warrior's blade. The warrior, on the other hand, remained silent, pursuing his deadly task with grim determination.

Taking advantage of a concerted assault by two of his friends, one of the Gnomes managed to get past the stranger's guard and stealthily approached Poe and Ligeia. His bloodied sword, and the expression on his face, left no doubt as to the nature of his intentions.

Poe automatically picked up a sword from a body on the floor and held it in front of him, in a grip made slippery by sweat, trying not to show the utter hopelessness he was feeling. This was nothing like the almost choreographed swordplay he had learned at school. As the Gnome raised his own blade to strike, he began to parry the blow. The force of the clashing swords sent vibrations of pain through his arm, all the way to his shoulder, but he did not drop the weapon.

The Gnome smirked. The creature was a skilled bladesman and, with a swift thrust, he sent Poe's own sword flying against the wall.

The Gnome prepared to deliver another, sure-to-be fatal, blow. Poe stood there, counting the last seconds of his life, his mind numb.

Ligeia made a quick gesture in the air, which merely produced a few, bright, blue sparkles. That was all her magic could achieve inside the Gnome Mountain's atmosphere of pure evil.

But, the warrior, who was still fencing with his own two opponents, saw the blue lights and, turning around in a flash, threw a dagger. The weapon flew through the air and came to rest embedded in the neck of the creature. The Gnome dropped his sword, brought his hands up to his neck, gurgled, vomited a bucketful of foul-smelling, dark-greenish blood, and then collapsed at Poe's feet.

"Thank you, Miss Ligeia," said the writer, dazed.

"You're welcome, Mr. Poe," said the Enchantress, "but truth be told, it is *him* to whom you owe your thanks."

However, by his brave and providential gesture, the warrior had exposed himself. One of the Gnomes seized the momentary advantage to plunge his sword into the stranger's right arm, his sword arm. The stranger pulled back, wrenching the sword out of his attacker's hand. The blade remained stuck in his flesh, piercing it through to the other side. Poe and Ligeia gasped, afraid that this might turn the tide of the battle against their ally.

But the warrior laughed the same glorious laugh as before. With his bare, free hand, he grabbed the embedded sword and wrenched it free. His wound bled profusely, but he did not seem to notice.

The disarmed Gnome and his companion stopped, mouths agape, almost paralyzed by the gory feat they had just witnessed.

The warrior seized the moment and used their momentary stupor to quickly dispatch the two creatures, one blade in each hand, smiting down the Gnomes simultaneously in a brief and amazing display of sword skill. One of the creatures fell with a sword sticking from his chest like an obscene appendage. The head of the other Gnome rolled macabrely across the stone floor.

The stranger then turned. He wiped his bloodied sword on his loincloth, and put one finger to his lips, making a "hush" sound. He then picked up two more swords, which he gave to Poe and Ligeia.

They continued running along the damp, stony corridors in silence, the warrior in the lead, until they reached an intersection. They faced two corridors, one leading to the right, and the other to the left. The stranger stopped and pondered.

"Which way?" asked Poe, while the warrior stood in concentration.

He finally pointed to the right, and that way they ran for a while, huffing and panting, with Poe and Ligeia trying not to fall too far behind. But, as Poe and Ligeia turned a corner, they almost slammed into the stranger, who had come to a sudden halt in the tunnel. Poe took a peek to see what had prompted their protector to pause, and what he saw caused him to inhale sharply.

Just ahead of them, the corridor led into a large cave, lit by huge overhanging braziers and decorated with hideous carvings. It was filled with Gnomes in ceremonial armor, armed to the teeth, all chanting what Poe now remembered had been described by his captors as the "sacrificial songs."

When the three humans appeared, the Gnomes turned around and the chanting abruptly stopped. Poe recognized Basso, the leader of the troop that had captured them in the mountains.

"Wrong way," said the warrior without the least touch of irony in the statement. Indeed, Poe found his matter-of-fact attitude slightly disturbing under the circumstances.

The Gnomes were growling and readying their weapons: gently caressing a mace, softly pulling a sword from its scabbard, eagerly polishing a dagger on a flint stone.

The stranger lost no time assessing their position. He immediately turned around, almost plowing into Poe, who was standing right behind him, and started running back in the direction from which they had come.

This seemed to signal the Gnomes to start in pursuit, urged on by Basso's loud shrieks.

Following the warrior, enveloped by the screams and maniacal sounds that were erupting behind them, Poe and Ligeia ran past the intersection and, this time, went left.

Left led to a steep, winding stone staircase. The warrior seemed tireless, but the young writer and the lithe Enchantress were soon panting and wheezing breathlessly. The spiraling stone steps felt truly endless. The blood pounded in Poe's temples. A red haze fell over his eyes like a curtain. Still, stopping was out of the question, as certain death was rushing at them from below. Helping each other, Poe and Ligeia managed to keep sight of the warrior, who gestured to encourage them to move faster. They climbed ever higher, the sound of their pursuers far too close behind, until they reached a platform that jutted out from the rock, suspended over a black void.

An eerie wind howled around the platform and cut through their clothing with the sharpness of a knife blade. The three humans fanned out on the terrace. They had reached a dead end and there was no way down other than the staircase they had just so painfully climbed.

The awful cacophony that emanated from the stairs made it clear that the mob of screaming Gnomes would be upon them in mere seconds. The fugitives noticed that a large, metal-reinforced wooden door separated the platform from the staircase. This the warrior slammed and bolted, hoping it would keep their attackers away, if only for a small while.

The gesture had been just in time, for almost immediately, the crashing sound of metal against wood was heard, as axe blows were frantically delivered to the other side of the door. Poe watched the door, wondering how long it would take until it finally gave way. Meanwhile, Ligeia had been inspecting the perimeter of the terrace, looking in dismay at the black void beyond.

"We appear to be trapped here," said Ligeia.

"What the blazes are we supposed to do now? Jump?" said Poe, and edge of bitterness in his voice.

At that very moment, the tip of an axe blade pierced the door. As if that was not enough, the warrior gave another of his loud, eerie cries causing Poe to almost fall off the platform with surprise.

Before the writer could react further, there was the sound of some great, unseen beast flying towards them from somewhere above in the unfathomable darkness.

"Yes," said the warrior.

"Yes, what?" said Poe.

"We jump," said the warrior as he stepped off the platform and fell into the great void below. Poe stared after him in shock.

"It now appears clear that this man is mad!" he said.

More axe blades pierced through the door. A big chunk of wood flew onto the platform and a snarling face appeared and grinned when he saw Poe and Ligeia standing huddled together on the edge of the abyss. The macabre hum of the sacrificial songs had begun again. The writer stood hesitantly, contemplating their choice of death at the hands of the cackling Gnomes behind the wrecked remains of the door and certain death if they jumped.

"I believe I would rather take my chance with the Gnomes," he said.

"We mustn't! We have to trust that man," said Ligeia. "He was sent by Montressor."

"You want to trust a madman who dove into a pit of flesh-eating fish?"

"Indeed!" said Ligeia, who seemed to radiate an aura of clarity and confidence. She seemed to be experiencing no panic nor anxiety, just a feeling of ultimate certainty about the right thing to do. She stepped towards the void and jumped.

In a clumsy effort to grab his companion, Poe leapt forward and he, too, fell into the blackness, screaming, just as the Gnomes finally broke through what remained of the door.

As they fell in the stygian darkness, time seemed to stand still. Only the whistling of the air whooshing past their ears, and the occasional light streaming out of an aperture in the Gnomes' mountain, enabled them to measure their speed. Poe was reminded of the fall of the proud Angels who had defied the Lord at the beginning of Time.

Suddenly, *something* rushed by, making a sound like a sail being battered by the wind; it was a massive, flying carpet, twelve feet in length. The stranger stood upon it, his arms extended, directing the carpet's flight through unseen means.

The warrior guided his carpet smoothly between Poe and Ligeia, carefully matching the speed of their descent. Then, he grabbed each of them by their collars held them thus, suspended in mid-air, in an impressive display of strength and concentration.

The warrior released the two onto the carpet's surface.

Poe wiped the sweat from his brow.

"Are you quite all right, Miss Ligeia?" he shouted to his companion.

"Yes, Mr. Poe, I am. This is truly wondrous!"

When he heard this, Poe rolled his eyes upward.

The carpet looped into an upward spiral that took them above the terrace from which they had just fallen, and then even further upward. Poe could see the enraged Gnomes below, but none of their arrows or projectiles could match the ascending speed of the magic carpet.

After a last loop over the top of the malevolent peak, they flew away into the darkness.

"You have not yet told us your name!" Ligeia shouted to the stranger to be heard over the wind.

"I am Gullivar Jones."

Ligeia

Once upon a time…

It happened that, during her initiation, the soon-to-be Enchantress Ligeia came to the city of Danjhar, one of the Tiny Kingdoms of the South, by the river Guli.

Ligeia was lithe and beautiful, with flowing black hair and striking violet eyes. She was sparkling and vivacious, and radiated a powerful energy that made those who approached her happier with their lot. More than one visitor who came to pay his respects left convinced that he, or she, had been blessed by the gods.

Ligeia was dressed in the traditional shimmering blue garment of the Enchanters of Seth. She had settled in Danjhar because she felt that there, she could best put to good use her natural gifts and the arts she had learned from her master, the powerful Montressor.

Upon her arrival, Ligeia quickly earned the trust of old King Laghren and soon became his adviser and confidant. Her influence was good, the kingdom prospered, and the citizens were happy.

One day, the King and the Enchantress were taking their daily walk in the palace's vast gardens, discussing affairs of state and the gossip of the court, when Ligeia felt compelled to depart from their usual itinerary and push further into the woods. Absorbed in the conversation, King Laghren did not notice, nor object.

Eventually, they came across a small building made up of sturdy reeds and almost entirely covered by clinging vines. An extraordinary silence reigned there. The leaves did not whisper in the wind as they did elsewhere. No bird dared sing in the foliage. One did not even hear the tinkling of the many fountains that decorated the King's gardens.

The dark, green vines that covered the small edifice had sprouted a few huge, crimson flowers that spread a powerful, heady perfume, contributing to the intoxicating atmosphere of the place.

"I have never been to this part of your gardens before," said Ligeia. "It is very beautiful, but rather strange. What is this building?"

The King remained silent for a while, then shrugging off any reservations he might have had, told his companion, "It is the Aviary of King Ghea the Magnificent, one of my ancestors. He was obsessed with birds. He used this place to breed and raise extraordinary new kinds of birds. My gardeners do not like to come here."

But Ligeia's curiosity had been piqued. She pushed the rusted door and entered the aviary. Inside, the silence was, if anything, even more oppressive than it had been outside. The small building was seemingly empty, littered with old, broken cages and discarded bird toys. Left untended, the grounds had begun to decay and nature was eagerly reclaiming the building.

Reluctantly, King Laghren followed Ligeia inside. The Enchantress' curiosity had been satisfied and she was prepared to leave, when suddenly the King let out a small gasp. Ligeia turned and saw the King pointing towards a corner of the aviary.

There, in a cage that looked new and not in the least rusted, stood the most beautiful bird the Enchantress had ever seen. Its feathers appeared to be made of the purest gold, and the white of its tail brightly shone in the darkness of the aviary. Ligeia could not understand how such a jewel of a bird could have escaped her notice, but then the bird began to sing a melodious trill, and she quickly forgot her concerns.

Entranced by the beauty and music of the bird, the King gently opened the cage and extended his hand. The bird flew out and landed on the King's arm.

Moving almost in accord with the bird's lulling song, the King and the Enchantress then walked slowly back to the palace.

The King had a new gold cage brought to his room for the bird. The cook was ordered to bring the finest seeds and a saucer of the purest water to feed the King's new companion.

From that day onward, King Laghren ordered that the bird be brought with him on all occasions. It stood there, in its cage, singing during council deliberations. And its music exerted a strange, compelling influence on all who listened to it. Matters of state rested unattended while the councilors listened to the wonderful trills in a transfixed state. Some sang softly under their breath, singing songs that had not been heard in Danjhar for generations–since the time of King Ghea, in fact.

As more and more of the court's affairs came to revolve around the wonderful bird, a certain torpor began to seep through the Kingdom of Danjhar. Taxes were no longer collected. Diplomatic missives with the mighty Confederation of Edora were left unanswered. Public works ground to a halt.

Of all who listened to the bird, only Ligeia and Thirios, the wise old Chancellor, seemed relatively unaffected.

"I have never heard a more troubling song," Thirios confided to the King, after a particularly unproductive meeting where all the participants had sat entranced listening to the wonderful songs. "Even I had to exert the last ounces of my will to restrain myself from humming. With your permission, Sire, I think the bird should be banned from the council chambers."

"Never," said the King. "This bird is mine and goes where I go." And he looked tenderly at the beautiful golden bird that sat in its cage.

"But, Sire, the kingdom..." begged the Chancellor.

The bird then sang another wonderfully inspired trill. The King, without taking his eyes off it, sighed deeply.

"His song is the most beautiful thing in my entire kingdom, and I can't bear to be separated from it." He then made a gesture of dismissal.

"A bird that sings so beautifully is not an honest bird," grumbled the Chancellor under his breath as he left. "He should get rid of it."

The following night, the King was deeply asleep when, suddenly, he was awakened by a voice calling him.

"Let me out, my Lord."

He sat up in his bed, rubbed his eyes and looked around the room, but saw no one.

"Let me out, my Lord," said the voice again. It was a woman's voice. A young woman's voice.

Now King Laghren was truly awake. For a fleeting moment, he considered summoning his guards. But the voice began again, begging him.

"Please, let me out, my Lord."

It seemed to come from the bird's cage.

The King took several hesitant steps towards the cage, not believing his senses. With a shaking hand, he opened the little door and the bird gently flew out.

Then in mid-air, it began to transform and change into a beautiful young woman. She had glowing, golden skin and radiantly shining silver hair. Her eyes were a deep emerald green and her smile was truly entrancing.

"I am Maliere," said the apparition in a trilling voice. "Will you marry me?"

And so powerful a spell had her beauty and her voice woven that King Laghren just nodded his head.

The next day, Ligeia came to the palace for the morning audience, as was her habit, and was surprised to see Maliere sitting to the right of the King, in the place of Chancellor Thirios.

"Where is the Chancellor?" she inquired.

"I am the Queen," replied Maliere. "The Kingdom no longer needs a Chancellor. I had him walled in a cell this morning. You must now obey me, as do all the others."

Ligeia looked at the King, but Laghren lowered his head and refused to meet her gaze.

"I will not," said Ligeia.

"Then wall her alive next to the old fool," ordered Maliere.

The guards came and escorted Ligeia out. Naturally, it was a simple matter for an Enchantress, even one as young as she, to cast a Spell of Oblivion. Mere minutes later, she was walking through the palace unhindered.

She decided to go looking for the Chancellor. She explored all the cellars, calling through the doors of the cells, but in vain. She then walked outside the walls of the palace. She was pondering where to look next when, suddenly, she heard a weak voice that seemed to come from beneath her feet. Bending down, she noticed a small crack between the stones that made up the foundations of the castle.

"Thirios? Is that you?" asked Ligeia.

It was indeed the old Chancellor, who told her how he had been arrested at dawn by the guards and, after refusing to obey Queen Maliere's orders, had been walled in a cell without food and water, condemned to die horribly.

Ligeia used a Spell of Replenishment to provide the old man with food and water. Then she decided to try to talk with King Laghren–alone.

But as she walked towards his apartments, she was confronted again by Queen Maliere and the guards.

"The King is sick. You can't see him."

Ligeia tried to force her way in using one of her spells, but Maliere seemed to be impervious to the Enchantress' magic. Having thus reached a stalemate of sorts, Ligeia turned and went back to her home in the city. But the Queen was now more convinced than ever that she had to get rid of the Enchantress.

She went out in the gardens and walked through the grounds until she reached the old aviary of King Ghea. There she sang a trill that no human throat could ever have sung. Two more birds, one silver and one bronze, came flying out of the shadows.

"You have to help me get rid of Ligeia, my sisters," said Maliere. "Tomorrow, I'll use my powers to send her here on some kind of errand. You must then capture her and kill her."

The next day, a guard came to tell Ligeia that she was summoned to the palace. She was led to Queen Maliere, who was sitting next to Laghren as before. The Queen was smiling and her singsong voice exerted a powerful attraction that even Ligeia found hard to resist.

"The King would like you to go back to the aviary and fetch him one of the beautiful red flowers that you saw the other day."

Ligeia left the palace, wondering what was behind the Queen's request. She decided to consult her master, Montressor, who had recently returned to Seth. She opened her sketchbook, and flipped through the pages until she came across a beautiful, vivid watercolor of her master. She then used a Spell of Communication to tell the Enchanter of the situation in Danjhar.

"I remember King Ghea the Magnificent," hummed the voice of Montressor in her mind. "He had the insane notion of binding some of the Demons into bird shapes! Ha! Ghea the Mad, he should have been called. I think I have come across a reference to this Maliere before. However, I must search the Great Library. Contact me again tomorrow, I'll have more information for you. In the meantime, you better find out what she wants, but be exceedingly cautious. These demons are not to be trifled with, and you're still only an apprentice."

Ligeia thanked her master. Reflecting upon his advice, she finally decided to take her horse and ride to the aviary. As she approached it, she whispered a Spell of Protection, then spurring her mount onward, holding tight to the reins with her left hand, she managed to pluck one of the crimson flowers with her right hand without stopping or dismounting. She saw that two women, one with silver-like skin and the other bronze, had been waiting in ambush for her. They tried to cap-

ture her with a net made of gold threads, but her strata-
gem had thwarted their attempt.

Arriving at the palace, she gave the freshly cut
flower to a guard.

"Tell the Queen that Ligeia has returned from the
aviary and here is the flower that she sought." Then she
rode away back to town.

The next day, Maliere again summoned Ligeia.

"The King now wants one of the bird toys from inside the aviary," she said.

Ligeia silently nodded. Outside, she again contacted
Montressor.

"I haven't yet managed to find the information I'm
looking for," said the mental voice of the Enchanter.
"But I can tell you that your Maliere is one of the
Xanaïs. They're dangerous demons..."

"I think I met two of her sisters yesterday, though
very briefly," smiled Ligeia wryly.

"I must locate the Scrolls of Seramize. She hunted
down and exterminated the Xanaïs during the Time of
the Dark Rain. Do not take unnecessary risks, Ligeia."

But knowing the nature of the threat she faced had
only strengthened the young Enchantress' resolve. She
put on a great cloak that covered her from head to toe
and walked stealthily back to the aviary. Once there, she
pulled up her hood and whispered the Spell of Invisibility. Immediately, she disappeared from sight.

Walking silently on the tips of her toes, she entered
the aviary. She clearly saw the two Xanaïs waiting for
her, this time clutching deadly golden scythes, fierce,
savage expressions on their faces. But the two furies did
not see her, nor did they hear her as she gently picked
one of the bird toys from the ground. Folded inside the

cape, the toy became invisible too, and Ligeia was able to walk away safely.

Back at the palace, she gave the toy to a guard. "Tell the Queen that Ligeia has returned from the aviary and here is the toy that she sought," she said, wickedly smiling.

This time, Maliere cursed her clumsy sisters; but even more, she cursed Ligeia.

Meanwhile, Ligeia had returned to her lodgings and was in contact with Montressor again, apprising him of her latest encounter with the deadly Xanaïs.

"I have found the manuscript I sought," said the Enchanter. "Seramize knew the secret of these creatures. Here is what you must do…"

Later, Ligeia, now disguised as one of the palace guards, proceeded towards the aviary. One of the Xanaï was standing near its entrance. The young Enchantress fearlessly approached the creature, pretending to be unaware of the danger.

"Lady, the Queen wants to see you," she said, playing the part of the unwitting man-at-arms.

"Who sent you?" said the Xanaï suspiciously.

"She asked me to come herself."

"And who might you be?"

"I'm her staff sergeant."

"Why didn't she come herself?"

"I don't know, but she muttered something about that accursed Enchantress, Ligeia."

"Very well," said the Xanaï after a thoughtful pause. "We will go, but we shall lock you inside this aviary. If we find out that you lied, little man, we will eat your eyes when we return."

The two Xanaïs locked Ligeia inside the aviary with a rudimentary spell. After they were gone, the Enchantress smiled and shook off her disguise. She then used the forbidden spells imparted to her by Montressor to gain entrance to the Xanaïs' hidden place, beneath the weave of the world.

She found herself inside a dark and confined space, in which burned the light of three small resplendent jewels: one was bronze, the other silver, but the most magnificent of the three radiated a pure, golden light.

"That must be Maliere's life," thought Ligeia. Grabbing one her silver daggers, she struck the bronze jewel. It shattered easily, as if it were the shell of an egg. She did the same to the silver jewel.

But the golden jewel, she took and buried inside her cloak. Then, slipping again through the weave, she stepped back inside the aviary.

The miasmic evil that had surrounded the place for so long had all but dissipated. The leaves were whispering in the wind, and even the shy birds had returned, singing a few tentative notes to celebrate nature's triumph.

Ligeia walked back to the palace, where she found Queen Maliere, pale and wan, in a prostrated state.

"I hold your life in my hand," said Ligeia, revealing the golden jewel. "I now ask you to free King Laghren of your spell, and leave this land. Go beyond the Nihan, or cross the Sarkean Sea if you wish, but never return."

"I will not. I am the Queen of Danjhar now, and the King will be dead before morning," raged Maliere. The Xanaï then stood up and summoning all of her evil powers, prepared to strike Ligeia where she stood.

But the Enchantress had merely to close her fist around the golden jewel in order to crush it.

As dust seeped between her fingers, Ligeia saw that, likewise, the Xanaï was turning to fine gold dust, and soon there was not even that, for the wind had blown her away.

"What happened here?" said King Laghren entering the room, looking like a man who had just awakened from a long and powerful nightmare.

"Queen Maliere is gone, My Lord," said Ligeia.

Later, once the Chancellor had been freed, the old man remarked rancorously, "a bird that sang so beautifully is not an honest bird. I am glad we are rid of her."

"But her song was the most beautiful thing in my entire kingdom," the King sighed deeply.

'Mid Dark Thoughts of the Grey Tombstone

The travelers had flown long hours through the seemingly endless night. The stars were far more numerous than in any night skies that Poe had ever seen, and the conspicuous presence of the two moons once more reminded him that he was no longer on Earth.

On ancient Mars the night was as deep, enveloping and palpable as a woolen blanket. It felt to the writer as if they were flying in a straight line, but he could not be sure and knew nothing of their destination. Gullivar Jones had mentioned the city of Melek, where he had friends, but that had been meager explanation. The warrior spoke little, ignoring Poe's entreaties, and finally they had settled into an uncomfortable silence, broken only by the soft whistling of the night air.

Ligeia had long since fallen asleep. The writer, too, began to feel the weight of the accumulated tension and concomitant exhaustion. His eyes became heavy and he had started to dose off when Gullivar Jones woke them. The warrior pointed towards a lone source of light in the darkness. At his silent behest, the magic carpet changed its course to fly towards it.

As they got closer, they saw that the light was a huge bonfire, a campfire burning brightly at the center of a cathedral made of giant, white pillars. Upon closer examination, the "cathedral" was revealed to be a long dead forest of giant, petrified trees, which had once reached high up into the sky, their leaves searching for the rays of the Sun. Poe had never heard of trees growing to such gigantic proportions, and had not believed such a thing possible before that moment.

A tribe of golden-skinned natives with green hair was gathered around the fire, partaking of various exotic foods. The presence of chariots drawn by horse-like creatures confirmed that these were wanderers.

Gullivar's carpet landed smoothly on the ground, permitting his riders to merely step off of it. The warrior then rolled up the carpet, and tied it to his back.

He humbly approached the oldest member of the tribe, who was sitting by the fire surrounded by others of his people, occasionally taking a puff on a long-stemmed pipe.

Gullivar made a short bow, then said something in an alien tongue; to his utter amazement, Poe realized that he understood. "Peace, Elder. May we share your fire this night?" The writer began to realize that maybe the creatures he had met until now had not spoken English after all, but that instead Ligeia had cast a spell enabling him to understand the local languages.

The Elder waved his arm in invitation.

"Welcome, Gullivar Jones of Nûr! May the gods be with you!"

Gullivar pointed at Poe and Ligeia.

"These Otherworlders are under my protection," he said.

The Elder nodded.

"If they travel with you, they too are welcome here," he replied.

Gullivar Jones nodded a last time to the Elder and walked to a spot apart from the others. Poe had the sense that a very codified ritual had just taken place, with certain forms that had had to be obeyed. He instinctively guessed that, from that point on, they were safe, or at least as safe as the golden-skinned men could make them.

The warrior unfurled a blanket on the ground, then sat down, pulled out a flintstone and began to sharpen several throwing weapons, all of which looked fierce and deadly.

Poe looked from Gullivar to the Elder and the other golden men lost in their silent contemplation of the flames. He shrugged in resignation, then walked over to the Elder, and bowed clumsily.

"Er, good evening! My name is Edgar Allan Poe," he began clumsily. The Elder kept puffing. The writer beckoned to Ligeia that she should come closer. "And this is my traveling companion, Miss Ligeia…"

As Ligeia stepped into the light of the fire, the golden men suddenly became animated and many of them moved closer. A hushed murmur spread through the crowd.

Then, as one, they bowed their heads to the young woman, while humming a low, tuneless mantra.

"In this hour of darkness, the Malachites' hearts rejoice to see that you have returned, O, Ligeia of Suman," said the Elder.

Ligeia looked uncomfortable. Her eyes darted right and left. Poe realized that she had not expected to be recognized so soon, and cursed himself for a fool to have mentioned her name. He might have inadvertently hurt their mysterious mission.

The sound of the mantra increased. In a strange and mysterious fashion, it looked as if it was starting to have an effect on the Enchantress. She began screaming.

"Elder! Please make them stop!"

Poe put her arm around the young woman's shoulders in a protective gesture, and looked pleadingly at the Elder.

"Stop, I beg you!"

The Elder made a gesture with his hand. The mantra immediately stopped. The golden men raised their heads again.

"We mean no harm, O Ligeia. You are much blessed."

"What is he talking about?" Poe asked Ligeia.

But the Enchantress didn't answer. No one said anything. They all stared at her, the expression on their golden faces unreadable. The atmosphere remained tense. The Elder finally gestured that the visitors should join him by the fire. Hesitantly, they did.

"We're from a place called Baltimore," said Poe. "That's on Earth. Can you help us?"

Nobody answered. The silence became oppressive. After a while, the writer decided to try again.

"Can you help us or not?"

"*He* will help you," said the Elder.

"Who will?"

The Elder pointed at the warrior, sitting apart from the rest of the tribe.

"Him? Who is he anyway?"

"He is Gullivar Jones."

"That tells me nothing."

"Do you want to hear the Lore of Gullivar Jones?" said the Elder in a voice heavy with ritual implications, almost like a priest asking someone if he wants to partake of the Holy Communion. Poe did not understand this, but nodded his assent.

The Elder immediately began to recite a long, po-
etic stanza in a resounding voice. "Hear the Lore of Gullivar Jones! Last of the Great Clan which once ruled the
Land east of the Desert of Tears! He who destroyed Phra
and fought the Noltoi..."

He stopped to take a puff on his pipe. Poe grabbed
the opportunity to interrupt him.

"I do not mean to be rude or cause distress, but I
would prefer to hear the whole story at another time. For
now, I would simply like to know if he can help us or
not."

The Elder was displeased at being interrupted. The
other Malachites also looked disappointed at not hearing
the rest of the story, although Poe had the certain impression that they all knew it by heart anyway.

"He will," said the Elder reluctantly. "However,
you must do what Montressor wants," he added, myste-
riously.

"What does that mean? What could Montressor
want from me?"

But the Elder would not say more. The writer
turned towards the other Malachites, but they too refused
to speak.

Poe turned towards Ligeia. "Miss Ligeia, please
talk to me. Has this anything to do with our 'mission?'
Why are we here?"

But the Enchantress remained as mute as their
hosts.

"Very well!" said Poe dejectedly. "It is clear I am
not to be told."

Gullivar Jones watched the scene and smiled enig-
matically. From somewhere beneath his cloak, he pulled
out a small flute and began to play.

Far to the West lay Seth. Circumstances had been difficult for the once great city since the evil Enchanter Rodrik-Usher of Mazan had conquered it. From his metal tower, he now ruled the South with an unbreakable grip of fear.

The top of Rodrik-Usher's grey tower stood silhouetted against a stormy, night sky crisscrossed by lightning. The crashing sound of thunder was familiar to the residents of Seth as the Arcane Mountains formed a buffer between the Desert of Tears and the Sarkean Sea beyond. Rodrik-Usher's tower vibrated beneath the blows of the storm, appearing to catch the lightning itself upon its oddly shaped metal extrusions.

In the belly of the grey tower were Rodrik-Usher's dimly lit dungeons. These contained row upon row of iron cages, all with slaves whose hands were manacled through holes in the bars, so that they seemed set out like pieces of meat on a butcher's rack. In some places, instead of hands were bandaged stumps. And not all the hands thus grimly displayed were human.

One of the slaves shrank back in horror as she saw a pair of repulsively withered hands, covered in putrid, decaying flesh, the bone showing in places, jut out of the darkness and grab hers. The slave was a young blonde woman with the fine features characteristic of the plains of Dorgé.

The awful hands began touching, examining and massaging her own. No matter how hard she tried to pull them back, she could not, for they were solidly held in place by the iron manacles.

"Beautiful. Just beautiful," said a sibilant voice in the darkness. It was the voice of Rodrik-Usher, who was also called the Damned.

The evil Enchanter stepped closer to the cage to take a better look. He was accompanied by his dread servant, the scarlet-clad, wraith-like Red Death, who was once, it was whispered, Andrevar, an Enchanter of Seth himself. Behind him stood two of his azure-clad soldiers, and the Jail Master, a hairy, bare-torsoed brute.

Rodrik-Usher moved on along the row of cages to inspect other hands, alternately praising and rejecting. Finally, he returned to the slave whose hands he had first examined. He made a quick, imperious gesture to the Red Death. In her cage, the woman began screaming. The Red Death raised his scimitar and, in an elegant arc, sliced off the chosen victim's hands. The scream of pain amplified, but did not manage to completely obscure the obscene, hissing sound of spilling blood.

Rodrik-Usher bent down to pick up the hands which had fallen into a wicker basket lined with white silk, now fast turning to scarlet as it soaked up the blood. The evil Enchanter quickly muttered an arcane ritual under his breath and the woman's hands appeared to decompose and melt over and onto his own like soft wax. Rodrik-Usher then began rubbing his hands together gently, as one would if covering them with a fine unguent. When he turned again to face the Jail Master, even that brute could not repress a shudder. No matter how many times he had seen his master's work, he could not accustom himself to the horror of it; arms that had moments before held withered, decaying flesh, now boasted a pair of fine woman's hands.

"Fresh, soft, sweet; feel the power coursing through them again," whispered Rodrik-Usher.

The woman was still screaming and crying in her cell, although more softly as she slowly bled to death.

The Enchanter turned to look at her, as if acknowledging her presence for the very first time.

"Thank you for these. I will use them well," he said. He then raised his stolen hands, which had once been hers, and sent out a bolt of eldritch energy, which struck the woman in the chest. Her screaming stopped abruptly as she collapsed in a lifeless heap inside the cage.

Rodrik-Usher smiled at the hands, pleased at the results.

"Perfect!" Then, turning to the Jail Master, he added, "I will return when Eelesh is high in the sky to select a fresh pair. Now, get rid of that!" He pointed at the bloodless body in the cell.

The brute bowed and led his master back to the door.

As the dread Enchanter was crossing the great hall, on his way back to his study, two of his men arrived, pushing before them a whimpering creature who was none other than Basso, the leader of the Mountain Gnomes. The Gnome was writhing and trying to break free of his captors' grip, while shrieking an unending flow of nearly incomprehensible babble.

Something in what the creature said caught Rodrik-Usher's ear, for the Enchanter suddenly halted and, after ordering his men to stop, turned to interrogate the captive.

"Two Otherworlders, you say, and you let them escape. How did that happen?"

The Gnome, realizing that he had landed himself in even worse trouble, fell to the ground and groveled. He babbled out a series of long-winded explanations in his bizarre, garbled tongue.

"Gullivar Jones, as well! What was he doing there?" interrupted Rodrik-Usher. Then, as the Gnome started to embark on another long-winded story, the Enchanter silenced him with a wave and demanded, "Yes, yes. The woman. Describe the woman!"

The Gnome did, to the best of his limited abilities, realizing that his life now depended on the whim of the dread Rodrik-Usher, undisputed lord of all he surveyed. Having finally run out of descriptions and excuses, the Gnome fell silent. A long pause ensued, while the Enchanter pondered what the creature had told him.

"This is interesting. Very interesting," said Rodrik-Usher finally.

The Gnome, seeing a shining ray of hope in this comment, volunteered his further services to go after the great Rodrik-Usher's prey. But the Enchanter distractedly waved his suggestion away. "No, right now, I feel you would be more useful to me as compost," he smiled.

Turning to the Red Death, he pointed at Basso. "Andrevar, take him to the Ring of a Thousand Agonies and have some fun with him."

Rodrik-Usher turned his back on the imploring Gnome as the Red Death and the soldiers dragged him away. His face now bore a dark frown, one that few of his courtiers had lived long enough to recognize.

In the camp of the Malachites, by the dying embers of a bonfire, Ligeia dreamed...

In that dream, a group of nine robed men, each holding a staff, were gathered as if in prayer, chanting.

Then, the scene became bathed in a deep, bright azure glow, and a loud rhythmic sound began to dominate the chanting. It reminded Ligeia of a giant heartbeat. Even though the booming sound drowned out the chant, the Enchantress could hear the voice of the nine men now repeating her name in cadence. It became so powerful, so overwhelming, that she woke up whimpering.

Had someone been watching her at the very moment she crossed the threshold from the land of dreams into wakefulness, he would have noticed a faint bluish glow in her eyes when she first opened them. But that, too, like the dream images, vanished; leaving only an odd aftertaste, no more than a cobweb of an impression in a corner of the young woman's mind.

Ligeia looked around her. Everything seemed peaceful. The Malachites were soundly asleep, and so was young Mr. Poe, who had proven to be so brave and so endearing. Yet, she could not suppress an uncontrollable if brief shudder as the last of the dream images faded away.

Just then, she saw Gullivar Jones, still sitting, still awake, still playing softly on his flute. Their eyes met. The warrior stopped playing, and put his index finger to his lips. Reassured, Ligeia lay down again, curled up in her blanket and went back to sleep.

This time, she did not dream.

Eventually, dawn came and with it, a beautiful, pale sunrise illuminated the horizon. In the daylight, the white pillars that were the giant petrified trunks of a once vibrant, ancient forest stood out in stark contrast against the rocky plain.

Everyone was awake and busily moving around. The Malachites were preparing to break camp. The men were harnessing their mounts while the women took their places at the heads of the chariots. The youngsters were packing supplies and burying all traces of their passage.

Ligeia went looking for Gullivar Jones, who was no longer at his post. She finally found him in conversation with the Elder. The warrior was dressed in full regalia, leather pants and shirt, boots and cloak.

"Thank you for sharing your fire, Elder."

"May the gods be with you on your journey, Gullivar Jones."

Gullivar bowed to the Elder.

At that moment, Poe walked over and, after making a warm if somewhat forced good morning to the warrior, asked if he was going to help them get home.

Gullivar pondered the question for a while, then said, "Eventually," and immediately proceeded to walk away, leaving the writer once again to ponder the meaning of his words.

"Do not be so eager to leave this world, Mr. Poe," said Ligeia. "We have much to accomplish here."

"Good morning to you too, Miss Ligeia," said Poe. "I presume you are referring to this mysterious 'mission' of yours?"

"Indeed, I am."

"I do not desire to appear rude, but I wish you were more forthright. Your uncle–pardon me, your mentor– Mr. Montressor appears to have lured me to your house under dubious pretenses. And you, in turn, brought me here. As I said, I would never dream of refusing my help, especially to a lady as charming as you..."

"You are too kind, Mr. Poe."

"...But I would expect a certain degree of forthrightness, and the assurance that you plan to return me to my own world, once your business here is concluded."

"Alas, Mr. Poe, such assurances are beyond my powers to provide, but I can swear by all that is holy that Montressor and I only feel the deepest respect and friendship for you. We would never do anything to harm you. And my teacher was most sincere in his praise for your work. You are a remarkable artist, Mr. Poe. Any world would be a much darker place without you in it."

Although Poe felt that, perhaps, he was being flattered by the Enchantress, Ligeia's face radiated such honest admiration and kindness that he couldn't bring himself to doubt her words.

"Thank you, Miss Ligeia," he said genuinely moved.

"As for your entirely legitimate concerns about the role we have to play here, I can only repeat that all will be fully revealed to you in due course. You must trust me for only a little while longer. Can you do that, Mr. Poe?"

"I... I think I can, Miss Ligeia."

"Very well. Then, let us rejoin Mr. Jones, whom Montressor has charged with escorting us."

In the meantime, Gullivar had unfolded his magic carpet, which was gently hovering a foot or so above the ground.

It was a large, strong rug of faded Oriental coloring, and looked as if it was made of camel's hair. The strangest thing about it was its pattern; although it was threadbare in places, the design still existed in solemn, age-wasted hues. It was much like a star map. In the center appeared a circle, such as might be taken for the Sun, while here and there, *in the field*, as heralds say, were lesser orbs which from their size and position could represent smaller worlds circling about it. Between these orbs were dotted lines and arrowheads pointing in all directions, while all the intervening spaces were filled up with woven characters halfway in appearance between Runes and Sanskrit. Round the borders, these characters ran into a wild maze, a perfect jungle of an alphabet through which none but a wizard could have forged a way in search of meaning.

Gullivar Jones gestured to Poe and Ligeia to step onto the carpet and sit down.

Hesitantly, Poe did so, followed by the Enchantress. The writer was surprised to find the fabric felt firm and unwavering beneath him. It felt not unlike being inside a canoe. He grabbed one edge of the carpet while Ligeia grabbed the other. Gullivar Jones stood up, like a captain standing at the prow of his ship and at his silent command, the carpet obediently took off. In no time, they were fully airborne. The Malachites' camp receded into the distance as the trio sped away.

They were flying over a giant "sea" of waving, flame-colored grass, which Gullivar Jones called the Burning Plains. Ligeia looked cold. She hunched up her shoulders, trying to protect her face from the biting wind. Poe, meanwhile, looked as if he still had not quite gotten used to the sensation–new to him–of flying. He looked mildly uncomfortable and had frequent attacks of hiccups. Jones still stood upright, peering ahead into the distance.

The monotonous landscape quickly bored Poe. Looking at the sky, he saw that it was remarkably empty and he suddenly realized that there were no traces of life anywhere, either above or below.

"I gather from your accent, Mr. Jones," said Poe, in an attempt to make conversation to while away the hours, "that you, too, hail from America. From the South, if I were to make a guess."

"And you would be right, Mr. Poe. I'm from White Lodge, Georgia. I was a poor Navy Lieutenant, with the honored stars of our Republic on my collar, and an un-deserved snub from those in authority in my heart, when I wished myself transported to this world. And thanks to this wondrous carpet under our feet, so I was."

"A most promising beginning for a story. I should like to hear more."

"That would take more time than we have, I'm afraid."

"Indeed?" said Poe. "How long have you been on Mars?"

"I have lost count, but by Earthly reckoning, per-haps a little over 150 years. A benefit of living here, you see."

"Truly amazing! So if I were to stay..."

"But you won't, Mr. Poe," said Gullivar, with an air of finality.

"How can you know this for certain?" asked the writer, puzzled by the warrior's tone.

"Because I come from the year 1905, and I know *your* story well, Mr. Poe..."

Suddenly, without warning, a fierce gust of wind buffeted the flying carpet. The writer wondered if Destiny itself had not intervened to prevent further revelations about what lay in store for him.

Before Gullivar or Poe could react, Ligeia lost her grip, cried out and fell.

Suddenly, the fiery grass rose up in the air to grab the young woman. The reddish matter stood revealed as the claws of horrid, crab-like creatures, which tried to grab the terrified Enchantress, who screamed in terror.

But Gullivar was even faster. He got the carpet to execute a loop-de-loop and, when it swooped down like an eagle after its prey, he managed to pluck Ligeia right out of the air, before she could hit the deadly ground.

Poe clung to the edge of the carpet for his life, but he sensed that, somehow, the wondrous carpet's magic was protecting him from the full impact of gravity. As for Gullivar Jones, he still stood, his knees slightly bent, his arms outstretched, riding the wind like Icarus reborn.

The monstrous, red claws kept rising up, writhing as the land crabs screamed in anger, trying desperately to capture their prey, but they were already higher than the beasts could reach.

In a matter of minutes, only a small bump in the rust-colored plain marked the spot where Ligeia had almost perished.

Gullivar gently deposited the Enchantress onto the carpet; the young woman was still shaking violently from fear. The warrior appeared moved by her terror, but was unsure of how to comfort her. He waited a moment for her to get her emotions under control, then awkwardly patted her hand.

All of a sudden, Poe pointed towards the horizon. In the middle of the grass stood an isolated stone mausoleum, attached to the ruins of a rampart that might once have been part of a massive fortification.

"What's that? Can we land there, Mr. Jones? I think Miss Ligeia could use a rest," he said.

"Agreed," replied Jones. "We have been flying for far too long. It will be good for us to stop for a while."

The warrior directed their flight towards the tomb. As they got closer, Poe realized that it was much bigger than it had at first appeared. It was covered with statues and carvings, and was surrounded by a permanent, misty fog. The remnants of the fortified walls created a terrace in front of the gaping doorway leading inside the monument. It looked like a perfect place to land.

The flying carpet did this gracefully, and its riders stepped onto the stones.

"Are you well, Miss Ligeia?" asked Poe.

The Enchantress did not answer, her eyes had glazed over and again glowed faintly blue. Her whole body grew rigid as she experienced another vision–the same one she had had the night before; the nine azure-robed men and the powerful blue glow, which called to her in a booming voice: "Ligeia! Ligeia!"

In her dream, Ligeia began walking towards the glow, while in the waking world, she walked towards the mausoleum's yawning entrance in a trace-like state, until she disappeared inside.

"What is happening?" said Poe. "Where is she going?"

"I don't know," replied Gullivar. "She just wandered off; we'd best go after her."

The writer had not waited for the warrior's advice and had already begun to run after his companion. Gullivar barely had time to look up and shout a warning.

"Mr. Poe! Wait! Don't go inside!"

He rushed after the writer, but it was too late; before the warrior could catch up with him, he had already stepped inside the tomb.

A huge slab of stone slammed down and closed off the mausoleum's opening. Gullivar pushed against the stone with all his considerable strength, but to no avail. The entrance was completely sealed off. He searched high and low for a hidden mechanism or some kind of pressure lever that would cause the stone to slide back, but there was nothing to be found; Poe and Ligeia appeared to be trapped within the edifice.

Having failed to enter the tomb from below, Gullivar decided to fly over it and look for an entrance from above; but as he unfurled his magic carpet, his senses suddenly alerted him to a new threat.

Grabbing his sword in his right hand, he whirled around and assumed a defensive position. What he saw almost caused his stern façade to crack. An 18-foot tall, black-furred, monstrous spider-like creature was clambering down the side of the tomb. Where its face should have been was the pallid torso of a man, his flesh albino-white. The man-thing portion of the spider had two arms that ended in claws, bulbous, bottle-green eyes and slobbering jaws. The monster left no doubt about its intentions, for it had no sooner set foot on the ramparts then it ponderously began to move towards the warrior, seven of its massive clawed legs touching the ground while the eighth was raised, ready to spear the impudent gnat who had dared profane its domain.

Gullivar eyed the creature carefully, measuring its strengths and attempting to evaluate its weaknesses. As it got within reach, the spider-monster made a surprisingly agile jump, trying to crush the warrior, or at least suffocate him within its unspeakable embrace.

But Gullivar had anticipated such a move, having fought the spider-swarms of the Noltoi and the Beast-Men of the River of the Dead. He nimbly sidestepped the creature and used the opportunity to sink his blade into its soft belly. The spider-beast made a deep, raucous roar of pain and anger, but to his horror, Gullivar saw little blood spill from the already-closing wound. The monster appeared to be almost invulnerable!

Meanwhile, within the intricately carved interior of the mausoleum, Poe was still chasing after Ligeia. Fortunately, the level on which they found themselves was comprised of only a handful of small tombs, radiating from a central shaft with a spiral staircase.

He caught up with the Enchantress in a large, empty tomb, barren of either sarcophagus or other fittings, with the exception of two vertical, gem-encrusted carvings on the wall, seemingly made of sapphires. Ligeia suddenly shook herself, appearing to be free of the strange spell that had controlled her. With eyes that contained just a hint of quickly fading blue, she looked at her surroundings in puzzlement.

"Why are we here, Miss Ligeia?" asked Poe.

"What are you talking about, Mr. Poe?"

"You were behaving very strangely and led us here with a great sense of purpose," said the writer. When Poe realized that the young woman was back to normal, he looked around uneasily and began to wonder about the tomb. "There's something unwholesome about this place," he continued. "I suggest we leave immediately."

He grabbed one of Ligeia's hands, telling himself that the urgency of the moment fully justified the impropriety of his action. But as he touched the young woman, she collapsed and fell at his feet.

Poe kneeled on the ground and bent forward to listen to her breathing, which appeared normal. The writer thought that she had again succumbed to whatever dark magic had drawn her inside this evil edifice, and resolved that they should leave it as soon as possible.

Carefully, he lifted Ligeia into his arms. He was a strong young man, and her small body felt inordinately light in his arms. Holding her gently, he started walking back the way they had come.

Behind them, the two carvings began to glow, creating a portal of light that bathed the tomb in an eerie, unearthly blue incandescence that seemed to kill all other shades and colors.

The image of Rodrik-Usher appeared through what Poe realized was another magical gateway. The evil Enchanter's face bore a benign, almost friendly expression.

"Ah! I've found you at last," he declared.

"What are you talking about? Who are you, sir?" asked Poe.

"I am Rodrik-Usher, a friend. I detect you are an Otherworlder. May I ask the same question? Who are you?"

"My name, sir, is Edgar Allan Poe. What do you want of me?"

"I want to help you, Mr. Poe. Your friend is sick and she needs my help. You must come to me quickly."

"And, pray tell, sir, why should you care about us?"

"I want to make up for the evil deeds committed upon you by Montressor, the scoundrel who banished you to this world."

"I see," said Poe, noncommittal.

"I can cure Ligeia and send you home, Mr. Poe," continued Rodrik-Usher, "but only if you trust me and not Gullivar Jones."

"Why? What has he done?" inquired the writer, becoming increasingly suspicious of the figure in the mirror.

Rodrik-Usher feigned surprise. "Surely, you've realized by now? Gullivar Jones is not your friend. In order for him to return to the land you call America, which he, like yourself, called home, someone else must take his place here. That is the reason Montressor, and this poor, misguided young woman, have lured you here, Mr. Poe..."

Meanwhile, on the ramparts outside, Gullivar Jones and the black-furred spider-beast were still locked in deadly combat. So far, the warrior's superior skill and agility had enabled him to escape from the monster's crushing embrace. But his repeated blows served only to enrage the creature further and did not appear to cause it the least bit of significant damage.

Gullivar's body told him that he could not hope to prevail in a test of endurance against the indefatigable monster, while his intuition warned him that the real battle was actually taking place elsewhere–very probably inside the tomb. Therefore, he had to gain the upper hand, or risk failing in his mission, and probably losing his life as well, although the latter was of minimal concern to a warrior of the Clan of Nûr.

As the monster again turned to grab Gullivar, the warrior slipped beneath its grasp, and with lightning speed, rolled under and between the creature's many legs. In passing, Gullivar made a stab with his sword into the monster's belly, hoping again that that part of the creature's anatomy would be more fragile than the rest of his carapaced body. His hopes were dashed in that respect, but he did have the satisfaction of hearing the spider howl in what seemed to Gullivar a definitely angrier voice. The Earthman smiled to himself, he had gained the position he sought, standing behind the monster, and the time necessary to jump on the creature's back.

Holding to the spider's human torso with his left arm, Gullivar delivered a powerful slicing blow to the creature's neck. Its head burst open, like an overripe melon, drenching his hand in foul-smelling pus. The spider-beast jumped violently into the air, screaming while attempting to shake the man off of his back. Even though its head was gone, its human-like arms bent backwards, trying to eviscerate the warrior with their claws.

Gullivar tried holding on by stabbing the monster repeatedly in the chest and the back, the way a mountaineer would plant a piton into a rock to keep a hold, but to no effect. The creature managed to grab his hand and tear away the sword, and was then able to sent Gullivar flying through the air until he slammed into the hard stone walls of the tomb, a few feet away.

The enraged spider-beast rushed towards the groggy warrior, murder and unholy hunger written in what remained of its face.

"You were always a sacrifice, intended to take Gullivar Jones' place on Mars," explained Rodrik-Usher in his smooth, unctuous voice. "Montressor traded you to him, in exchange for his help."

The most effective lies are always the truth seen through the distorting prism of evil. No one knew this better than Rodrik-Usher, whose rule extended from Seth to the far lands of Dorgé.

To someone like Poe, who felt he had been lied to and exploited his entire life, it should have been a simple matter to heed the evil Enchanter's words and act accordingly. Yet, the writer could not bring himself to easily trust the sinister figure standing before him.

"Why should I believe you, sir?" he asked.

Rodrik-Usher smiled benevolently. "Montressor is cunning," he said. "He has cast a Spell of Enslavement over young Ligeia. The poor thing has had her memories tampered with by that abominable man. But I plan to restore her to her rightful place..." (*I must not overdo it,* he thought. *The Otherworlder may be naive, but he is no fool.*) Then, the evil Enchanter showed his withered hands. *It is good that I did not yet get a new pair*, he thought. "Look! This is Montressor's work," he added. "He destroyed my beautiful hands. (*More truth, but with a slight omission.*) Step through the Gate. Come to me and I will send you home," he begged.

I don't trust him, but I don't see what other choice I have, thought Poe. *At least, this gives us a chance of getting out of here.*

Still not convinced, the writer turned towards Rodrik-Usher again. "What exactly does Montressor want with Miss Ligeia?" he asked.

There was a small pause while the evil Enchanter quickly weighed how much truth ought to be used. "He believes she is in league with a demon far, far more powerful than..." he began.

As he heard this, Poe made up his mind. The verbal attacks the strange man had directed at Montressor and Gullivar Jones had not really bothered him. But Ligeia was something else. Poe had come to know the young woman and felt he understood her true nature. It was not even in the realm of possibility that she was in league with any demon. Every fiber of his being now sensed that Rodrik-Usher was lying. Further, he now knew for certain that they were in a deadly trap.

Unaware of the writer's dawning realization, Rodrik-Usher continued, "All I want is to get you home safely and take care of the girl." The Enchanter smiled what he hoped was an ingratiating smile that would be convincing enough to persuade Poe of his sincerity. "You have my sacred word that I will help you as soon as you step through the Gate." *He is mine!*, he thought.

If Poe could have looked at the other side of the Gate, he would have shrunk in horror at the sight of Rodrik-Usher's blue-garbed soldiers preparing to seize them as soon as they crossed through.

Still, the writer must have had a notion of the fate in store for him, for he said very politely, "I am most grateful for your offer of help, sir, but all the same, I think I will take care of Miss Ligeia myself and find my own way home. Now, if you will excuse me..."

He turned around and began to walk back the way he had come. Suddenly, Rodrik-Usher's voice snapped like a whip, no longer kind and mellifluous.

"I did not give you permission to leave, Mr. Poe."

Poe found that his feet no longer obeyed his will. In fact, not only was he unable to step forward, but he found himself turning against his will and walking back towards the Gate.

"I am sorry," he said, trying to somehow gain enough time to reclaim control over his body. "I thought we were finished."

"Oh no, we are most definitely not finished, Mr. Poe," said Rodrik-Usher, gloating. "Come to me," he added, crooking one of the fingers of his ghastly hand.

This is most definitely not good... thought the writer, as he took another step towards the Gate.

Outside, Gullivar Jones, battered and exhausted, had managed to roll out of the way of the monstrous spider-beast just in time to save his life. He found himself backed up to the very edge of the ramparts.

Many feet below, the horrible red crab creatures that made up the Burning Plains somehow sensed that fresh prey might be coming. The flame-colored claws rippled and began to form a hungry, quivering mass under the walls.

When the monster again lunged towards him, certain now of its kill, Gulliver threw himself over the edge, falling towards the rapacious crabs below.

But with a lightning-fast gesture in mid-air, the warrior unfurled his flying carpet and landed safely on its surface!

The spider-beast was not so lucky. Moving too fast to stop, it lost its balance and went over the side of the ramparts.

At the last minute, it managed to grab onto the edge of the crenellated walls with one claw, and hung there, trembling.

Gullivar quickly flew over the ramparts, then past and behind the tomb. When the carpet emerged on the other side, the warrior was no longer on it.

Having found a window entrance on an upper floor, he desperately raced down the spiral staircase, looking for Poe and Ligeia.

Gullivar burst into the room just as Poe, still holding the Enchantress, was about to walk through Rodrik-Usher's Gate. The evil Enchanter saw the warrior at the same time the Earthman screamed loudly, imploring the writer to stop.

"Quick! Come through the Gate!" shouted Rodrik-Usher.

But suddenly, Ligeia woke up. In a flash, she became aware of the situation and, shaking off Poe's embrace, got back to her feet. Hastily, she uttered a Spell of Repulsion. An invisible hand slammed into the writer, sending him reeling backward into the opposite wall.

"Miss Ligeia! No!" screamed Poe.

Inside his sanctum, a seething Rodrik-Usher unleashed a magical bolt at the Enchantress through the Gate. Blue fire erupted from two of his bony fingers, and like living sapphire snakes, the flames zoomed forward towards the young woman. She found herself surrounded by a ball of azure fire. Poe saw her body become entirely rigid. The tip of her toes barely touched the floor as she was dragged inexorably towards the Gate.

Gullivar pulled a small, glowing ball from beneath his cloak and threw it into the magic portal, at the same time that he grabbed hold of Poe.

"Run!" he shouted.

The ball hit the Gate just as Ligeia was being pulled through it. Rodrik-Usher held his hand forward and shouted a Spell of Neutralization, but nothing prevented the ball of light from growing larger and brighter. He finally had to step back and his silhouette disappeared in the golden shine.

A huge, silent explosion of light engulfed the room.

When the light eventually subsided then vanished, the room was as empty as it had been before. On its walls, two pieces of crumbling sapphire that had once been carvings, and were now no more than dust, fell softly to the floor.

Andrevar

Once upon a time...

On the western edge of the Desert of Tears, on the flanks of Mount Arcane, lay the city of Seth, home to the Elders of the Golden Race, who had once retreated to this isolated location after the Time of the Great Fear.

The city was an odd jumble of towers and spires, mismatched levels and crooked temples, which had been built, layer on top of layer, over the centuries. None, save perhaps its Great Librarian, knew what structures lay beneath its foundations.

Seth was not beautiful, nor did it convey the same impression of raw temporal force as Qiml or Galehault. Yet, from it radiated an aura of imperceptible yet very real power.

To Seth came those seeking ancient knowledge and enlightenment. The journey was arduous, for only one road led to the city. It crossed the Desert of Tears, and the Burning Plains before that, but that was good because enlightenment should not be too easily come by. To Seth also came those seeking power and mastery of the forgotten sciences. These seekers were treated with the same equanimity as the harmless academics, for in Seth the man-made laws did not always apply.

The sole authority recognized in Seth, if such a thing truly existed, was that of the Great Librarian and that of the Brotherhood of the Nine, the highest and most powerful Enchanters of the city.

To Seth had once come Rodrik, son of Usher, Baron of Mazan, a young man already filled with seething hatred and boiling rage. Rodrik-Usher had been tutored by Andrevar, one of the Nine, until the time had come for him to go out in the land, to prove himself as Enchanter.

Then Andrevar had passed on, as must all in the end, even Enchanters of Seth. Sanahujee of the Lute was appointed to take his place among the Nine, instead of Rodrik-Usher, and no more was heard of the latter for many years, to the satisfaction of many.

The storm clouds often broke over the port of Alsabeh by the river Zebi, releasing torrents of rain that washed its great harbor clean of the debris left by the mighty trading junks of Edora. One night, the storm seemed to be focused on a dark, shiny, jewel-encrusted tower that had been erected at the behest of the necromancer Rodrik-Usher, who had established himself in the city.

Rodrik-Usher's influence in Alsabeh had steadily grown over the years, which many resented. Yet, if any resident wished that the lightning would rid them once and for all of his pestilence, he kept these thoughts well buried deep within the recesses of his own mind. There were those who swore that the evil Enchanter had developed the power to read men's thoughts.

If the hatred that the citizens of Alsabeh felt for him bothered Rodrik-Usher, it did not seem to affect him. The tall, pale Enchanter was in his sanctum, bathed in a sinister, blue glow, making mystical passes over a shard of blue crystal. Next to him was a pulpit on which rested an ancient tome, one that he had purloined at great personal risk from the forbidden shelves of the Great Library of Seth.

"Perfect," muttered the Enchanter, pausing to check something in the book. "Do I have everything I need? No, I need the blood of a simorgh..."

Rodrik-Usher gestured towards one of the shelves and a small glass vial came flying into his hand. Cautiously, the Enchanter uncapped it and allowed a single drop of a black, viscous liquid to fall onto the blue shard, where it was absorbed with a hissing sound.

"Oh, Seth, you shall soon rue the day you let Rodrik-Usher tread your putrid halls, for you shall be mine now, to do with as I wish," whispered Rodrik-Usher gleefully. Then, he moved his hands softly over the blue shard while muttering words in a tongue so ancient it had not been heard since the Time of the Great Fear.

As he spoke, a blue vapor seemed to seep from the shard, then grow higher and taller. It began assuming the form and consistency of a vaguely human figure, one made of fine blue mist, animated by its own unholy life. The mist creature began swaying back and forth, while Rodrik-Usher erupted in maniacal, high-pitched laughter.

Meanwhile in Seth, the Enchanter Montressor, one of the Nine, was in residence at his tower, an occurrence rare enough that it had the city buzzing. For it was known that Montressor preferred the company of mortals to the society of his peers.

The tower was generally left in the care of Montressor's factotum, a ferret-headed creature answering to the odd name of Pym, whom the Enchanter had brought back from one of his journeys into the Other Worlds. When his master was absent, Pym kept the tower in shining order. But the return of Montressor also heralded the return of chaos: dishes with uneaten food left out on chairs, books littering the floors, strange artifacts forgotten under the furniture, and a seemingly endless stream of visitors, all eager for news of the outside world. And there were the boxes.

The boxes contained items that Montressor had gathered from all parts of the world, known and unknown, and brought back with him to Seth to enrich his collection of odd and perhaps someday useful objects. Last time the Enchanter had visited Seth, it had taken Pym several cycles to catalog it all.

Presently, the ferret-like creature was opening a box wrapped in nondescript green paper, which his master had only labeled *ztak*. As he opened the box, Pym was blinded by a powerful flash of light. *Ztak indeed*, he thought.

After he had recovered his sight, Pym bent forward to examine the inside of the box. It contained several handfuls of small, white, pearl-like pebbles. The factotum took one of the pebbles in his hand and decided to go looking for his master to ask him under which category it should be filed.

Pym went down a flight of stairs, then crossed the great dining hall, which was currently completely overtaken by more boxes, then went up another flight of stairs and down a corridor until he reached his Master's quarters.

Behind a closed door, he could hear Montressor singing what only someone from a place far, far from Seth would have recognized as an aria from Gounod's *Faust*.

Pym knocked on the door. The singing stopped, and one could hear the shuffling sounds of the Enchanter walking to the door. Montressor was dressed in his favorite blue bathrobe and was holding a toothbrush.

"Yes, Pym, what is it?"

At that very moment, the pebble exploded again in a bursting flash of light.

"Don't tell me. I know why you've come," said the Enchanter after recovering the use of his sight. "This is a pearl from the bottom of the Sarkean Sea, found inside a monstrous fish that was beached near Cape Sahil. I traded a merchant of Suman a second-hand copy of a map to the Fountains of Gade for a boxful of them. Put it with the other sea items, and mark them *handle with care*. It wouldn't do to have them all going off at once."

Satisfied with his master's decision, Pym returned to his filing.

In his jewel-encrusted tower in Alsabeh, Rodrik-Usher sat holding the shard of blue crystal, testing the powers of the blue mist creature he had created.

Finally, satisfied with his servant's prowess, he decided that the time had come to put his great plan in motion.

Under his mental guidance, the blue mist creature left the tower, as if carried by the night winds. It wandered briefly under the twin moons Nooma and Eelesh in the skies over Alsabeh, testing its ability to move. Then, gaining confidence, it zoomed forward towards the south.

Had a madman been crossing the Desert of Tears, or a lone mountaineer the Arcane Mountains, no more than a blue blur would he have seen, for Rodrik-Usher's creature moved at the speed of thought.

Finally, it came in sight of Seth itself, and paused while Rodrik-Usher used his mind's eye to reacquaint himself with the City of Enchanters.

One tower stood out proudly among the jumble: a tall, metallic spire, which sported strange metal protrusions. Rodrik-Usher knew that it was home to Prospero, the Great Librarian of Seth, appointed leader of the Nine. The creature wavered in its direction, then turned back. *No need to disturb Prospero–yet*, thought Rodrik-Usher.

Instead, the blue mist turned towards a more modest tower that was the home of Sanahujee of the Lute. Sanahujee was a shy and retiring Enchanter, whose sole claim to fame was the authorship of a treaty that was considered the definitive study of the musical arts from the Time of the Great Rain to the Time of Ashes.

The mist creature slid stealthily under a bolted window and seeped into the tower. It moved cautiously through a number of different rooms, carefully examining every artifact, looking for magical defenses or hidden booby traps. But it found none. In his trance, Rodrik-Usher sniggered at Sanahujee's naiveté.

Once, and only once, was the mist creature forced to hide, when two servants on a late night errand rushing back to their quarters might have spied it. Rodrik-Usher was not yet ready to be exposed, and he mentally ordered the mist creature to pour itself into a crystal trumpet while the two men ran by.

Eventually, the misty thing extricated itself from the trumpet, pulled itself back into shape and resumed its progression. The layout of Sanahujee's tower was most traditional, and Rodrik-Usher quickly located his goal: his former rival's sleeping quarters.

The mist creature slipped under the door and silently entered the room. Sanahujee was deep asleep at the center of a large bed, buried under a pile of blankets (for the nights were ever cold in Seth) and surrounded by a nest of pillows.

The mist creature slithered up to the bed, then a blue appendage covered the Enchanter's face. It was all over in a matter of minutes.

The death of one of the Nine was always cause for agitation in the otherwise placid Seth, where most of the excitement usually derived from esoteric academic quarrels. Sanahujee's servants had reported finding their master's body dead in his bed, and an extraordinary council of those of the Nine currently in residence had been called by Prospero, the Great Librarian, a tall, gaunt man whose eyes bore witness to the wisdom of the centuries.

Attending the council were: the rotund Montressor, the delicate Fortunato of Samar, the stout and stocky Whorle, the aged Lady Roché, ever wrapped in her blue robes, and Baron Karyuff of Ibhad, a tall, lanky man. Montressor apologized on behalf of Ligeia, presently occupied at his request in the Nihan Mountains. And all knew that Valdemar, the Ninth of the Nine, spent most of his time on the Other World.

"I examined the body," said Karyuff, "and applied every Spell of Discernment I know. I found nothing wrong. It must be a natural death."

"Enchanters just don't pass on in their sleep like that," roared Whorle. "It's not normal."

"Perhaps he had a weak heart, or…"

"No weak heart," interrupted Montressor. "I took tea with Sanahujee a fortnight ago, and he told me he had just been seen by Master Bargel, who had pronounced him fit as a fiddle."

"Master Bargel is not an Enchanter," said Karyuff defensively. "Perhaps he failed to locate a small flaw of the heart, or an engorged blood vessel in the brain."

"I'm inclined to agree," said Lady Roché in her aged, yet still strong, voice. "I myself have caught Bargel in error more than once. He is getting on in years and ought to be replaced."

Seeing Montressor wince, Prospero made an appeasing gesture. "Why don't we reserve judgment for the moment? We have more pressing matters to discuss, such as Sanahujee's replacement."

"I nominate Zenobia," said Whorle.

"And I, Ponnoner," piped Fortunato of Samar.

"Good choices both," agreed Prospero, "but there are others equally worthy of consideration. Let us gather again in a fortnight and each present a worthwhile candidate. Then we will make a choice."

As the Enchanters parted company, each to attend his or her own business, Montressor took Prospero aside.

"A word with you, if I may, Great Librarian," he said.

Prospero gestured him into a private alcove.

"What is it?"

"A thought occurred to me. If Sanahujee has indeed been the victim of some evil machination, which I agree remains only conjecture so far, then there would be only one obvious suspect, wouldn't there?"

A long silence followed. Then Prospero uttered the name that Montressor had not dared pronounce.

"Rodrik-Usher. Is that who you mean?"

"Indeed. He was passed over for Andrevar's seat when his Master died, because we all felt that, despite his exemplary behavior, there was something sinister about him. I sometimes thought that he was Andrevar's revenge for having himself been passed over as Great Librarian during the Time of the Great Fire. It would have been just like Andrevar to do this to us. He was a spiteful old merkul, may the gods forgive me."

"And what happened to Rodrik-Usher?"

"No one knows exactly. I confess that I haven't paid much attention to him. I hope this is not a mistake I'll come to rue. Once, I heard he was in Qiml, consorting with Maurdhaine..."

Prospero winced, for the reputation of the evil Queen of Qiml was known to all.

"Yes, and more recently, I heard he was in Alsabeh, but as you know, my interests tend to lie northward, so I didn't pay it any attention."

"What do you suggest we do?"

"We can do nothing at this stage. If it turns out that it is indeed Rodrik-Usher who has returned to exact vengeance, we will know soon enough, I fear. Meanwhile, I would advise being most vigilant. I intend to take certain dispositions myself."

In his jewel-encrusted tower in Alsabeh, Rodrik-Usher listened with great interest to a voice that spoke from the shadows. "So Montressor already suspects," he said with a cackle. "Pah! Let that fat buffoon believe as he will. My blue slayer is already on the move. By the time the Sun rises on Seth, they will all realize their doom is upon them."

The next morning, the body of stout Whorle was similarly found dead in his bed. No visible cause could account for his demise.

"I admit I was wrong yesterday," said Karyuff, sounding peeved. "But still I have found no signs of any magical attack."

"Neither have I," said Roché. "I think both Sanahujee and Whorle have succumbed to a purely natural agent."

"Do you mean to say that they were poisoned?" asked Fortunato of Samar in a whiny voice. "I can't believe it. This is far too preposterous!"

"Yet it is a strong possibility," said Roché. "We are looking into it."

"Whether magical or natural, we appear to be facing a concerted attack by an enemy determined to eliminate us all," said Prospero.

"Kill the Nine Enchanters of Seth! That is even more ridiculous! Who would do such a thing?" protested Fortunato.

"Rodrik-Usher, for one," piped Montressor.

A long pause followed, during which dark thoughts were pondered by all those in the room. Finally, even Fortunato harrumphed his acquiescence, daring not to put his feelings into words.

"Mind you, it is only a hypothesis at this stage, nothing more," added Prospero.

"If I may be so bold," said Montressor, "there is one thing we could do. All of us here could cast a Spell of Fiery Protection upon the city. That should effectively do away with any kind of magical threat that someone such as Rodrik-Usher could likely muster. That would leave only poison to be faced, and I'm sure, now that we've all been forewarned, we can each come up with our own means of dealing with that."

"A sensible precaution, I agree," said Lady Roché.

"Hear, hear," said Fortunato.

"Fine by me," said Karyuff.

"Well then, since we're all in agreement, let us get to work," said Prospero.

In his jewel-encrusted tower in Alsabeh, Rodrik-Usher received the information with a chuckle. "A Spell of Fiery Protection will be useless against the magic that I control, the magic of the Keepers," he said, brandishing the blue shard. "The only matter to be decided is, whom among the Nine shall be next to die?"

The evil trill of his laughter filled the tower, while in far-off Seth his interlocutor repressed a shiver.

The next morning, it was the body of Fortunato of Samar that was found dead, just as the others had been. This time, the mood in the Council Room of the Great Library was ominous. Only three of the Nine were left in Seth to answer Prospero's summons: Montressor, Lady Roché and Baron Karyuff.

"How can it be magic?" said Karyuff, visibly exasperated. "No magic can breach the Spell of Fiery Protection."

"No mundane magic," said Montressor.

"What do you mean?" said Prospero.

"I can tell by the frown on your face that you have already divined my thoughts, Great Librarian," replied Montressor. "The magic of the Keepers can defeat the Spell of Fiery Protection."

"But Rodrik-Usher, if indeed it is he who is responsible for this, could not possibly have access to the magic of the Keepers," said Lady Roché.

"Not true. Andrevar could have secretly inducted him to the Blue Crystal before he died."

"Andrevar was one of us. That would have meant breaking his most sacred oath!"

"Andrevar was a spiteful man, jealous of our Great Librarian. Even if he did not willfully induct Rodrik-Usher, Rodrik-Usher may have forced him to do it. Andrevar was not quite himself before he died. We attributed it to old age or senility, but perhaps it was something else. We will likely never know the truth now, but it certainly is a possibility."

"A very real possibility indeed," said Prospero, his head lowered in shame. "I have a confession to make. This morning, I personally checked the forbidden shelf of the Library, and one of the tomes is missing. It should have been discovered before, and for this, I bear great responsibility."

"Even if it is Rodrik-Usher whom we face," said Karyuff, still unconvinced, "and he is armed with knowledge of the Keepers' magic, which I still find nearly unbelievable, he does not have access to the Blue Crystal."

"He may not need to, if he was able to acquire a fragment, one of the Blue Shards for example," said Montressor.

"All the Shards were destroyed aeons ago! You yourself saw to it, Great Librarian," said Karyuff.

"Not quite. One was thrown into the Sarkean Sea off the coast of Qiml, if I recall correctly," said Montressor. "It could have been found. By Maurdhaine of Qiml, for example…"

"And Rodrik-Usher was seen in Qiml," said Prospero pensively.

"Let us assume that Rodrik-Usher does have the surviving Blue Shard. The four of us still control the Blue Crystal. We can set up defenses that even he won't be able to break," said Montressor.

"Four Enchanters have never tried to use the Crystal," said Prospero. "There has always been at least five."

"We don't have a choice. It's too late to call Ligeia back from the Nihan, and Valdemar is damned unfindable. We four will have to do. The fate of Seth is at stake!"

In his jewel-encrusted tower in Alsabeh, Rodrik-Usher was unrolling a scrolled map before a triumvirate of blue-clad soldiers.

"The blue slayers are ready to move, my Lord," said one of the men. "We have three legions standing by at the edge of the Burning Plains, awaiting your word."

"I expected no less, General Zumar. My signal shall come soon, very soon. There is but one final arrangement that needs to be made..."

The next morning, the body of Lady Roché was discovered, not dead in her bed like the others, but her throat slit with what appeared to be a ceremonial knife.

"We can no longer command the Blue Crystal," said Prospero, "and we do not have the time to induct new Enchanters. I have just received word that three legions from the west are marching against the city."

"Mere soldiers against our marshaled power?" said Karyuff. "That is a joke."

"I do not agree," said Montressor. "If these are indeed Rodrik-Usher's men, they are backed by the power of the Blue Shard. It will take all our combined strength to just keep at bay whatever monstrosity he has already unleashed. We will be defenseless against an army of that size."

"Do you have a plan?" asked Prospero.

"I think I do. The men are not the problem. Rodrik-Usher is. If he wants the power of the Blue Crystal, he must come here. Let him do so. If we can dispose of him, then getting rid of his mercenaries will be child's play."

"This goes against my nature, but we shall do as you suggest, Montressor. We shall wait for Rodrik-Usher."

In his jewel-encrusted tower in Alsabeh, Rodrik-Usher laughed when he heard the voice of the shadow relay the conversation that was taking place at that very moment in Seth.

"Ha! I smell the legendary cunning of Montressor!" said Rodrik-Usher. "I would wager that he already suspects far more than he is telling you, my friend. But this time, it is we who are playing games with him. I shall indeed come to Seth, but to rule it forever more!"

"First, there is a pressing task to which we must attend," continued Montressor.

The Enchanter stood and began pacing the council room. His face bore an unusually serious expression, and he kept his normally agitated hands folded within the sleeves of his blue robe.

"From the start, I have felt that Rodrik-Usher could not have achieved all that he has without help from inside. And what better help than from one of us, one of the Nine." He then turned towards Karyuff. "You, Baron Karyuff, are from Ibhad, one of the Tiny Kingdoms. And Rodrik-Usher's mother was Maline of Ibhad. That would make you, what, cousins? What has he promised you?"

Karyuff jumped up his chair, his face red with indignation. He waved an angry fist at his portly accuser. "This is a lie! How dare you accuse me!" The two Enchanters glared at each other in fury.

At that moment, a pearly laugh filled the room, a laugh that had been repressed for far too long, a laugh of pure joy, a laugh of pure evil.

"Oh, Montressor, Karyuff! If only you could see your faces now," said the voice of Prospero, Great Librarian of Seth. Except that it was also not the voice of Prospero. From behind his ordinarily wise eyes, an ancient, evil intelligence lurked.

The two Enchanters turned in unison, mouths agape, unwilling to believe their eyes.

"Prospero?" stuttered Montressor.

"I am not Prospero, my friend. I have not been Prospero for a very long time. I am Andrevar! You have all been, oh, so very easy to deceive."

The truth suddenly hit Montressor with the force of a crushing blow in the very depths of his soul. How could he have been so blind? He remembered Andrevar being passed over for the position of Great Librarian. He remembered Andrevar not being himself before his death, a condition blamed on senility. He remembered the missing tome from the Great Library, and the Blue Shard thrown into the Sarkean Sea, where it could later be recovered.

Montressor's understanding was final, full and crushingly complete. It was easy to imagine the honey-sweet words of Rodrik-Usher, tempting his once-noble aged master, perverting him, twisting him, and then, the two of them plotting together the exchange of bodies…

Karyuff's thoughts had followed the same line of reasoning as Montressor's. Impulsive as ever, the Enchanter leaped forward to attack the man who had betrayed them.

But Andrevar was ready. From between the cracks of the stone floor, where it had waited, unseen, the blue mist devil creature materialized and wrapped itself around Karyuff. The Enchanter gasped, struggled, but in vain. In mere seconds, his lifeless body dropped to the floor.

"I shall miss you greatly, my good Montressor," hissed Andrevar. "But you understand that there is no room for one such as you in the new regime."

"Oh, I understand all right, Andrevar. And I confess that I made a mistake, one that will haunt me for a long time. But you and your associate have also made a mistake. You see, I recalled Ligeia from the Nihan as soon as this affair began, and she has not been idle… But that story is for another day, another day that, I am happy to say, you, Andrevar, will not be here to see."

As he finished speaking, with a quick gesture, Montressor violently threw to the floor a handful of the small, white pearls that had once been found inside a fish and that he had kept hidden in his sleeve.

A blinding flash of light, brighter than the explosion of a hundred stars, filled the room as a colossal *ztak* sound shook Seth to its very foundations. Under its sheer brilliance, the blue mist creature evaporated like dew in the sun. In Alsabeh, Rodrik-Usher screamed as his mental link with Andrevar was destroyed in a blinding instant.

When the servants eventually dared enter the council room unbidden, Montressor was nowhere to be seen. They found only a black charred husk on the floor, blind, inchoate and yet not dead. It was the shell of the man who had worn the name Prospero, but had once been born Andrevar.

Meanwhile, in his jewel-encrusted tower in Alsabeh, a recovered Rodrik-Usher became further enraged to discover that someone had stealthily gained access to his tower and stolen the Blue Shard from the secret chamber where it was kept. Its protector, a giant creature brought at great expense from the putrid marshes of Zekar, had been killed with a small dagger made of pure silver.

The mark of Ligeia!

Rodrik-Usher's rage was prodigious, and several hundred residents of Alsabeh died that night in the typhoon that the necromancer summoned. Still, in the morning, the survivors were relieved to see the evil Enchanter leave, they hoped forever.

The jewel-encrusted tower vanished as if it had never been. The ground upon which it had stood remained vacant for many years, until a foreigner from Brange bought it to build a palace. It burned down the first night, killing the man, his family and slaves. After that, no one ever built there again.

Rodrik-Usher entered Seth riding at the head of his blue legions. Left without Enchanters, the city elders welcomed him tepidly. To all appearances, Rodrik-Usher was victorious, having become the first supreme Lord of Seth in the entire history of the Golden Race. Yet, within his dark heart, he felt only seething rage, because he knew that, somewhere, Montressor and Li-geia were plotting against him.

The Melancholy Waters Lie

Another magical gateway stood in lonely isolation in a long-forgotten oasis in the Desert of Tears. The meager rivulet of water that had once provided a haven for the occasional wanderer had eventually run dry, leaving a small, crusty, salt pond behind.

The two carved posts that indicated the presence of a Gate suddenly began to glow. The light increased in intensity, easily dwarfing that of the afternoon Sun, until a powerful *whooshing* noise was heard and Poe and Ligeia appeared together, thrown to the ground, looking dazed.

As the light subsided, they discovered a strange sight: only Gullivar Jones' upper body had been transported through the still faintly glowing Gate. At his waist was a small patch of light. It gave the appearance that his upper half was floating alone in space. His lower body had remained stuck on the tomb side of the Gate, his legs kicking, as he tried to push himself through to the other side.

Poe approached the trapped Gullivar.

"What did you do?" asked the writer.

"I saved you," replied the warrior. "I threw a magical *ztak* given to me by Montressor into the Gate in order to disturb its function. It seemed that I was only partially successful," he added with a rueful smile.

Poe and Ligeia began pulling Gullivar, but they soon realized that, as the Gate faded, the warrior was inexorably being pulled back to the other side.

"You have to push me back," he said. "Otherwise, when the Gate fully closes, it will cut me in half. Quick! I will catch up with you later! But be careful about—"

Ligeia gave a mighty a shove on the warrior's shoulders, which caused his head to be swallowed by the patch of light, and cut off his last words.

As Gullivar disappeared, so did the light.

"I wish we had had time to listen to his warning," said Poe. "It might have been important."

"It might have cost him his life, Mr. Poe," said Ligeia. Then, energetically, she continued, "We have no time to waste. We must be on the move."

Back in the tomb, Gullivar Jones landed on his rump. The patch of light flickered out of existence. The warrior remained lost in silent thought for a moment. Only his clenched fists betrayed his anger and frustration. Then, he stood up and walked outside.

There, he casually glanced at the claws of the black-furred spider-beast which still clung to the edge of the ramparts, while the crab-grass below it rose ever higher into the air.

Gullivar stared at the trembling monster, betraying no emotion. He mounted his flying carpet, and, without looking back, took off.

The creature shook one last time, then suddenly fell, leaving behind a disgustingly soft, meaty sound.

Minutes later, only its claw remained, still clutching at the air, totally still.

Meanwhile, in far-off Seth, in Rodrik-Usher's metal-grey tower, which stood silhouetted against a waning afternoon Sun, the evil Enchanter, wearing a new set of hands, sat on his throne, mulling over dark, Machiavellian thoughts.

The loud sound of a gong reverberated throughout the palace, then a set of double-doors opened, and the Red Death, leading a squadron of azure-clad soldiers, entered.

They were dragging behind them several Malachites, including the Elder who had welcomed Gullivar. The golden-skinned men were in chains. Their bodies were covered in bruises and cuts. Some were bleeding beneath hastily applied bandages. It was clear that they had not been captured and taken to Seth without a fight.

"I hear you have seen Gullivar Jones, Elder?" said Rodrik-Usher with false civility.

The Elder remained silent. His attitude conveyed that they even though they were prisoners, their spirits remained free and unbroken.

"You know that your people only travel the southern routes by my sufferance. I could wipe out your miserable tribes as easily as I snuff a candle. Tell me about the Otherworlders, and I will let you live."

But the Malachites persisted in their silence.

"How dare you and your worthless pack of dogs plot against me?" exploded Rodrik-Usher, all pretense of courtesy discarded. The Enchanter stood and started pacing, occasionally waving an angry fist at the golden-skinned nomads.

"You think you can defy my will? You are fools! I rule the South and soon the entire world as well. You are nothing but insects to Rodrik-Usher!"

The Enchanter turned towards the Red Death.

"Take them to the Place of Silence, while I decide their fate."

The Red Death and the soldiers dragged the Malachites away, hitting them with the butts of their lances to move them forward. Any who stumbled and fell because of their chains, were kicked mercilessly until they got up and rejoined the rest.

Eventually, they reached a set of huge, double doors made of sculpted bronze, secured by an intricate wheel-and-key locking mechanism, guarded by two cloaked guards, wearing strange, visored helmets.

When they saw the Red Death approaching with the Malachites, the guards opened the complicated locks, quickly and smoothly performing a series of complex maneuvers.

The double doors slid open silently, and the Malachites were ushered into what was known in Seth as the Place of Silence.

It looked like a square, empty room, with no windows and no other openings, both floor and walls were composed of slick, white marble. The ceiling, however, appeared to be made of blue crystal. Running along the perimeter of the floor all around the room was a line of black mosaic. The light inside was dim, yet it had no apparent source. It looked cool, quiet and peaceful.

The doors closed behind the Malachites. They cautiously begin exploring the empty room.

"Do you think he will spare us?" asked a young man.

"Not Rodrik-Usher the Damned! He only wishes to prolong our suffering," replied the Elder.

Suddenly, one of the Malachites was pulled up to the ceiling by an invisible force. He was almost squashed by the incredible pressure as he hit the blue crystal with a loud thud.

He began to scream. The Malachites watched in horror as the young man's body began to melt and liquefy, turning into a sickening puddle of blood and flesh, which refused to fall as nature would ordain it, but instead was slowly absorbed by the ceiling itself, which now glowed a dull, throbbing purple. A sound, not unlike that of a monstrous, inhuman heartbeat filled the room.

At this horrible sight, all the Malachites except the Elder ran towards the doors, and started banging on them, begging to be let out.

But the purple glow only intensified, and, one by one, the golden-skinned men were pulled to the ceiling, where they dissolved horribly.

Outside the room, the guards remained impassive as the banging and screaming was rapidly replaced by complete, ominous silence.

After a time Rodrik-Usher approached the guards, they immediately opened the locks allowing the doors to once again slide smoothly open.

It was as if they had opened a doorway into the heart of the fieriest volcano of all the Yamur. A violent, pulsating purple light filled the room. The hissing sound of coruscating energy drowned the alien heartbeat, yet could not completely suppress it. Raw heat blasted through the opening, as well as the pungent, disgusting odor of boiled flesh.

Despite their cloaks and visors, the guards turned away for self-protection. Rodrik-Usher, the Lord of Seth, untouched, unscathed, walked into the room, silhouetted against the inferno.

Silently, the doors closed behind him.

In the Desert of Tears, many miles to the East, Poe and Ligeia were trekking through the desert. They were exhausted.

"Any idea where we're going, Miss Ligeia?" asked Poe.

"Not exactly, Mr. Poe," replied Ligeia, "but I'm sure that, if we keep walking in this direction, we're bound to find some kind of settlement."

"I hope that they will prove less barbaric than some of those we have so far encountered, for without the aid of Mr. Jones, I fear we are fairly vulnerable."

"Speak for yourself, Mr. Poe. I do have certain abilities."

"I apologize, Miss Ligeia. I meant no offense."

"None has been taken, Mr. Poe."

"I certainly am very grateful that you acted to save my life when that villainous Rodrik-Usher had me under his control."

"And I thank you for rushing after me when he had me spellbound," she smiled. "We seem to be managing well enough, after a fashion. We're bound to find a way out of the desert soon."

"Look!"

In the direction Poe was pointing were another small oasis and a Gate. He and Ligeia ran towards them, hope filling their hearts. The oasis did contain some water, and a couple of palm trees, and they were at last able to quench their thirst and eat a few dates to staunch their hunger.

After they had rested, they looked at the Gate. It appeared very similar to the others they'd seen. They inspected it from every angle, but it obstinately remained inert.

"Do you know how to make it work?" said Poe.

"Certainly. I am, after all, an Enchanter of Seth," replied Ligeia.

She began singing a soft melody, but at first, nothing happened. However, as she placed her hands on the Gate, her eyes shimmered with the same bluish glow that had haunted them before and, for a brief second, she heard inside her mind the distant sound of a powerful alien heartbeat.

The Gate suddenly came to life. It vibrated and began to glow softly. Poe was elated.

"My congratulations, Miss Ligeia! I was wrong to have ever doubted you."

The Gate now seemed fully operational. They looked at it carefully.

"I will try it," said Poe.

He took a step towards the opening.

"Remember, Mr. Poe. The Gates are one-way," said Ligeia. "So, just a peek."

The writer put his head through the Gate and it re-emerged out of an ancient stone wall with the usual carvings on it, half-erased by time.

It was about 8 p.m., and a thousand joyful noises were bursting forth from the Boulevard Montmartre–the rendezvous of popular pleasures that has a special place in the memory of every Parisian. The crowds were pressing around theaters whose advertisements promised laughter or tears. Merchants selling cheap baubles added to the ambiance, and even those who did not have three *sous* to get into the latest play by Paul Féval were able to pass their time for free in front of the booth of some successor of the famous clown, Bobèche.

Poe pulled his head back.

"It looks like Earth, but I'm not sure where it is. It certainly doesn't look like Baltimore. Would you like to take a look?"

"Why not?" said Ligeia.

She put her head through, looked around, and then pulled back.

"I'm not an expert, but it looks like it might be Paris."

"Then, that's settled. We'll give it a try. Anything is better than this awful desert."

As they crossed the Gate, Poe wondered briefly if he would ever get home, but the thrill of adventure more than overcame his nagging homesickness.

On the other side, they sniffed the air. It was a mixture of dung and smoke, filth and grease, cheap perfumes and warm chestnuts. Still, it was Earth, and the writer stamped the pavement as if he had just gotten off a boat and needed to feel firm ground beneath his feet.

They had emerged in a small cul-de-sac just off the notorious Boulevard Montmartre. The noise and movement that gave such a unique appearance to the old Boulevard did not, however, extend very far from it. The Château-d'Eau on one side, and the neighborhood of *La Galiote* on the other, were both relatively deserted. Soon, Poe and Ligeia found themselves in the midst of decrepit houses and sordid hovels. Ahead of them was a narrow back-street which led, after a long and tortuous course, to the Rue du Faubourg Saint-Martin.

"Monsieur Poe, Mademoiselle Ligeia, this way," said a rich tenor voice coming from behind them.

They turned around and saw a tall, young, distinguished Frenchman, with piercing dark eyes.

"I am Edgar Allan Poe," said the writer. "Who might you be, Monsieur?"

"I am Auguste Dupin," replied the Frenchman. "I recognized you at once, Monsieur Poe, but I haven't had the pleasure of meeting your lovely companion." He then performed an elegant *baise-main* on Ligeia's hand.

"How could you recognize me, Monsieur? I have never set eyes on you before in my life," said Poe.

"It is true that you do not know me–yet."

"Yet?"

"You are in the year 1840, Monsieur Poe. Our mutual friend, Monsieur Montressor, instructed me to wait for you, at this very spot, at this appointed time."

"1840? Montressor? How could he know?..."

"I am not privy to his secrets, alas. My task in this matter is a relatively simple one. I am to take you and Mademoiselle Ligeia to another Gate, very near to here. I was told that your journey is of the greatest importance. So, if you will kindly follow me..."

Dupin turned around and led Poe and Ligeia through a maze of darkened alleys, until they reached a miserable thoroughfare located between the Rue Richelieu and the Rue Saint-Roch. That street had no official name, except at the point where it cut through the Faubourg du Temple, behind the Maltese workshops. There, a placard identified it as the Rue du Haut-Moulin–but everywhere else, it was popularly known as the Rue Morgue.

The first house in the Rue Morgue, as one entered it from the Rue Richelieu, was a sleazy café whose sign bore the bold pun: *Estaminet de l'Epi-Scié*. This establishment, which had an infamous reputation and was frequently raided by the Police, had a facade facing the Boulevard because of a sharp turning in the street.

Dupin stopped in front of it, and gestured to Poe and Ligeia to wait for him there. From where they stood, they could see the lights of a billiard-room through the red curtains of two windows. One could play pool there, according to a small, hand-written placard set beneath the red lantern, which told passers-by the price of *glorias* and *demi-tasses*: 10 and 20 *centimes*.

Dupin pointed towards a set of double-doors, leading to an enclosed courtyard, located just behind the café. "We only need to get into this courtyard, and you will be on your way," he said. "At this time of the night, someone is bound to come out sooner or later on some kind of errand."

"The Gate is located inside the courtyard?" asked Ligeia.

"Yes. I don't mind telling you, it has caused us some problems in the past. Things have come out of it, that should not walk on this planet. Only last year, a murderous–but I speak too much."

After a few minutes, the door opened and a man of Herculean build, whose wan and miserable face was half-hidden beneath his untidy hair, came out. He wore a leather apron covered with dark, brown spots that could only be blood.

He saw the Frenchman and stopped. His eyes narrowed, then relaxed.

"Dupin," he muttered, by way of salute.

"Marchef," replied the Frenchman. "*Il fait jour*. I have some business inside."

"I don't like your kind of business, Dupin," said the Marchef. "Give me an honest blade and I'll do a honest day's work. None of that heathen magic stuff. It's not Catholic."

"You might be surprised to learn that I agree with you, my good Monsieur Coyatier," said Dupin to the Marchef. "But sometimes, there are unpleasant things we must do which cannot be avoided. Please give my regards to the Colonel."

With those words, Dupin walked inside the court-yard, ushering Poe and Ligeia after him. Inside, it was dark and filthy. The narrow space was cluttered with wooden crates and wine barrels.

"Monsieur Poe, would you help me to move these barrels, please?"

As the writer and Dupin rolled a couple of barrels away from the wall against which they had been stacked, Ligeia ran her fingers on the grimy, sooty surface.

"The Gate is there," she said. "I can feel it!"

"I had the barrels put here to prevent any more in-trusions," explained Dupin. "After you have gone, I will block the passage again. *Bon voyage, mes amis!*"

After they had crossed the Gate, Poe and Ligeia found themselves on a forest path that took them down-hill past masses of conifers. As they reached the bottom, in the distance, between the trees, they saw the sparkling reflections of the Sun on the waters. From its size, they knew they were definitely back on Mars.

"But when are we?" said Ligeia. "We might be too late–or too early."

"If Montressor instructed this Monsieur Dupin to take us to that specific Gate, he must have known it would deposit us just where we must be. Your mentor seems to know what he is doing."

"That is true, but I can't help wondering..."

Suddenly, in the distance ahead of them, on the shore of a reddish sea, they spied the silhouettes of two men fishing.

"People!" said Poe. "We'll find out where–and when–we are."

They hurried towards the two men, but as they got closer, Poe began to feel nervous.

These were not men, but *beast-men*. The writer had once seen an orangutan brought back from the Far East, and the creatures he beheld remind him of that beast– except, possibly, more savage.

"Miss Ligeia, I think we should..." he started.

But before he could complete his sentence, the two beast-men's faces broke into slow and hideous grins, displaying sharply filed teeth!

Suddenly, a small horde of wild-eyed beast-men jumped out from behind the trees and pounced on them.

"Oh, Dear Lord! Not again!" thought Poe, just before a sack was thrust over his head.

The village of the beast-men (they called themselves the Metg, which meant "Chosen People" in their native tongue) stood on a desolate corner of Cape Cheref. It was a primitive village that few ever visited, due to the Metgs' general bad behavior and repugnant eating habits. Lying scattered on the village ground were piles of skulls, skinned bodies and other gruesome things, remains of the Metgs' last foray.

Many times had the Kings of Danjhar, Bukar or Den-Cha embarked on an expedition to solve the Metg "problem" once and for all, but every time, the crafty beast-men had managed to elude their enemies in the cave-riddled mountains and wild forests of Cape Cheref.

The survivors had returned to their burned-down village, rebuilt their tree huts and gone on as before.

As the tightly bound Poe and Ligeia were being carried into the village, a Metg child sucking a thumb–not his own–watched the spectacle with a hungry gaze.

In the center of the village, several Metgs were busy erecting another Gate. The two carved totems were their most prized sacred possessions. After they had been properly sanctified and planted at the correct distance, Rehio, their tribal Chief, began to sing a spell, transmitted by rote through the generations.

Soon, the image of Rodrik-Usher appeared in the glowing Gate. The Enchanter made a gesture and the Metgs removed the bags covering Poe and Ligeia's faces.

"You see, Otherworlder, in this world, all roads lead to Rodrik-Usher," said the Enchanter maliciously.

"I am indeed glad to see you, sir," said Poe with a forced smile. "As you can see, Mr. Jones is no longer with us, and I would now be open to pursuing our earlier line of conversation."

The writer was under no illusion as to what grisly fate was in store for them with the Metgs and hoped that the Enchanter would provide a moderately better alternative.

Rodrik-Usher laughed. "You are indeed a wilier rogue than I thought, Mr. Poe." He then turned to Rehio. "I only want the woman. Throw her into the Gate. The man, you may dispose of as you please."

Poe looked horrified as he realized that he had quite possibly doomed both himself and Ligeia.

"Thank you, O Great Enchanter," said Rehio, bowing. "The Doriô will be pleased!"

"The Doriô?" said Rodrik-Usher, raising an eyebrow. "What an excellent idea."

Meanwhile, two Metgs approached Ligeia and began dragging her, very much against her will, towards the Gate. The young woman kicked and clawed, but her hands were tied and her mouth gagged, leaving her powerless against the beast-men.

"What do you want with her?" shouted Poe. "Let her go!"

Ligeia fought even harder, and suddenly, her eyes began to glow blue. She again started hearing the same alien heartbeat—except that, this time, everyone in the village seemed to hear it as well.

The Metgs looked at her in fear and immediately released her. They stepped back in panic. Several of the beast-men fled in terror. Poe thought he heard the name "Ligeia" muttered throughout the crowd, like the whispers of leaves in the wind.

When he saw what was happening, Rodrik-Usher's face contorted in fury.

"Remain where you are!" he ordered. Then, raising his arms in a magical gesture, he loosed a bolt of eldritch, blue flame, which struck down two running Metgs, turning them to stone. Their momentum caused them to fall, and they crumbled into chunks when they hit the hard ground.

"She is only a woman, you fools! Obey me, or I will destroy you all."

The Chief stood, thinking for a second, then gestured commandingly at the beast-men.

"Obey the Great Enchanter! At once!"

Carefully at first, as if testing the waters of a shark-infested pool, then acting together as a mob, the beast-men leapt onto Ligeia, and knocked her unconscious.

They threw her limp body through the Gate, into the eager, waiting arms of Rodrik-Usher. The Gate then glowed more brightly, and vanished.

Poe, his head down, looked utterly crushed.

Hours later, when night had fallen, Poe was still tied up inside one of the beast-men's huts.

Suddenly, the curtain of beads marking the entrance of the hut was noisily shoved aside. The Chief and several villagers, all dressed in ceremonial garb and bearing torches, entered.

"It is time!" he said. "The Doriô awaits!"

The beast-men unceremoniously dragged Poe outside. He was dumped into a small skiff, with two Metgs already aboard.

This does not seem to be a positive thing, thought the writer.

Rehio got into a larger, more sumptuous boat, decorated with garlands of wild flowers and equipped with a combination foghorn and gong.

The rest of the beast-men, bearing torches and spears, sat in a smaller group of canoes, and soon, the little fleet left the shore to navigate the dark waters.

The two Metgs rowed until the skiff reached an island located not far offshore. It was very small, no more than a patch of land, merely a piece of porous, grey rock, covered with green, slimy moss.

The two Metgs dumped Poe on the island's ground. Then they struck their spears into the island, which seemed to vibrate slightly. At that, they ran hurriedly back to their skiff and rowed as fast as they could to rejoin the main fleet.

The Chief blew on the horn and struck the gong. The sound carried far across the dark waters, resonating in an oddly ominous fashion. All the Metgs began a monotonous and repetitive ritual chant.

On the island, Poe caught the word "Doriô" several times and wondered what new nightmare was going to come next.

There seems to be an awful lot of bad singing going on this world, he thought, dryly.

Suddenly, the dark waters around the island began to roil and churn. With a massive splash, a multiplicity of undulating tentacles broke the surface of the waters, and tried to seize the writer.

Poe screamed in horror as he heard a bellowing roar and saw the top of the Island slowly splitting apart, like a cracked nutshell, revealing a huge opening, lined with rows upon rows of terrifyingly pointed teeth!

Poe grappled his way out of the ropes that bound him and tried desperately to escape the tentacles' grasp, but there was no place to run. The writer knew it was only a matter of moments before the tentacles grabbed him and shoved him into the Doriô's hungry maw.

Almost as if it were answering the Doriô's roar, a piercing cry suddenly echoed in the night sky.

Poe heard a loud splash, as if something had dropped from the sky into the water. His eyes searched the darkness, which was barely broken by the torches of the singing Metgs. As the heaven-sent object burst back to the surface of the sea, Poe's heart leapt with joy. It was Gullivar Jones!

The warrior hacked off several tentacles with his sword, causing the Doriô to roar again, this time in pain. Then, the Earthman set foot on the "island."

"I am glad to see you, Mr. Jones," said Poe.

Gullivar remained silent as he handed the writer a sword. Together, they began to fight back.

Never in all of the Metgs' long history had such a sacrilege taken place. The beast-men were incensed at the profanation occurring before their very eyes, none more so than Rehio, who was screaming at the top of his lungs. They began throwing a hail of spears at the intended sacrifice and his rescuer, but they were too far away, and the weapons splashed harmlessly into the water. The Chief motioned to his men to row closer to their god.

Meanwhile, Gullivar and Poe fought side by side, hacking away at the hideous sea monster. A tentacle surreptitiously appeared from below and succeeded in wrapping itself around Poe's arm. Gullivar went to his rescue, but slipped on the mossy "ground" and fell. His head landed at the edge of the Doriô's gaping mouth, and he was immediately caught in a web of smaller tentacles. He hacked and slashed, but to no avail. He was rapidly being pulled inside the hungry maw. Poe, seeing the plight of the brave warrior, managed to struggle free and ran to his rescue, slicing at the tentacles until the Earthman was free.

As the Metgs rowed closer to the "island," the Doriô's wild thrashings looked ever more frightening to them. Caution and terror soon replaced their religious fervor. The Chief was oblivious to the changing attitudes of his followers, and continued to rave and utter horrible curses. Some of the Metgs half-heartedly tried to row to help the Doriô, but each time they approached, they were driven away by the flailing tentacles.

Rehio at last noticed that his authority over the beast-men was waning. He ordered his own boat to go forward, waving his sword at those who dared defy him. Yet, by so doing, he unwittingly attracted the Doriô's attention. Enraged that another puny creature had come to attack it, the monster scooped up the unprepared Chief and dropped him into its gaping mouth.

The Metgs interpreted this in the only way they could: the Doriô was angry at them, quite understandably so, and their Chief had paid the price. Reacting with panic seemed a perfectly justified reaction, which they did, fleeing back to their village, screaming in terror, rowing as fast as they could.

On the "island," Gullivar took advantage of the distraction caused by the Doriô's capture of Rehio to plunge his sword deep into the beast's throat.

The Doriô screamed mightily, and spewed forth a flow of putrid, black blood. Still bellowing, and severely wounded, the monster began sinking beneath the reddish black waters.

Seeing that the massive beast would drag him and his companion down to the depths, Gullivar screeched his now-familiar cry, and the magic carpet appeared, gliding out of the night air, silhouetted against the two moons.

Before Gullivar and Poe could become fully submerged, they each managed to grab hold of the carpet and flew away.

The Oasis of Shuffa was a beautiful spot on the edge of the Desert of Tears, south of Alsabeh. It had once been used by the miners and prospectors who had spent months in the Arcane Mountains digging for ore and precious gems, before trailing back to the markets of Chemane and Melek to sell them. Such traffic, however, had slowed to a mere trickle since Rodrik-Usher had extended his grip across the South, and now the Oasis was virtually abandoned.

Its main feature was a beautiful waterfall, over-looking a small, blue lake whose waters were said to have remarkable restorative faculties. It was there that Gullivar had taken Poe, flying across the Straits of Dan-jhar. They had reached the Oasis a short while before dawn, and had rested throughout the morning. They were, at last, able to wash themselves and their blood-stained clothes.

While Gullivar was washing in the lake, enjoying the splash of the crystal-clear, pure water against his skin, Poe pulled off his torn shirt and began washing it energetically.

Suddenly, the warrior pressed his arm, with its still fresh wounds, against the writer's raw forearm, causing him to jump and cry out.

"Mr. Jones! What are you doing?"

"We have fought and shed blood together, Mr. Poe. We are now blood brothers. It is the way of the warrior," Gullivar replied. After a beat, he added, "I have had no such brothers for a long, long time."

Poe felt himself moved, "I am honored, sir. I could not feel safer in the company of my own, Earthly brother."

"We are not truly safe until we complete Montres-sor's mission," said Gullivar. "Now we must rescue Miss Ligeia together."

"Indeed..."

Gullivar nodded his appreciation, silently.

"How did you find me, Mr. Jones?" asked Poe as he dried himself with a rough, woolen blanket.

"My carpet sometimes is capable of more than mere flight."

Poe felt that he would never understand all the mysteries of this strange world on which he found himself.

Maurdhaine

Once upon a time...

The ancient city of Qiml stood on the estuary of the mighty river Arlas, south of the snow-capped land of Qiml, far to the north, beyond the fertile plains of Dorgé and the swampy marshes of Zekar. It was dominated by its huge palace, built on top a mound that some said pre-dated even the Time of the Dark Flame. Qiml's trading ships were known in every port, plying their routes from Kesh to Alsabeh. So were its Black Wardens, the feared envoys of its Queen, the lady Maurdhaine, whose beauty was legend and whose wrath was feared from the edge of the Sarkean Sea to the mighty peaks of the Nihan Mountains.

A stranger flew once across the skies of Qiml, before turning back over the reddish waters of the Sarkean Sea, and slowly approaching the city from the west. His skin was burnished, ageless as an old sword that has seen too many battles. His hair was an unusual pale blond. His features were set in a grim, determined expression, and his hooded eyes captured even the most minute of details. The stranger flew a magic carpet. He was dressed in unmatched leathers and skins, variety providing no clues as to his origins.

After a final, leisurely pass across the sky, the man settled to land on a low tower, near the great marketplace. He dismounted and calmly rolled up his carpet before taking a flight of stone steps down to the street.

The markets of Qiml were justifiably famous throughout the Northern Lands. Folk came from as far away as Brange and Samar to trade in exotic furs, pelts, spices, weapons, gems and the occasional poison. The man crossed the market, seemingly uninterested in the bustle that went on around him. The experienced traders cautiously made ample room to ease his passage. Some thought that he might be a freebooter from Kesh, or a pirate from Sahil Island. Others believed him to be a rover from the Yamur Mountains. Others, even more experienced or better traveled, thought he might come from farther South, possibly even from beyond the Nihan, or the great Desert of Tears. All gave him a wide berth, because of his stature and presence.

The man entered a tavern located on the edge of the market. It was the busiest time of the day, when happy traders drink to celebrate their successes, and unhappy ones to drown their sorrows. Yet, even in a place such as this, the stranger experienced no trouble securing a comfortable position at the bar. It only took a glance for two Samarian men-at-arms to obligingly squeeze aside to accommodate him.

The man ordered a drink, then began to question the bartender.

"A good day," he began.

"It could be better," replied the bartender cautiously.

"I am new in Qiml."

"I can see that."

"What employment might there be for wanderers these days?" The term was a more pleasant euphemism for mercenary throughout the Northern Kingdoms.

The bartender eyed the stranger warily. Experience had taught him caution.

"Qiml has finally settled its border quarrel with Zekar," he eventually uttered. "But good soldiers are always in demand... Still, most of the trading caravans have already left, and there won't be anymore until after the Season of Snows. So opportunities may be scarce just now."

Apprised of this fact, the stranger merely shrugged and thanked the bartender with a coin. He finished his drink while taking in the sights of a beautiful dancing girl flaunting her charms on a nearby table. He did not linger long.

After visiting several other taverns, and making similar inquiries, which led to identical results, the warrior considered his options. He had spent most of his money buying food and drinks in the taverns. He pondered whether he should leave Qiml now and travel south. At one of his stops, he had been told that the brigands of Kesh were in a state of quasi-revolt, and perhaps opportunities would abound there.

As the man made his way through the narrow streets of Qiml, walking in the omnipresent shadow of the great palace, he spotted another tavern sign–the *Eye of Lorre*, named after the faun-like divinity of the folk of Qiml. Shrugging, he decided to try his luck one final time.

The tavern was small and plunged in deep shadows, lit only by a fireplace decorated with old swords and shields. The air smelt of stale ale. This was not a place where people came to dance, laugh or be merry, but one where drinkers pondered their fates moodily, over pots of smoking bleane. As the stranger crossed the room, he noticed that it was mostly empty, save for a few lost souls lost in drunken reverie.

The bar was tended by a red-haired girl, with a pretty face and sparkling emerald eyes. From her accent when she welcomed him, the man guessed that she came from Savaria. She smelt fresh, like her native prairies, a pleasant fragrance that cut through the musty air like a beam of sunlight piercing the clouds.

The stranger asked for a drink and repeated his inquiry. Not surprisingly, the girl knew of no employment opportunities for wanderers in Qiml at the present. Or so she claimed, for the man detected an odd reticence in her reply. She had begun to suggest that he ought to travel south when, suddenly, the owner of the tavern appeared, carrying two jugs of alberry wine, entering through a metal beaded curtain that separated the bar from the back room.

"My name is Logay," he introduced himself. Then, frowning, he turned towards the girl, "Jhavane, why did you not inform this good sir of Bossior's request?"

"I guess it slipped my mind," she sulked.

Logay harrumphed. "Someday, it'll slip my mind to pay you, girl. Go and clean the kitchen."

Jhavane left, and Logay addressed the stranger. "Bossior is the Queen's very own Master of Arms, and a good customer of this establishment, which is how I came to be in possession of this information," he whispered conspiratorially, even though there was no one who could hear him. "The Queen is looking for a new bodyguard, to fill the ranks of the Five; it's a very elite corps. You look amply qualified for the job to me," he added, sizing up the warrior with an expert glance. "Besides, truthfully, the job is more like a sinecure."

"What happened to the previous holder of the position?" inquired the stranger.

"Bossior only told me that the job had recently been vacated. But I would think he merely got a better offer from those brigands in Kesh."

Jhavane returned, carrying an assortment of clean bowls and cups. The stranger noticed that she seemed to purposefully avoid his eyes.

"Thank you," he thanked Logay. "This seems worth looking into."

"Why don't you go now?" suggested Logay. "If I know Bossior, tomorrow he'll have the criers on it and the line of applicants will stretch from the palace gates to the statue of Stemos."

The warrior nodded, and left the tavern. After some thought, he decided to follow Logay's advice and walked uphill to the palace's gates. It was a huge citadel of stone and metal. Unlike most palaces, it had an austere look about it, being unadorned with any carvings or sculptures.

In the declining light of the day, with the two moons rising, its great iron gates exuded an air of quiet, obdurate hatred towards the world, the kind of hatred that ugliness often feels towards beauty. It was from here that Maurdhaine, Queen of Qiml, ruled.

Upon entering, the wanderer felt surrounded by the presence of an obstinate looming evil, like a beast refusing to heed his master's voice, meeting him instead with waves of silent loathing. Still, the hour was late, and passing a damp night under the skies of Qiml held no charm.

The warrior hailed a gnome-like guard, who at first looked upon him with deep suspicion, but whose eyes cleared when he heard the name of Bossior. The guard confirmed that there had indeed been a recent vacancy among the Five who comprised the Queen's elite guard, and offered to take the wanderer to the Master of Arms.

The man followed the gnome as he climbed a great stone stairway lined with war trophies and portraits of the ancient Kings and Queens of Qiml. The wheezing guard eventually took the stranger to a training hall where a short, stout man was practicing swinging an axe at a wooden dummy. Bossior was thick, large, with a brutish face and glinting, cunning eyes. Seeing the two men approach, he laid down his battle-axe and wiped the sweat from his brow with a rag.

He curtly dismissed the guard with an imperious nod, then took a long, hard look at the warrior. The man weathered the inspection without the least sign of a flinch. Then, Bossior asked the stranger for his name.

"Gullivar Jones," replied the man.

The Master of Arms frowned, his eyes narrowed, and he took a second, harder look at the wanderer who stood before him.

"I've heard of you," he finally said after a long silence. "You fought Ar-Hap at the Golden Citadel, didn't you?"

"A long time ago."

Another long silence followed. "Hmm... I heard about that fight. It was a good fight. You must be a good man. I was told you're from the South. We don't often see folk from the South here. What brought you to our climes?"

Now it was Gullivar's turn to remain silent.

"I was looking for something," he finally uttered reluctantly. "I didn't find it."

"Hmm…" said Bossior, his face suddenly broken by an evil, cunning smile. Then he immediately added with a wave of the hand, "Don't worry. In Qiml, a man's business is his own. It's enough that you are here. Did you come because you want to join the Five?"

"That depends."

"The job's easy and the pay's good. You'll do well."

"I could use good pay."

"Very well then. Let me show you your quarters, then I'll introduce you to the Queen at tonight's dinner. The Five always dine with the Queen. It's a tradition. But let's hurry, there isn't that much time."

Bossior led Gullivar Jones to an upper floor of the palace, using a series of ever-narrowing flights of stairs, leading to a dark corridor that, in turn, took them to a sparsely furnished yet attractive room. Through a window, the Earthman could see the vanishing light of the Sun setting over the Sarkean Sea.

"This will be your room," said Bossior. "Tomorrow, you can instruct the men to bring your belongings to the palace. Now, we must get to the dining hall at once."

Backtracking, the two warriors eventually reached the great dining room, a damp and dark room smelling of the grease of countless meals caught in musty tapestries. It was lit by too few candelabra. A cadre of the same gnome-like servants Gullivar had seen before was serving the food.

At the head of a long dinner table sat Queen Maurdhaine. She was a tall, not unattractive yellow-skinned woman, with silver hair. She did not look old, rather ageless. Her eyes were like angry emeralds set in the burnished gold of her face.

Bossior first introduced Gullivar ceremonially to the Queen, who looked at the Earthman as one would inspect cattle on the auction block. Finally, she nodded and waved her hand. "I hope this one will prove better than your last selection, Bossior."

"It is my most fervent hope, My Lady," replied the Master of Arms.

Then, Bossior introduced Gullivar to the other four diners: Lhimat, an old, wizened swordsman whose vacant eyes were fixed in a glassy stare; Valyre, a strong, lithe, black woman from Den-cha, who greeted the wanderer with a smile fraught with obscene promise; Burdiay, a young, impassive wrestler from the Nihan; and finally K'ulze, a large, vulgar Keshite who was presently tearing chunks of greasy meat off a bone. It was he who first broke the strained silence, inviting Gullivar to sit next to him.

"You fought in Zekar; I can always tell men who fought in Zekar," he started. "You must look at my trophies sometimes. Did you know that I was behind the victory at Marek's Tower near Gridbhan?"

"Way behind," interjected Valyre with heavy sarcasm.

The remark infuriated K'ulze who began to argue loudly with the black woman, until the Queen shut him up with a few curt words.

"Bossior, this food is barely edible," she complained. Gullivar guessed that the Master of Arms' duties also included that of intendant.

"Good suppliers are hard to find, My Lady."

"I should have you whipped like a dog. Perhaps it would teach them all a lesson. Thieving merchants! Next cycle, I want my Wardens to exact a treble levee on them! You hear me!"

"As you wish, so will it be, My Lady," replied Bossior. But never before had Gullivar seen such pure hatred radiate from a man as he now saw from the Master of Arms.

The dinner continued in glacial silence. No one appeared interested in saying much beyond uttering a few utilitarian grunts. Suddenly, something seemed to grip Lhimat. He began shaking violently, spewing gruel everywhere, and babbling incoherently about *eyes*, before finally collapsing face down on his plate.

Bossior apologized to the Queen, remarking that Lhimat had been training very hard lately, obviously too hard. Maurdhaine shook her head in bemused tolerance, smiling faintly, the way a teacher would at a favorite student's harmless prank.

With a twin clap of his hands, Bossior summoned two guards who dragged the poor wretch out of the hall.

That first night in the palace, Gullivar Jones slept restlessly. He was visited by monstrous, amorphous visions, such as he had never before seen. Once during the night, he awoke, his nerves still tingling with vivid if only half-remembered pain. There was a reddish-colored film before his eyes. He brought his hands to his face, and they appeared covered in blood. He was crying tears of blood. An irrepressible scream formed in his throat—then he awoke again, for that had also been a dream.

There was no blood on his hands, and his eyes were uninjured. However, a single red spot on his pillow, where his head had lain, opened a yawning chasm in the depths of his bowels.

160

The Earthman heard another scream. For a moment, he wondered if it was yet another dream, but he got up and walked to the door. There, he stopped as he reached the handle. In the pallid light, something had caught his piercing eyes. A word. A name was scratched on the mantelpiece: "Galdane."

Outside, the corridors were dark and empty. Gullivar walked slowly down the steps to a great moonlit hall, but he heard no further noise and saw no suspicious sights.

Dawn brought small succor. Gullivar Jones decided that he would learn more about the name carved on his door. But it was nearly midday before he finished training.

"Who told you that name? Why do you want to know?" Bossior did not welcome Gullivar's inquiry, and indeed rebuffed the warrior. Only Gullivar's insistence caused him to finally relent and reveal what Gullivar had suspected, which was that Galdane was the name of the member of the Five that had preceded him. But no matter how hard the wanderer tried, he could not extract any more information from Bossior than a mere "He went away. That's all I know."

Gullivar wandered through the palace. The guards had obviously been instructed to ignore him, and no one tried to stop him or interfere with his exploration.

Eventually, his steps took him to a round room that occupied a small turret in the palace's eastern wing. But was it mere chance, or some strange influence that drew the wanderer to that room?

There stood a small, undecorated altar, upon which lay a statue. It was like nothing Gullivar had ever seen before: a bulbous form, elongated, with odd appendages, terminating in suction-like mouths. The statue seemed made of neither metal nor stone, but something which was between, and was covered in a shiny substance that could have been oil, grease or some kind of monstrous ichor that seemed to seep from the very object itself.

Gullivar put a cautious finger on the thing, and felt it hum softly under his touch, in an endless vibration that was like a mockery of true life. The warrior reacted to it as a young bird reacts to its first snake, his very being recognizing a thing even though his eyes had never before beheld it.

"What are you doing here?"

That was Queen Maurdhaine's voice, coming from just behind the Earthman's shoulder. It would have caused most men to jump back in fright, but Gullivar merely turned and stared at her.

The Queen threw a sheet over the thing. The wanderer noticed an odd respect in her gesture.

"This is something I am studying. Your clumsy meddling could have damaged it. Go away. I will talk to Bossior about this."

With a nod of the head, the warrior turned and left. He decided to leave the palace, remembering that his original purpose had been to learn about the mysterious Galdane, but he was not unhappy to seek relief from the palace's oppressive atmosphere.

In the street, at the bottom of the hill, the suffocating environment of the palace seemed entirely unreal. Gullivar breathed long and deep, almost as if he were cleaning his lungs of the miasmic atmosphere that held sway within the Queen's dwellings.

He decided that the best place to find answers was Logay's tavern. The ever-so-helpful innkeeper recognized him as he entered and asked the Earthman if he had called at the palace as he had suggested the day before. Gullivar nodded, but something in the wanderer's sour face must have betrayed his feelings, for Logay launched himself into a rambling panegyric of the job.

"That is not why I came," Gullivar cut him off as Logay was waxing about the alleged generosity of the Queen. "Did you know my predecessor–a man named Galdane?"

"Galdane? Galdane?" muttered Logay. "He may have come here for a drink once or twice. They all do, you know. A regular stop, we are. But I can't say I really made his acquaintance."

At that moment, a burly man walked in carrying a barrel of ale. Logay apologized to Gullivar, telling him he had to attend to his supplier. Gullivar nodded, and sat down in a corner of the room, nursing his drink. Eventually, Logay left the tavern. Then the person he had really come to see stepped from the back room. The red-haired girl named Jhavane.

"Logay has been lying to you," she whispered.

"That is no great surprise."

"Bossior is his brother."

Gullivar took in the information and pondered it in his mind, turning and twisting it like a Rivan puzzle.

"That would explain why he was eager to send me to the palace," he finally said.

"There were others before you. Wanderers same as you. Galdane was one of them. They all went to the palace, and they were never seen or heard from again."

Gullivar guessed that Galdane had at one time meant something or other to the girl, but said nothing.

"I overheard Bossior talk with Logay," she continued. "They say the Queen is a Xanaï, who escaped the wrath of Seramize. When he smokes the red root, Logay becomes loquacious. I will try to find out more. Tomorrow is my day off. Meet me at the blue fountain, at the eastern corner of the market, and I will tell you what I've learned."

That night, dinner at the palace was, if anything, even more bizarre and repulsive than before. The Queen was in a foul mood. During the day, she had received a messenger from Rodrik-Usher, the Lord of fabled Seth, the City of Enchanters to the south. Whatever communication had passed between them had not pleased her.

"I loaned that Mazan bastard the Blue Shard–how could he lose it? And to that creature, Ligeia! Bossior, where is the food?" Impatient at not being served sooner, Maurdhaine threw the contents of her goblet into the Master of Arms' face. Gullivar saw the seething anger in the eyes of the man, but his reply was a coolly polite, "Right away, My Lady."

Then, Lhimat had another seizure, but no one seemed to care or notice. No one dared lift a finger to help him, not while Maurdhaine continued to rant against "the foul wench who killed my sister Maliere." The old swordsman rolled on the floor, frothing and foaming, unattended.

Meanwhile, Valyre and K'ulze began to lasciviously paw each other, muttering obscenities in each other's ears. The black amazon began to emit small, animal-like grunts, as the Keshite caressed her with his food, leaving his fingers in her mouth after he had fed her morsels of meat. No one gave any notice. Gullivar thought that the scene looked almost ritualistic.

At last, Lhimat lay still on the floor. Again, at Bossior's command, two guards came and dragged the body away.

The second night, the fragile boundaries between Gullivar's consciousness and the mysteries that suffused the Palace of Qiml crumbled farther away. The Earthman was plagued by wave upon wave of nightmarish visions. As his brain burned, he tried to shut out the dreams, but in vain. He cursed the white-hot flow of blood that seemed to want to escape from his body through his burning eyes.

Finally, he awoke again, his body covered in a sheen of cold sweat. Seeking the cool refuge of the dark corridor outside, he walked through the door, only to be mockingly reminded of his as yet unguessed at fate by the name scratched on the lintel.

On the floor below, Gullivar noticed a door standing ajar. Viscous light spilled through the opening, laying upon the darkness like oil on water. Approaching silently, the warrior stole a glance inside the room thus revealed. It was filled with weird weapons and sculptures, but none were as disturbing as its two occupants. Valyre and K'ulze were engaged in some kind of personal, loathsome ritual. Their eyes kept wide open through pins hanging from hooks attached to their flesh, they took turn licking each other's eyeballs, all the while making mewling sounds.

Gullivar climbed heavily back to his room, pondering the true meaning of the scene he had just beheld. Had that been what had happened to Galdane? Had he gone insane? Become a monster like the others? What had been his final fate?

The next morning, as Gullivar trained at spear-throwing in the palace courtyard, he saw Bossior accompanying two guards carrying what looked like a body wrapped in a sheath of red cloth. A scarlet chariot was waiting in the front courtyard, escorted by two semiarchs, colorful traffickers in corpses that were the tradition in the northern regions. Gullivar felt no surprise, as death seemed a natural visitor to the palace.

"It was Lhimat, wasn't it?" he inquired of Bossior upon the man's return.

For a minute, it seemed that the Master of Arms would not answer him, and just walk by. But finally, Bossior nodded and said, "Yes. He killed himself during the night. It is very sad, for he was once a great man."

It seemed to Gullivar that Bossior's compassion was merely feigned, but he said nothing. Putting his spear back on the rack, he moved closer to the courtyard to listen to the two semiarchs.

His acute hearing enabled him to hear one remark that he had never seen anyone take their life in such a horrible way. The other replied about a case he'd once seen in the Lower City. Ghoulishly they began to compare notes.

Moved by intuition, Gullivar raised his head and saw Queen Maurdhaine watching as the two men carted the body away on their red chariot. Her face was inscrutable.

Gullivar met Jhavane at the appointed time near the blue fountain. Side by side, they walked silently from the market to the nearby city gardens. The bright, sunny day made the horrors of the palace seem even more unreal.

"According to Logay, Bossior believes that the Queen is a Xanaï," she finally began. "She merely changes her shape and her name, but in one guise or another, she's been ruling Qiml since my ancestors crossed Direwood and came over the great marshes of Zekar. She is Maurdhaine today, but she was Melsche yesterday, and Margal, and M'osale of Grance before that, and so on, stretching back to the Time of the Dark Rain. Bossior believes that she made a pact with creatures even more ancient than she, Horrors from before the Time of the Great Fear, who still live, deep inside the Mound upon which the palace was built. They're the ones who saved her from Seramize. Their excrement and foul ichors are part of the mortar that bind the very stones of the palace. They're the true Lords of Qiml, may the gods have mercy on us!"

Gullivar had listened in silence, with great attention to Jhavane's story. Queen Heru, his lover, had imparted him with the sacred words that no Horrors from before the Time of the Great Fear could withstand. The sacred words that had been entrusted to her people, she said, by the Keepers themselves. And the knowledge of these words carried responsibility. Gullivar knew that he had not come to Qiml seeking this task, but perhaps he had been drawn there by some higher purpose after all. In any event, his duty was clear. It was part of him. It was in his blood. He sighed, and in that sigh, Jhavane guessed that he had made a decision.

"Do not return there. Please. It is an evil place," she begged as she grabbed his arm.

But the Earthman gently released her grip. "I am under a most solemn vow," he said. Then, he turned and stepped back. He never knew if red-haired Jhavane, who had loved Galdane and could have loved him, cried as he walked back to the palace in the falling dusk.

That night, the dinner went on in complete silence, save for the gnawing of the food. Gullivar retired early, preparing himself for the anticipated ordeal.

As Eelesh, the second moon, started his descent in the eastern sky, a squadron of guards burst into Gullivar's room and pounced on him. Soon, the Earthman was in chains and dragged out of the room. As he was pulled through the corridor, the warrior saw Bossior grimly surveying the proceedings.

"You know what you must do, Man of Nûr," whispered the Master of Arms.

When he heard this, Gullivar, who had anticipated his capture, and indeed let himself be chained, putting up just enough resistance to convince his captors they had prevailed, realized that there were wheels within wheels here. Bossior knew who he was, and more so, he knew from where he came.

As the Earthman pondered this, he was dragged deeper and deeper within the bowels of the palace. One of the guards led the way, holding a torch. Bossior brought up the rear. They went down a flight of stairs carved into the very rock. They passed dungeons infested with vermin, and traveled down tunnels that looked as if they had been dug by inhuman hands. From the length of their journey, Gullivar guessed that they were now deep within the ancient mound upon which the palace had been erected.

They finally arrived in a small cavern, filled with an eerie phosphorescence, not unlike that of a deep sea glow. The air was fetid, in spite of the burning of zandrune-filled holders.

The guards tied Gullivar to a x-shaped cross that stood erect in a corner of the cavern. At the opposite end, Gullivar saw a pitch-black pit, a hellmouth leading to some unfathomable abyss.

Maurdhaine stood at the center of the room, dressed in ceremonial robes, embroidered with mysterious runes. K'ulze and Valyre, clad in the same vestments, were by her side. Next to the pit was a small stone altar. On it was the strange sculpture that Gullivar had spied in the eastern wing turret.

Maurdhaine walked towards Gullivar, and lightly raked his half-naked body with her nails. Her eyes were glassy, and the wanderer guessed that she was under the influence of a powerful root.

"It is time for you to perform the job for which you were hired, wanderer. You must meet the Soul Reaper. I had not planned to break you so early–normally, certain drugs are used to make the exchange more... pleasurable." Here, she licked her lips. "But Lhimat's death has forced my hand. The Soul Reaper needs nourishment, and Lhimat was but an empty husk at the end, and Burdiay is not yet... mature enough. You will provide a soul fresh, vibrant and richly-flavored, one that will greatly please the Reaper."

Had Maurdhaine been more observant, she would have detected a thin, wan smile on Gullivar's lips. But she turned around, letting Valyre and K'ulze come on either side of the wanderer, to apply the hooks and strings that would pull his eyes wide open.

"The windows to the soul," snickered K'ulze. "I envy you, Gullivar, although without the drugs, you may just go mad!" The Keshite burst out in a mad cackle.

"The time has come," called Maurdhaine from the other side of the room.

The Queen began performing a strange and obscene ritual rubbing the otherworldly statue on the altar. She caressed it, licked it and whispered to it in an ancient language known only to the Elders of Seth.

The fetid smell that had filled the cavern became ever more intense and the phosphorescent glow intensified. Then, a low, throbbing sound was heard.

The Soul Reaper crawled out of the pit. It resembled the sculpture that Maurdhaine worshipped, but was indeed much larger. Its pallid body pulsated with unholy life, greenish veins throbbed on oozing, grey skin. Its appendages lashed the air, adding a whipping rhythm to its inhuman wheeze. It slithered past Maurdhaine and Valyre and K'ulze. The Keshite and his companion, lost in the madness of the adoration of their awful master, had fallen to the ground and were pawing his body and licking the ooze off their fingers, while mewling in ecstasy. Maurdhaine stared, entranced, at the Horror from before the very Dawn of Time.

Only Bossior watched intently, a grim look of anticipation on his face.

You know what you must do, Man of Nûr, he had told Gullivar. The warrior steeled himself for what he knew was to come. In his mind, he recited the 12 prayers that Heru had taught him, and prepared himself for the task at hand.

The Horror extended its serpentine trunk towards Gullivar. Out of it came two obscenely pink and quivering tendrils that came to rest on Gullivar's pinned-open eyes.

Everyone held their breath.

Suddenly, the Soul Reaper released a screeching sound that may have been a scream of rage or of pain. It lashed wildly, in rage, crushing Valyre and K'ulze under its quivering mass as it thrashed furiously around the room.

Maurdhaine looked on, awe-struck as she saw Gullivar burst from his chains with a mighty effort. The warrior was unhurt, unscathed. His face was filled with total determination.

Facing the creature palms forward, he uttered the words that Heru had taught him. The words that were part of the very fiber of every man, woman and child born of the Golden Race on this world. Two words that had been passed on for generations. Two words that caused even Maurdhaine to shudder and cover her ears in pain.

"KANAMA KALAJERAMA!"

The Horror shuddered, as if it had been physically hit by a power greater than itself. Gullivar stepped forward and repeated the words again, but as he did, he knew that he was but delivering a mercy blow, for the Horror was already dying.

Maurdhaine stumbled backwards, displaying naked fear for the first time. As the creature turned towards her in its dying gasps, she uttered a small whine, then attempted to flee. But Bossior remembered old accounts yet to be settled. With one mighty push, he sent the Queen reeling backward, into the Horror's deadly embrace.

Soon, the creature dissolved into a foul-smelling, acid goo that also disposed of Maurdhaine, the Xanaï Queen of Qiml.

"I guess Qiml has gotten itself a new King," said Gullivar, looking at Bossior warily, thinking that perhaps he might be counted as an undesirable witness to a secret of state.

The two men eyed each other for a moment. Then Bossior smiled, and extended his hand to the Earthman.

"I thought I might take a stab at it, yes," said the Master of Arms.

"If this plan of yours is an example of your skills at governing, I am sure you will do very well indeed," replied Gullivar, dryly.

"I know you claim to come from the Other World, the Blue Star itself. But I believe you were sent here by the gods themselves."

"Perhaps."

They had reached the upper section of the palace. Dawn had broken over the city and the long night of Qiml was over. Following Bossior's lead, Gullivar found himself in the same courtyard where he had been training only the day before. Bulging supply bags were waiting there, a testimony to the Master of Arms' generosity.

"All of Qiml owes you a debt, Gullivar Jones. Still, it would not be good for you to stay any longer. Let me repay you with some news, however. As Maurdhaine's chamberlain, I learned that Rodrik-Usher the Damned is moving in the south. Maurdhaine was a Xanaï. She knew many secrets. She may have given him information about your people."

Gullivar nodded. The time had come for him to return home to Heru. He unfurled his magic carpet and was airborne in a matter of minutes. After a last loop over Qiml, he flew straight east towards Savaria, never looking back.

Dim Vales and Shadowy Floods

In Seth, the fabled City of Enchanters, Rodrik-Usher beheld with pleasure his newest hands: golden-skinned and decorated with the subtle ritual tattoos of the Malachites. He let his fingers run gently over Ligeia's tear-streaked cheeks. The young woman, held in chains, surrounded by azure-clad soldiers, shrank back at the villain's touch.

"How do you like my humble abode, Ligeia?" One of the nails raked the Enchantress' skin, without drawing blood. "I never dreamed that that fool Montressor would have dared to send you back here."

"What do you want of me, Rodrik-Usher?"

"I have craved your blood for more time than you can dream of, child, for it is magic blood. You drank from the cup of the Phra-kan. When I feed you to the Blue Crystal, I will have access to power on a scale unimagined... I will be like unto the Keepers themselves!"

Rodrik-Usher's eyes glinted with madness; a small sheen of perspiration made his brow shine. With a gesture from his left hand, he summoned the Red Death and pointed at the young woman.

"Why postpone this happy event? Andrevar, take her to the Place of Silence now."

The Red Death dragged Ligeia away. Rodrik-Usher got up and followed them, lost in reveries of godhood.

Minutes later, Rodrik-Usher and the Red Death stood outside the heavy metal doors of the Place of Silence. Inside, a sharp, piercing scream was heard, unmistakably Ligeia's, as her voice rose, it was brutally cut off. Only silence ensued.

Rodrik-Usher frowned briefly, and then gestured impatiently to the two cloaked guards to open the doors.

When they had done so, they could not suppress audible gasps of surprise. Even Rodrik-Usher took an involuntarily step back.

Inside the Place of Silence, the room was alive with energy; not the fiery, volcanic, coruscating purple radiance they expected to see, instead it was a deep, peaceful blue glow. Dominating the scene was the pulsing sound of an impossible heartbeat. But it was the sight of the young woman herself which froze Rodrik-Usher and his men on the spots where they stood.

Ligeia stood slightly crouched, head down, miraculously unscathed, at the very center of the room. If it had been physically possible, one would have said that she had just stepped out of a blazing oven, because she was surrounded with a shimmering heat aura, like a mirage, and her image looked slightly frizzed around its edges.

Suddenly, she raised her head and opened her eyes, which glowed a deep, sapphire blue.

Outside, the guards moved several more steps back and grasped their weapons in fear. Rodrik-Usher however, pursed his lips, and appeared more annoyed than frightened.

"I should have known it would never take her against her will. She is stronger than I thought."

The evil Enchanter stepped into the room and, acting in a deceptively fatherly way placed his incongruously golden hand on Ligeia's shoulder.

"I didn't want to cause you needless pain, my dear, but you leave me no choice..."

The cell was deep, deep below ground. Only a few men in the history of Seth knew of the existence of the lower levels of the Seth of old, which had first been erected during the Time of the Great Fear. There lay the bones of ancient Horrors, mingled with the blood of the Enchanters who had defeated them. There were preserved the most dangerous relics of ages gone by, and the secrets that successive generations of Great Librarians had chosen to entomb forever. There did Rodrik-Usher keep the fruits of his most private experiments.

The evil Enchanter walked ahead, ankle-deep in dust, in a foggy maze of ruins and debris, smelling of the musty remnants of death and decay. Ligeia, who was being dragged in her zombie-like condition by the Red Death, followed him. They reached the edge of a large tank filled with bubbling, black tar, built in an enclosed space that may have once been a temple.

Inside the tank were several slowly writhing, tar-encased figures, their faces frozen into terrifying masks of terror, mouths gaping in silent screams.

Rodrik-Usher clapped his hands. The surface of the tank bubbled some more and then a huge humanoid figure covered in boiling tar emerged. It had dark, fish-like eyes, without pupils, and a thin, gash of a mouth.

"This is your new subject, Nekrosian," said Rodrik-Usher. "Show her the ways of madness. Destroy her spirit. Rip away her soul, but do not kill her."

The thing that had been called Nekrosian waded through the tar towards Ligeia, and opened his arms to take her, as in an obscene embrace.

Later, Rodrik-Usher and Andrevar watched the Sun setting over the peaks of the Arcane Mountains from the windows of the Enchanter's metal grey tower. To their right was the vast, barren horizon of the Desert of Tears, engulfed in encroaching darkness. The Enchanter turned towards the creature who had once been his master.

"If Montressor sent Ligeia back to Mars, that means that he must, at last, feel ready to challenge me. Yet, after that coward ran from me last time, I made sure that the use of the Gates would be forever denied to him. Still, it does not pay to underestimate Montressor, as I've learned. He is wily and cunning. The only place where he can return, if he has found a way to cheat the Keepers' science, is the Master-Gate at the Pyramid of Kamor... Andrevar, go there and kill anyone who approaches it."

The Red Death nodded and strode away.

After a long flight through a thundercloud filled sky over the unending Desert of Tears, Gullivar Jones and Edgar Allan Poe saw the peaks of Kamor rise over the horizon. Poe was now dressed in native clothes and looked healthier and stronger.

The mountains were desolate, parched orange rocks that rose abruptly from the ground, almost as if an underground giant had pushed his fist through the desert floor. The peaks were short and jagged, nearly impossible to climb, broken only by narrow gorges, canyons and massively huge boulders of weird shapes and configurations.

Gullivar navigated his flying carpet between the rocks with an ease that still astounded Poe.

"Are we on our way to rescue Ligeia?" shouted the writer.

"The two of us would not stand a chance against Rodrik-Usher. Only Montressor can help."

"I welcome the thought of seeing him again. To be frank, I have a few things I should like to say to him." Poe looked at the sky, which grew ominously dark, even though the Sun was still high on the horizon. "It looks like a storm's coming."

"The weather will be the least of our problems," said Gullivar.

The sky began filling with lightning, as the thunderstorm, caught between mountain and desert, finally erupted. Water poured down in thick, almost sheet-like waves. Fortunately it did not last, for almost as quickly as the storm had broken, it dissipated.

They emerged, drenched, from a canyon and, in front of them they beheld the Pyramid of Kamor.

Only Gullivar could recognize in this tall, pointed spire erected above a blocky foundation, mounted on giant steps, the architecture of the Keepers. It was obvious to all that the place had been uninhabited for a long, long time, for it was now mostly in ruins. They stood at the center of a natural, crater-like depression that lay hidden within the mountains.

"That was once the home of my adopted people," said Gullivar. "They tended to the Keepers' needs and lived contentedly."

"What happened?" asked Poe.

"The Elder Melnach once told me that, one day, the Keepers left and the Demons came. Evil men from the

East who were their servants accompanied them. They killed many."

"Why?"

"Because, back then, we were free. The few who remained eventually moved to Nûr and rebuilt. But even that was taken away by Rodrik-Usher. And I was unable to return in time with that which might have saved them."

The warrior said no more, and Poe dared not ask further questions. Gullivar gestured to him to prepare to land. The carpet banked and started its descent towards the Pyramid.

Suddenly, the Red Death flew out from above and behind the stormy clouds and jagged peaks. He was mounted on a huge scarlet dragon, covered in dark-red scales and spikes, with a long tail barbed with stingers and huge front claws that could tear and rend. The beast's evil, jet-black eyes shone, reflecting the clouds above, and its frothing, fiery mouth gaped to let out smoke and reveal two rows of razor-sharp teeth.

The Red Death carried a samurai style sword in his black-gloved hand. Many more deadly weapons hung on his person or from his saddle.

He flew silently towards them at high speed. With a swipe of his sword, he struck the flying carpet before either Gullivar or Poe could react.

Acting as if it had been wounded, the magical rug plummeted towards the ground. But at the last minute, it halted its descent.

"Get off, Mr. Poe," said Gullivar. "Quickly!"

The writer then realized that the carpet had only been following the silent instructions of its master.

"Only I can fight the Red Death," added the Earth-man. "Trust me. I want to avenge the deaths of my adopted people more than I cherish life itself. If I do not return, go inside the Pyramid and make use of this."

Gullivar removed a small key from a chain around his neck and gave it to the writer.

Poe jumped on the foundation of the Pyramid, his landing cushioned by the mossy vegetation. He then looked skyward as Gullivar zoomed back up into the air.

The Earthman grabbed his sword and prepared for battle. He and the Red Death observed each other, measuring their respective strengths and weaknesses. Several times they flew straight at each other, exchanging and parrying deadly blows that made their swords clang and sparkle. Poe was reminded of images of medieval jousts he had seen illustrated in books. But the warrior of Nûr and the Red Death proved too evenly matched, and neither could manage to wound or unseat the other.

The Red Death then pulled a bolo-like weapon from his saddle, swung it rapidly in the air, and threw it at Gullivar. The wanderer was caught unprepared; the bolo wrapped itself around him, causing him to drop his sword, which fell to the ground below.

The Red Death gleefully seized upon his opportunity. Steering his mount in a deadly ballet-like move, he positioned himself to deliver a crushing deathblow to the immobilized Gullivar, who in the meantime was desperately trying to extricate himself from the bolo.

At the last moment, as the Red Death struck, the front half of Gullivar's flying carpet rose up and caught the blow that would surely have killed its rider.

This action gained the warrior enough time to free himself. The Red Death was hot in pursuit and attempted several times to land more blows, but Gullivar managed to evade them by doing a sudden flip-flop in the air. He even succeeded in briefly flying upside down, holding onto the carpet with one hand, passing beneath his foe, and delivering a powerful blow to the belly of his enemy's mount with the other.

Gullivar was slowing, however. He had begun to lose blood from some of his wounds, and small, red, almost black droplets of fluid streamed in the air behind him. With the Red Death still after him, the Earthman steered his carpet towards a huge storm cloud.

As the warrior disappeared into the billowing, dark mass, the rumbling of thunder was heard. When the carpet emerged from the other side of the cloud, the Red Death saw that it was empty. He rubbed his eyes in disbelief. It looked as if Gullivar Jones had vanished!

The Red Death cautiously flew down towards the carpet, unsure of what was happening.

Suddenly, Gullivar jumped out of the cloud, holding on to a piece of carpet, which he had cut away from the rest.

The warrior's prodigious leap landed him on the back of the Red Death's mount.

A fierce fight began between the two opponents. Gullivar and the Red Death hit, choked, stabbed, gouged, and bit each other. The two men wrestled in mid-air, locked in a deadly embrace. The dragon-beast tried to help his master, vainly attempting to bite the warrior of Nûr.

The battle focused on possession of the Red Death's sword. Each combatant tried to wrest it from the other, at one time, both having a grip on it with his powerful hands.

Suddenly, a particularly loud thunderclap sounded in the air. Gullivar glanced away for a split second, then looked back at the Red Death, and, with a cryptic grin released his grip on the sword.

The Red Death, smiling, raised the sword high in the air, ready to split Gullivar in two.

Suddenly, a bolt of lightning hit the sword, just as the warrior had anticipated.

Gullivar leapt off backwards in the air, as both the Red Death and his mount exploded into flames, their charred remains falling to their doom.

But Gullivar, too, was falling.

His magic carpet, torn and tattered, strained mightily to reach him in time. With a final burst of energy, just as the ground was growing dangerously near, it caught up with Gullivar.

The Earthman then dropped on its surface, banked down and landed near Poe.

The writer, seeing the number and severity of the warrior's wounds, expressed his concern.

"They don't matter," replied Gullivar. "We do not have much time. Rodrik-Usher sent the Red Death here because he suspects our intentions. We must act quickly."

The warrior led Poe inside the pyramid. They climbed down a flight of steps and entered a larger, inside space, that housed a much smaller pyramid. A vast, circular area had been dug all round it. It reminded Poe of an arena.

Gullivar and Poe went down another flight of steps and crossed the ring. The writer could not help noticing that, in places, it was littered with human bones and dark spots that might have been congealed blood.

The central pyramid sported a single, metal door with a lock. Poe took the small key Gullivar had given him and opened it.

Inside, Poe discovered, to his surprise, that the inner pyramid was so chockfull of cogs, gears, wheels and springs that he thought for a moment they had entered a giant clock. Above their heads, a pendulum, affixed to the apex of the pyramid, hung motionlessly. Just underneath it, in the very center of the pyramid, stood a dais, that held a man-size, oval, mirror-like object, made of a dark-green metal that might have passed for bronze, but wasn't. The air was stale, everything was still and a fine layer of undisturbed dust indicated that no one had set foot inside this edifice for many years.

"Where are we?" asked Poe, indicating the whole room.

"I don't know," replied Gullivar. "Montressor once called it the Control Room. He told me it was the Keepers' way station. Something they left on this world before they went away, in case they would one day have need of it, like a life raft."

"Do you know how to make it work?"

"No, but Montressor does. The only thing required now is for you to activate it, Mr. Poe."

"Me? But I don't know anything about it."

"It's very simple. Montressor told me what you had to do..."

Gullivar pulled open a small metal panel and began poking and prodding inside the machinery. He took out a small, round metal ball.

"Please hold this."

Poe did so, then almost immediately let it fall.

"Ow! It stung me!"

At once, a soft hum began to fill the room, and suddenly, the pendulum began to swing back and forth and the gears, the cogs and the wheels sprung into life. It was as if the clock-like mechanism had just been rewound. On the dais, the oval, mirror-like surface brightened and began to glow with a blue light.

Gullivar put the ball back inside the cabinet and shut the metal panel. "This is the Master-Gate," he remarked.

A series of surreal images began to appear in rapid succession on the oval mirror, as if it was sorting though a collection of postcards. Suddenly, it shimmered brightly, as if it had found what it sought, and a short, plump figure wearing a bright blue and yellow robe stepped decisively through the Gate.

"Finally. I was beginning to be concerned," said Montressor.

The Gate silently closed behind the Enchanter as he turned toward Poe. "So, how is the book going, my young sir?" he asked mischievously.

Poe caught his breath in anger and had to control himself from grabbing the small, stout man standing before him.

"Montressor–how could you...?" he stuttered, indignantly. "We were almost killed–and Miss Ligeia..."

"Calm down, Mr. Poe," said Montressor. "And don't worry; I do not believe my ward is in any immediate danger."

"What do you mean, 'you do not believe?' "

"I mean that I *know*. I am sorry I involved you in this situation, but I assure you that I had no other choice. I imagine that you feel that you are owed a modicum of explanation?"

"That, sir, is quite the understatement. I am waiting."

"I wonder where the best place to start is... Well, shorter is always best, as I tell my writers. A long time ago, Ligeia and I fought Rodrik-Usher. We lost, and were forced to flee to your world." Montressor paused.

"Mind you, since then, I've come to like it there. Especially the food."

"The point, sir, please, come to the point."

"Yes. Frankly, I would have been happy to stay there forever, but I kept an eye on what was going on back here. That's how I learned that Rodrik-Usher, in his folly, had embarked on a massive campaign of slaughter and conquest. I had to do something about it. I couldn't just sit back and let that genocidal maniac butcher his way through my world. Plus, some other information came into my possession, which revealed a connection between Mars and Earth. But I will tell you more about that later. In any event, I began planning my return. But then, I made a discovery: Rodrik-Usher had anticipated that I might, someday, come back to challenge him, and he had found an ingenious way to stop me from using the Gates. He had taught them to recognize my genetic pattern and, on that basis, deny me access..."

"Genetic pattern?"

"Hmm. Yes. My blood, if you will. The only place where the Gates could be reprogrammed was here. I would have to come here and re-enter my blood into the mechanism. But how could I do this if I was stranded on Earth? Rodrik-Usher thought he had me stumped. You can appreciate the dilemma."

"A quandary indeed. You had to come to Mars in order to return to Mars. Impossible on the face of it."

"I thought so for a while, until it occurred to me that someone of my own bloodline, who wasn't myself, might be able to travel through the Gates, come here, and reprogram the system in my stead."

"I fail to see how–"

Suddenly, Poe stopped as the truth began to dawn on him.

"Oh no, you don't mean to say that–"

"I'm afraid so, my boy. Your father, David Poe, was my son–before I learned of my predicament, of course. He was happy to live his life as human. Your mother, Elizabeth, was an absolute darling, and I felt terrible when she passed over from pneumonia. You were only four at the time. After that, David insisted, very much against my own advice, to help me. One day, he walked through a Gate, fully intending to come here to reprogram the Master-Gate. He never returned. To this day, I do not know what happened to him. I had no choice but to wait for you to grow up, but this time, I made sure you would not travel alone. I sent Ligeia with you, as she has her own role to play in all this, and I arranged for Mr. Jones to protect you both.

"You have now more than fulfilled your mission, Mr. Poe. I can send you back home through this Gate right now, if you want. And my promises of literary glory were not empty either. Your *Tamerlane* will be published, if not by me, then by a friend of mine in Boston."

Poe was torn by conflicting emotions. A storm of jumbled thoughts and feelings roared through his brain. It was almost too much to process.

"But–what about Miss Ligeia?" he finally said.

"Mr. Jones and I plan to rescue her, of course. Her part in this matter is, as I said, yet unfinished."

"I would like to come with you, sir."

Montressor looked at Poe with squinted eyes and the writer felt himself scrutinized to the most hidden, deepest recesses of his soul.

"Are you sure this is what you wish to do?"

"It is," he said firmly.

The Enchanter sighed.

In Seth, Rodrik-Usher sat on his throne, lost in a dark reverie. "Andrevar has not returned. The darkness is slipping away," he thought.

A blue-clad guard entered, bringing Ligeia with him. She walked like a zombie, her eyes blank, and her face totally expressionless.

Rodrik-Usher looked at her attentively for a few seconds. He purposefully, but lightly, passed his hands–now a well-tanned, hard-working pair–over and in front of the young woman's face. She began screaming uncontrollably.

"The Nekrosian has done well," he muttered. The Enchanter repeated his hand gesture, and Ligeia went totally silent in the middle of a scream, returning to her trance.

"Very good," said the Enchanter. Then, he turned towards the guard. "Gather the eight other Enchanters. Tell them the ceremony will begin soon."

"Mr. Jones, I must have a talk with you, as well," said Montressor.

"I'm standing right here," said the warrior, grimly.

"I'm given to understand that you blame yourself for the death of the people of Nûr, because you failed to find and bring back the Blue Shard that had been cast into the Sarkean Sea off the shores of Qiml, is that correct?"

"Yes, that's right."

"You shouldn't."

"I don't understand."

"As you surmised, the Shard was found by Maurdhaine... By the way, congratulations for the job you did on her. The world is a better place without that evil

Xanaï. She sold the Shard to Rodrik-Usher, but it was retaken by Ligeia in Alsabeh later, and she took it to Nûr. Alas, it failed to stop the advance of Rodrik-Usher's blue legions, which were protected by spells far mightier than anything we could summon. We were lucky to be able to destroy it before Rodrik-Usher could reclaim it and escape. So, as you see, you bear no responsibility at all in the fate that befell your adopted people."

"So... I didn't fail... Heru didn't die because of me..."

"Indeed not. Had you been there during the attack, you would have undoubtedly perished with your folk–a most pointless sacrifice, in my opinion."

Gullivar pondered over what the Enchanter had just revealed to him. It had lightened his burden, but not quenched the thirst for revenge that he now felt stronger than ever.

"So what do we do now?" asked Poe.

Montressor winked, "Well, young sir, we go to rescue Ligeia, what else?"

Seramize

Once upon a time…

Far in the northern lands, west of the snow-encrusted peaks of the Nihan Mountains, nestled between the rivers Arlas, Chel and Gavene, lay the fertile valley of Brange. There lived Dromu, a poor farmer. He owned nothing but a small, miserable plot of land, which grew barely enough maize to feed his wife and three children. Few were the days when a roasted grouse, cooked with juicy peppers or crackling *ycorns*, graced their table. But Dromu was not a demanding man, and he thanked the gods for what he genuinely thought was his good fortune.

One day, as the leaves had begun to fall and the winds of the Nihan heralded the first days of the gatherings, a stranger knocked on his door and inquired whether the farmer needed any extra hands for the gatherings. The year had been good, and Dromu knew there was much labor to be done–perhaps too much for him and his family–but in the past, he had found that he could not pay the wages usually asked by the itinerant workers who traveled south from Savaria.

"I am poor and unable to pay you," Dromu told the man, "but if you wish to stay and work, you will have shelter and a seat at the table as if you were one of my own."

The man had flown all the way from Qiml on a magic carpet, barely stopping at Catan and Miserne to resupply himself. Now, he knew that to travel south through the icy highlands of Mhurruk during the season of snows was ill advised. The offer appealed to him. He agreed to stay and help Dromu until after the first snow melt.

The stranger's name was Gullivar Jones.

He was lean and athletic; his skin was burnished as old bronze that had been hammered a thousand times and his face bore an indefinable exotic expression. His eyes had a hooded slant, hiding a flame that few would care to face. Like most wanderers, his clothes were a jumble of rags collected from lands as diverse as the flowers of the field.

Gullivar was fast as a mountain fox and tough as an old wolf. He worked hard, and his only distraction was playing upon a small flute that he carried in his vest. Dromu was pleased, and thanked the gods for sending him the man.

When there was a heavy job to be done, Gullivar never tried to boost his strength with drink, unlike the northerners. He simply applied more energy and toiled with stubborn strength until it was all but done. One day, Dromu showed him a secret shown to him by his father, and which had been held in his family for generations. Spotting a tuft of the dark blue-greenish grass called germande, he took a handful and began to chew it. It was bitter, very bitter, but as the farmer told Gullivar, if he had the strength to withstand its bitterness, the germande would fill him with more strength than the mountain, and more courage than thunder.

Life on the farm was good. The crops were turning a soft gold, and with Gullivar's help, Dromu could look forward to the best gathering he had had in years.

But that part of Brange belonged to Baron Massoch, a coarse, evil man, known for his wild hunts which spared neither men nor beasts. A score of days before the gathering, the Baron's hunt came to Dromu's land. The Baron had been in pursuit of a great ferch since the first hours of the morning, and he was in the darkest of moods. His great hound, Abad, a fierce brute with purple teeth and blood-injected yellow eyes, led the hunt on an increasingly wilder chase. With his spurs, the Baron tore at the flanks of his mount, pressing ever onward, paying no heed to his followers, who were reeling from exhaustion. He and his pack ran through Dromu's field as if it was not there, trampling the ripe maize beneath their horses' hooves, crushing it into dust. When the roaring of the dogs and the yells of their masters had passed behind the hills, Dromu's crop was gone, and his land looked as if a thousand plows had tilled it a thousand times.

Dromu did not curse the gods, though even the holiest man could not have blamed him for doing so. The situation was bleak. With no more seeds to plant, and no maize to gather, starvation loomed before them. Against his wife's advice, Dromu decided to set off to petition the Baron, hoping that the nobleman would indemnify him for the damages. Gullivar traveled with him to the Baron's castle but, at Dromu's insistence, remained outside.

That day, the ferch that Baron Massoch had been hunting had succeeded in escaping, thus the Baron's mood was even more somber than usual. He heard Dromu's complaint, then looked over to the evil, yellow eyes of his great hound Abad, and flew into a dark rage. He struck the farmer with his spear, killing him on the spot.

It was Gullivar's task to return Dromu's body to the farm, which he did with dignity. When the poor farmer's corpse had been consigned to the gods, and the ritual period of mourning observed, the Earthman asked the farmer's widow if she wanted revenge against the evil Lord who had killed her husband. He gave her to understand that he had certain skills that could be brought to use in this matter. But the widow wisely turned him down. She told him she had decided to abandon the farm and return with her children to her family, who lived in Zekar, west of the Arlas.

Left alone on the empty farm, with little food to last till the season of snows, Gullivar decided he would try to cross the highlands of Mhurruk after all. So he packed up his few belongings, unfurled his magic carpet, chewed on a tuft of germande, and once again flew south.

He followed a brook upstream, until it reached the edge of the forest of Direwood, on the first slopes of the Nihan Mountains. From up in the sky, he beheld a most remarkable sight: on every road, from every corner of Brange, came men carrying plows. Yet, the gatherings were almost over. His curiosity piqued, the Earthman decided to land and learn the reason for this rare occurrence. Spotting an old man who had come from collecting wood in the forest, the wanderer stopped him.

"Good day, Old Father," he said. "Are you the only one not carrying a plow today? Where are all these men going? Is it some kind of pilgrimage of plows?"

"Almost, stranger," the Old Man replied. "You've heard of Baron Massoch who destroyed all our crops with his damned hunts? And who had all who dared complain whipped?"

"Whipped–or murdered, as I have reason to know."

"Well, we sent a delegation to Catan to see King Guillem of Savaria, asking him to stop the Baron. The

King heeded our pleas and ordered that, as punishment for what the Baron did to our lands, his castle be torn down to the very ground, and that, furthermore, its ground be tilled under a hundred times and sown with salt, so that nothing ever again grow upon it. I would have loved to go with the others, but I am too old to till. Still, blessed be the King."

"His justice was swift and good. You are fortunate indeed."

After bidding the Old Man farewell, the Earthman continued on his way and, near dusk, found himself in Direwood near the place known as the Canyon of Chel. To eke out his supplies, he had not eaten all day, contenting himself with playing his flute to silence his stomach's grumbling. Suddenly, he spotted a small clearing, occupied by a lonely house. He flew over it, and from its surroundings, saw that it was a Woodsman's home.

He landed again, and knocked at the door. The man who answered was clearly the woodsman himself: his face and hands were black with soot. He was a short, stout fellow, with a crafty look. Gullivar noticed that his eyes shone brightly, like two, hungry flames, in the midst of his dark face.

"I seek hospitality and work," said the Earthman.

"I'm a woodsman. I know your wandering kind. Men like you generally don't take to living alone in these woods. They don't like the dirt, or the grime, or looking like a rock troll, as I do. But there is plenty of work to be had for one who is not shy of these things."

"Since I only look to work here until after the season of snows, these things do not bother me. What would you have me do?"

"Help me cut the wood and prepare the stacks for the burning; when I set off with the donkey to sell the charcoal, you can take care of the house, the sheds and the hen house. Pay particular attention to the small, white bird inside. Let it eat anything it wants, but never a snail, a worm or any other sightless creature. If you do that, I'll flay you alive, understand?"

"It doesn't seem too difficult. What is the pay?"

After some haggling, they arrived at the figure of one bronze coin every fortnight. The Woodsman showed Gullivar a cot near the fireplace. The wanderer set his belongings in a trunk, rolled up his carpet, and stayed and helped the Woodsman.

The season of snows came and went, and the first flowers made their first, shy appearance, heralding the season of mists. Gullivar had, by then, earned a dozen bronze coins and was thinking of again embarking upon his journey south. But, one afternoon, a beautiful carriage rolled slowly into the clearing. The driver moved cautiously because one of the carriage's rear wheels had been damaged during its crossing of the Gavene that marked the boundaries between Brange and Savaria. A finely dressed lord and a beautiful lady got out and walked towards the house. When he spied them, the Woodsman told Gullivar:

"Greet those people politely, but tell them you're alone. If they ask, I'm away selling coal."

Then, the Woodsman left through a back door, which led to the hen house, which held a dozen chickens and pigeons, as well as the small, white bird. The wanderer, made curious by such unusual behavior, stole a glance through the keyhole. He saw the Woodsman put the white bird beneath his left arm.

Treating it like a baby more than an animal, the Woodsman petted it with his right hand, while singing a strange lullaby:

"*Night before me, day after me,*
Let no mortal eye see me!"

At that instant, the two strangers knocked on the door, and Gullivar could see no more. He went to the door and opened it.

"Good afternoon, wanderer," said the lord. "Are you alone here?"

"Yes. My master is away," replied Gullivar. "Can I be of assistance?"

"Indeed you can. My lady here is tired from our journey and would dearly love a glass of fresh water."

While Gullivar fetched the water, the lord continued.

"Do you know where we might find a wheelwright to repair one of our wheels, and maybe an inn to spend the night?"

"As for the wheelwright, I couldn't say, but there's an inn just past the Canyon of Chel, near the bridge."

After drinking her glass of water, the lady seemed in a hurry to leave, so the lord handed the Earthman a few copper coins to thank him for his hospitality, and the two returned to their carriage, which soon departed as cautiously as it had come.

Almost immediately, Gullivar heard steps in the hen house. He rushed to the keyhole but, at first, saw nothing but the empty house and the sleeping birds. Then, he heard the Woodsman's voice sing:

"*Day before me, night after me,*
Let any mortal eye see me!"

And, suddenly, the Woodsman stood there, in a dark corner of the house. He put the white bird on the ground. Then, it appeared to Gullivar that he hid four heavy bags behind the birds' feed, but the light was failing and it was difficult to tell.

The Woodsman entered the house and asked the Earthman who the visitors were and what they had wanted. Gullivar told him the little he knew. The Woodsman seemed to be in a good mood, and praised the lord for his generosity. He ordered the wanderer to bring some wine from the cellar to celebrate his good fortune. Gullivar, who had had time throughout the snow season to learn how miserly his employer was, was puzzled by the Woodsman's sudden generosity. But he hid his doubts and kept his own council.

When he returned from the cellar, he noticed that his master had been into the hen house again, but could not divine his purpose. With a crafty expression on his face, the Woodsman grabbed the wine jug that Gullivar had brought and told the wanderer that, if he wanted a drink, he would first have to dance. Seeing Gullivar's puzzlement, he repeated his instructions very seriously.

Intent on discovering the purpose of this farce, Gullivar decided to play along with the Woodsman and tried some steps of a minuet. The Woodsman nodded his approval gravely and began pouring some of the delicious white wine into a cup, while telling the wanderer fancy yarns about Direwood, including a particularly foolish story about a lady troll who had purportedly fallen in love with him when he was young.

Gullivar quickly understood that the Woodsman was trying to make him drunk, so he stopped drinking while pretending to swallow pint after pint. He seized every opportunity when the Woodsman was not watching him to surreptitiously pour his wine beneath the table–an act made easy by the Woodsman's nervousness.

It was obvious that it was not wine but something else that was on the man's mind and Gullivar recognized in the Woodsman's eyes the same dark flame that he had noticed upon his first meeting with the man.

So malicious was that look, that the wanderer could not help but repress a shudder.

In the Woodsman's house, Gullivar laughed, sang and thumped the table. He slurred his speech, and pretended his fingers could not find the holes of his flute, all while he wondered what dark plan his master plotted against him.

Suddenly, the Woodsman stood up.

"The season of mists has come," he told the Earthman, "and I know you've made up your mind to go. I, myself, will no longer need your services. But you've been a good worker and I want to thank you. I'm not rich, but I can teach you a trick to make money. Take this broom and hit the cupboard."

Gullivar got up, pretended to stumble, and affecting the stupidest air he could, did just as he was told. To his unfeigned surprise, sparks flew in the air, becoming two gold coins, which fell ringing and spinning on the stone floor.

"Good," said the Woodsman. "Now try hitting the fireplace."

Gullivar did as he was bid, and two more gold pieces fell. He quickly realized the Woodsman had put these there while he was down in the cellar.

"Very good," said the Woodsman. "These four gold coins are yours." Then, after a brief hesitation, he added, "Now that you're rich, you'll no longer need my few bronze coins, will you?" And the Woodsman had Gullivar give him back his salary. After which, he offered him a last drink to speed him on his way, then went outside.

The Woodsman insisted on accompanying the wanderer on foot through the Canyon of Chel to the Inn, singing loudly and forcing the wanderer to join him. As they approached the Inn, he said, "Ask for their finest room, and pay with gold. Order more wine. If they ask, tell them you're no longer in my employ because I went off to marry a lady troll."

Then he hurriedly scampered away. Gullivar approached the Inn alone, pondering over the meaning of the night's strange events. In the end, he decided to do exactly the opposite of what the Woodsman had said. He knocked on the Inn's door. The Innkeeper, who had been awakened by the loud singing, came to the door grumpily, expecting to find a drunkard. Instead, he was pleasantly surprised to see a wanderer with all his wits about him.

"Were you the one making all that racket?" he asked.

"No," Gullivar replied. "It was a drunken lout who insisted on keeping me company through the canyon, but I got rid of him. I need a place to spend the night."

"You've come to the right place. Do you have any money?"

"Not a copper, but I can do a good day's work for you in the morning, if that's acceptable."

"Wait a minute! I recognize you! You're the Woodsman's apprentice, aren't you? Why are you here?"

"I spilled some wine. The old miser got mad and fired me."

"Are you sure you hadn't had a little too much to drink?"

"Do I look like someone who drinks?"

The Innkeeper had to admit that Gullivar did not, and thus reassured about his guest's sobriety, allowed him to spend the night in his barn.

The next morning, the wanderer went to look for the Innkeeper. He was busily preparing breakfast for a party of merchants traveling south. The Earthman offered to help, but the man instead inquired, "You worked for the Woodsman, so you know about cutting wood?"

"I guess I do," replied Gullivar.

"If you know about cutting wood, maybe you could help our wheelwright repair the wheel of a carriage that is stuck here."

Gullivar remembered the lord and the lady who had stopped at the Woodsman's house the day before to ask for a glass of water. Their carriage had damaged a wheel as it crossed the mountains. Their brief visit had begun the puzzling sequence of events that had led the Woodsman to dismiss Gullivar, and the wanderer was quite curious to find out more.

"With pleasure," he told the Innkeeper, and left to fetch tools.

The carriage had been stored in the stable. There, Gullivar met the driver, whom he had briefly seen during his masters' halt at the Woodsman's (and who did not recognize him) and the local wheelwright, who had just finished forging a new, metal circle for the damaged wheel. Gullivar went to work helping the two men, scraping and polishing the new wood until it fit perfectly.

After several hours of hard toil together, the three men began to enjoy a hearty relationship, swapping jokes and confidences. Gullivar grabbed this opportunity to inquire as to the identity of the driver's master and mistress, but the loyal man would not divulge their secret. However, what he told the wanderer more than made up for it.

"What I can tell you," the driver said, "is that, yesterday, someone stole four bags of gold which we were carrying. Thanks to your help, they can now leave to try to replace them. Otherwise, my masters' journey will have been in vain, and it will cause great unhappiness in the land..."

"Four bags of gold, you say," asked Gullivar. "How did it happen?"

"No one knows. The strangest thing is that nobody came near the carriage all day. The four bags were safely stored in a trunk beneath my master's seat when we left at dawn. When we arrived here at nightfall, they were gone!"

"Did you stop along the way?"

"Half-an-hour for lunch in the mountains, where we neither saw nor met anyone, and ten minutes at a hovel in the forest for my lady to get a glass of water. But I stood on guard all the time and saw not a soul."

Gullivar then began to piece the mystery together: the Woodsman's mysterious disappearance and reappearance, the white bird, the gold coins, the rush to make him drunk and send him on his way with a ludicrous story and a few gold coins in his pocket, the very image of a wanderer brash enough to somehow steal a treasure and foolish enough to brag about it.

"Tell your Master that I must speak with him," said Gullivar to the driver.

Something in the warrior's voice must have impressed the driver, and the repairs on the damaged wheel were almost complete, leaving the carriage in condition to travel again. So, the driver went and quickly returned to tell Gullivar that his master would see him in the common room.

The Lord was sipping hot kanel wine cooked with almond shells, when Gullivar came to talk to him. He recognized the wanderer whom he had met the day before, and asked why he wanted to see him. After saluting and introducing himself, the Earthman showed the Lord the four gold coins that the Woodsman had given him.

"Do you recognize these coins?"

"Yes. This is King Guillem's profile. The coins that were stolen from us were exactly the same. Where did you find those?"

"I think I can now explain what happened to you, and even identify the thief," said Gullivar.

The Lord then rose and hugged the wanderer.

"If you can do that, then we're saved. The Kingdom is saved. I am Phaine, High Lord Chamberlain to King Guillem, and the Lady traveling with me is Queen Brune herself. The King is being held prisoner at the Keep of the Two Orbs deep in the Nihan Mountains. The four bags of gold we were carrying were his ransom. If we don't pay it by the day after tomorrow, he and his daughter, Princess Aelia, will be put to death. The Queen became almost mad with grief when she found that someone had stolen the ransom. Our only hope was to reach her father, the Jubarque of Samar, but his kingdom is on the other side of Direwood, past the great marshes, and with our broken wheel, we'd lost all hope of traveling there in time to save the King's life."

"What happened?" inquired Gullivar.

"Baron Massoch sought revenge against King Guillem for ordering his castle razed. He took advantage of the fact that the royal family was spending some time alone with but a small retinue of followers at the Keep of

Two Orbs, a small, isolated castle in the Nihan. He attacked it with his soldiers, and took us by surprise. He massacred all our men, but made us his prisoners. Then, he sent me back with the Queen to collect a ransom. If it is not paid by the day after tomorrow, he'll nail the King and young Princess Aelia's hands and feet to the ground, and have horses run a plow across their bodies."

"Well, I know who stole your gold: the Woodsman at whose house you stopped yesterday. But by now he's probably hidden it in a secret place in the forest."

"I could summon soldiers to seize him and force him to talk."

"You don't have time. Besides, I know the kind of man he is. Force would lead you nowhere. He is too crafty. But if you follow my instructions, I think I see a way to save your King."

Later that day, the Lord Chamberlain knocked on the Woodsman's door, pretending to make inquiries about the stolen gold, while the Earthman hid behind a tree. As the wanderer had foretold, the Woodsman behaved humbly. He claimed that he had not been present the day before, and when told about the ransom's disappearance, blamed it all on his apprentice, whom he said was a drunk and a madman, and whom he had just dismissed.

While the Chamberlain kept the Woodsman busy, Gullivar sneaked into the hen house from the back and stole the white bird. Then, he ran back into the forest and, soon afterwards, rejoined the Chamberlain in his room at the Inn. The Lord was somber. Dusk had come and he knew that they had only two more days to save the King and the Princess–and no gold.

"Don't worry," said Gullivar. "I now have the means to rescue your King."

The Chamberlain thought the wanderer had lost his mind. He saw a bird, of admittedly an unusual hue, but a bird nevertheless. However, Gullivar placed the white bird under his left arm and, as he had seen the Woodsman do, petted him with his right hand while singing:

> *"Night before me, day after me,*
> *Let no mortal eye see me!"*

"Where are you?" the Chamberlain said. "You've disappeared!" And from what seemed like empty space, Gullivar's voice said, "It works! The King is saved now!" And he sang:

> *"Day before me, night after me,*
> *Let any mortal eye see me!"*

And, immediately, he reappeared before the Chamberlain's startled eyes.

The next morning, soon after dawn, the Chamberlain's carriage arrived at the Keep of Two Orbs. It had been named thus because it had two burning jewels, one of ruby and a smaller one of sapphire, which decorated the top of its tallest tower. The castle had once belonged to Phra-kan, and it was there that Montressor, the legendary Enchanter of Seth, had finally defeated that mighty demon. It was surrounded by tall granite monoliths, which were said to be the Seven Servants of Phra-kan, turned to stone by Montressor. It was an impressive place, fit for a King.

Gullivar had carefully explained his plan to the Chamberlain. Then, he used the white bird's bizarre magic to become invisible. When the first of Baron Massoch's men stopped the carriage, they saw only the Chamberlain. The drawbridge was lowered to allow the carriage inside. The Chamberlain stepped out, careful not to close the door behind him.

"Where is the gold?" the Baron asked.

"It was stolen just as we were bringing it, but if you grant us three more days, my lady and I can get more from her father, the Jubarque of Samar."

"No! It is a trick!" shouted the Baron. "My word stands! Tomorrow at noon, your precious King and his little broodling shall perish!"

Then, he ordered his men to escort the Chamberlain out. Many of the men thought that their liege would not be too saddened if the ransom was not paid, as he would obviously enjoy torturing the King and his young daughter, but their long years spent in the employ of their dark master had hardened their heart and, wisely, tightened their lips, and so they remained silent.

When the High Lord Chamberlain had left, Gullivar Jones had not stayed inside his carriage. Instead, invisible to all, he had remained behind in the Keep of the Two Orbs, and explored it until he felt reasonably familiar with the lay of the place, and had found King Guillem and Princess Aelia's room. Two sentinels guarded it.

Gathering some dust from the floor, Gullivar gently blew it across the sentinels' face until they burst into a fit of sneezes. The wanderer took that opportunity to discretely push the door open and slip into the room, causing the guards to blame the drafts and slam the door shut behind him.

Once inside, Gullivar whispered, "I'm a friend. Don't be afraid. I've come to rescue you."

King Guillem naturally rubbed his eye and looked everywhere for the source of the mysterious voice. But not so Princess Aelia, who was sixteen and quite beautiful. She was still of the age when one believed in guardian spirits, and was thrilled that one had come down from the Sphere Invisible to their rescue. After some hurried explanations, the Earthman gave a vial containing a fine, white powder to the King.

"I can take the Princess today," he said. "I shall have to come back for you tomorrow. Take some of this powder tonight in a glass of wine, and have no fear. Now, kiss your daughter and we'll be on our way."

Gullivar then grabbed Aelia and carried her in piggyback fashion. As soon as the princess's feet left the ground, the magic of the white bird surrounded her, and she, too, became invisible. King Guillem shook his head in wonderment at this prodigy, then, as the Earthman had instructed him to do, opened the door to go talk to the guards. This, of course, enabled the crafty wanderer to leave the room, unseen and unheard.

Gullivar crossed the castle, taking every precaution to not touch anything or anyone, waiting for doors to be opened whenever necessary. He had to wait for a good hour until the drawbridge was lowered as the guards changed watch. During that time, the princess began to weigh heavily on the wanderer's back, but he could not release her without risking both their lives.

Finally, they were out of the Keep. Gullivar ran past the stone monoliths towards the woods. There, nearly out of breath, and safely out of sight, he dropped the Princess to the ground and rested. But he knew they could not linger, as the Baron had posted patrols throughout the neighboring area. So, with the princess once more on his back, Gullivar began the long run towards Direwood, the white bird's strange magic protecting him from the Baron's men.

Meanwhile, at the Keep, the Princess's absence had finally been discovered. The Baron flew into a black rage and cursed his men roundly.

"You allowed that thieving Chamberlain to infiltrate a spy into the Keep! You will all be punished! No meat and wine for two days! The guard will be doubled, and if I catch anyone failing in his duty, I'll personally skin him alive!"

Baron Massoch frothed, while Abad, his great hound, watched him with bloodthirsty yellow eyes. Abad was an incarnated Horror from the Underworld of Mars, and it was he who had always compelled the Baron to ever-greater wickedness. Seeing another opportunity to grab one more piece of the Baron's soul for his demon lords, he darted his evil eyes towards the cursed nobleman who, beneath the beast's malignant influence, blasphemed so horribly that even his more hardened men blanched.

"May I be consigned to the Deepest Pit if I let these two escape! I'll die a happy man if Thunder smashes that bitch Aelia and the King's spy!"

And Thunder, who was an old friend of Abad's evil masters, heard the Baron's curse and responded in kind. A storm began rolling in from the North, where all evil lived, and gathered over the mountains...

Meanwhile, Gullivar was running for his life, still carrying Aelia on his back, avoiding the horsemen that the Baron had sent in pursuit. The Princess's weight was heavy on his shoulders, and he now stumbled often, yet continued to carry his burden as he jumped from rock to rock, crossed streams, and avoided the strangelings which lived in the mountains.

"I'm ashamed to cause you so much pain," whispered the Princess, who could hear the Earthman's wheezing, raucous breath. "You should just abandon me here and escape."

But the warrior just gritted his teeth and continued to run. Near an ancient, crumbling stone wall, Gullivar spotted a tuft of germande. He remembered Dromu's advice and pulled up a handful, which he began to chew. The awful bitterness of the herb spread throughout his body, invigorating him and granting him new strength. His strides became more assured, and his breath steadier.

But suddenly, the storm broke, seeking them throughout the canyons and the valleys.

"Strike here!" said Thunder to Lightning. And Lightning struck, causing rocks to shatter. "Splinter this tree!" ordered Thunder, and Lightning did, ripping the wood asunder. "Wreck this cabin!" "Destroy this boulder!" And all the while, Gullivar continued to run, protected from the storm's fury by the invisibility of the white bird, until finally, the storm's energies were all expended, and it was forced to abate.

After crossing the river Orsage, Gullivar Jones knew he was safe. He put Aelia back on the ground and, together, they walked to the meeting point where the Lord Chamberlain was waiting for them. Queen Brune's joy at finding her daughter was marred only by the fact that she knew her husband was still in the clutches of Baron Massoch, and that he would die on the morrow if not rescued.

"It will be more difficult with the King," said Gullivar, "because now, they'll be on their guard, and he is too heavy for me to carry. But I think I've come up with a plan..."

And the wanderer and the High Lord Chamberlain retired to plan the King's rescue.

The next morning, the Baron was awakened by a low growl from Abad. The Baron, confident in the strength of his forces, and believing that the ransom would never be paid, was looking forward to the harrowing death he had promised King Guillem: crucified on the ground, his body would be wracked by the blade of a plow. Then, with the King dead, he hoped to rally other barons to his cause, and perhaps open for himself the road to the throne of Savaria. His dreams of blood and avarice were shattered when a guard quakingly told him the King appeared to have died in his sleep.

The Baron swore a foul curse and rushed to the King's room. There, his drawn face the pallor of death, his lips black, lay the still body of King Guillem. Being thus thwarted of his revenge was too much for the Baron. He screamed until his face became crimson with blood. The men cowered before their lord's rage; only Abad licked his yellow lips with a purple tongue, for he knew the hour was near when he would be able to carry away the prize he had sought for so long: the Baron's soul.

Finally, the Baron did what he had always done in the past when confronted with obstacles to his will: he went hunting. Gathering his hounds and a few, frightened followers, he blew his horn, ordered the drawbridge to be lowered and, at a hell-bent pace, left the Keep of Two Orbs.

An hour later, the Keep's sentinels beheld a most extraordinary sight. On the road leading to the Keep walked a fully-grown fatted ox. They took it to be an animal that had escaped from its master's barn, perhaps because of the dreadful storm which the Baron had summoned the day before. Deprived of wine and meat because of their master's orders, the guards were delighted by their find. Lowering the drawbridge, they went out and led the animal inside.

What they could not have known was that the ox had been bought from a local farmer by the Lord Chamberlain at Gullivar's request, and led to the Keep by the wanderer, now invisible and back within the castle's walls.

The unwitting guards took the hapless animal to the stables, where they slaughtered and skinned it. They then dragged the carcass to the kitchens and ordered the cooks to prepare the meat.

While all this activity was going on, Gullivar returned to the King's room. The body had been left untouched. The Earthman delicately lifted an eyebrow, looked into the King's pupils and smiled with satisfaction. The powder he had given to King Guillem the day before had acted as it was meant to do. To all eyes, the King appeared to be dead. Yet, he was only plunged in a deep, catatonic slumber.

With a mighty heave, the Earthman lifted the King's body, which became invisible as soon as it left the ground. He then carried it back to the stables, which were now deserted. The weight of the King was terrible, and Gullivar well knew that he could not afford to drop his burden. Fortunately, the distance was short, and he was able to make it. Once in the stables, the warrior began to work in earnest on his plan.

Meanwhile, outside, the guards were taking advantage of the Baron's absence to enjoy a repast such as they had not had in many a month. The meat of the fatted ox, cooked to perfection, was succulent. Soon, it was all gone, and a careful observer would have noticed a rosy glow to the men's cheeks that had not been there before.

A few hours later, the blaring of the trumpets and the baying of the hounds signaled the return of the Baron's hunt. The soldiers quickly rid themselves of whatever remains there were of their meal. In the stables, Gullivar became tense for he knew his time had come.

The Baron was, if anything, in a fouler mood than before, having failed to catch anything. The horses were overexcited, sensing their master's anger; the dogs were frustrated to not have had their share of flesh and blood. Abad's lips quivered; his yellow eyes glinted; he was frothing with anticipation: the Baron's soul would please his demonic lords, and he could look forward to a better incarnation next time.

The drawbridge was lowered to allow the hunt inside. As the Baron entered the Keep's courtyard, a ghastly music was heard: the thin, wailing sound of a flute, playing the *Cantabile Macabre*–the Music of the Dead.

Then, a gruesome spectacle made its appearance. First, there was the freshly cut head of the dead ox, still dripping with blood. Its eyes bulged with fear, its lips hung loosely, covered with flies, its hair was matted with clotted blood, and its horns were soiled with offal. The stench was abominable. The grotesque head appeared to float in the air, being stuck at the end of a pitchfork, which dragged on the ground but otherwise enjoyed no visible means of support. The awful thing was pulling a chariot upon which, lying on the blood-smeared hide of the ox, was the corpse of the Dead King. A candle, whose pale flame cast strange shadows upon the King's face, burned at the head of the carriage. And as if that abominable sight was not enough, the sinister, overpowering *Cantabile Macabre* clawed at the ears and froze the hearts of the onlookers.

Sheer terror struck everyone. Panic spread like wild fire. The horses reared, breaking skulls and crushing bones, throwing their riders and trampling their bodies. The dogs broke their leashes and, screaming, turned against their masters, tearing into their flesh, drinking blood from severed jugulars. The soldiers, in their blind desire to flee, unsheathed their swords and hacked each other in a frenzy of fear and savagery.

Baron Massoch was thrown to the ground and trampled by his horse, but he did not die. His doom came when the great hound Abad looked into his eyes and there, he saw the fate that was in store for him. His scream was cut short by the gurgling sound of the blood which erupted from the Horror that had been Abad, as it tore his head from his body and took it back with him to the Seventh Circle of the Pit. The rest of his body was hacked to pieces, the same fate that he had intended for his prisoners.

And so, the macabre cortege of the King's body triumphantly left the Keep of Two Orbs unhindered, while the few survivors scattered on the winds of madness and despair.

Later, and much farther away, when he was sure he could no longer be caught or detected, Gullivar threw away the ghastly ox head and pitchfork, and sang:

"*Day before me, night after me,*
Let any mortal eye see me!"

Then, visible once more, he crushed some germande in a cup of water and forced some of the potion between the King's lips. The bitterness of the herb made the patient shiver and chased away the paralyzing cold that the drug had poured into his veins. The King opened his eyes, sneezed, saw he was free and hugged his savior.

They eventually returned to Direwood, where the Chamberlain was waiting for them, with an escort of soldiers he had had time to summon. Queen Brune and Princess Aelia saw the King and their hearts leaped with joy. The royal family fell into each other's arms, and much laughter and happiness was shared by all that day.

After Gullivar's daring and ingenious rescue of the King and his daughter, there was much pomp and celebration in the capital of Savaria. The Courts of the Kingdom gathered to offer the warrior title and fortune, but faithful to the vow he had once made to Princess Heru of the Golden Race, he refused all offers of wealth and ennoblement. Indeed, as the season of mists was now well underway, Gullivar prepared to yet again take the road south. But before he could pack his few belongings, he was summoned by the King.

"A strange thing has happened," said Guillem. "Something which I hope you can help me fathom. As soon as we returned to Savaria, I dispatched a squadron of my finest guards to arrest the Woodsman of Direwood, he who had stolen the four bags of gold that were to be my ransom. When my men reached his house in the clearing of Chel, they found it deserted..."

"Surely, upon hearing of your deliverance, he fled, fearing your rightful justice," the Earthman said.

"Perhaps, but that is not likely. My men were most thorough in interrogating everyone in the province. A Woodsman, even disguised, carrying four bags of gold is not easy to hide. Yet, no one saw him go. It is as if he has vanished from the face of the Earth. Do you think he had a second white bird to protect him with the same spell of invisibility that you used to rescue me?"

"I do not think so. I cared for all his animals throughout the season of snows, and I know he had only one such bird."

"Then, it is most assuredly a mystery. One that I should like to see resolved. You appear to have a good head for conundrums of this nature, and I wonder whether you could be persuaded to find its solution. Besides, I would like to recover the four bags of gold..."

"The matter does intrigue me, and I would be happy to look into the Woodsman's disappearance."

"If you can solve this puzzle, you will have once more earned my gratitude. I shall instruct all within my kingdom to remain at your disposal."

Thus did Gullivar Jones again fly to Direwood, accompanied by two of the King's men. Yet, search and question without cease, he could find no trace of the Woodsman or the four missing bags of gold. Thus was a fortnight spent in fruitless investigation, until a day came when the Earthman thought that he, too, would be forced to return to Savaria empty-handed.

On the last of the days Gullivar had given himself to find the key to the mystery, one of the local peasants breathlessly appeared to tell him that the Woodsman had returned.

Gullivar and his men rushed to the house in the clearing and saw that the informant had indeed been right: the Woodsman was back in his house, looking dirtier and craftier than ever. The wanderer confronted the man, who seemed embarrassed at seeing his former apprentice before him, but somehow less so than Gullivar would have believed.

"Don't lie to me this time, or I'll have you arrested," said Gullivar. "Tell me what you did with the King's ransom."

"Do I look like a man who has a buried treasure," replied the Woodsman wearily. "I no longer have it. If I did, I wouldn't be back in this hovel."

"What did you do with it?"

"It's a long story, but one I see I will have to share with you. Maybe *she* meant for this to be..."

"*She*? Who is *she*?"

"You will learn that soon enough. Now, listen. When I thought I had gotten rid of you at the inn outside of the Canyon of Chel, I buried the four bags of gold near a great oak, deep in the forest. I did not dare spend it, knowing that would attract attention. A few days later, word came that you had rescued the King, so I decided to leave quickly before they sent guards to arrest me.

"I headed north, planning to escape through the Nihan, using roads known to few but smugglers. The next evening, I had reached the place known as the Rock of Despair. It is a lonely peak, avoided even by the strangelings who live inside the mountains. It bears the sculpted faces of the Fallen Ones, and I heard it said that it was there that their souls were chained to the rock, after they took the side of the Black Beast when it rose against the Lords of Life before the Great Fear. At the Rock's feet, there is a lake with waters of unparalleled clarity, which the strangelings call the Pool of Tears, because they say it is made of the Keepers' tears. It is an accursed place, avoided by all but the bravest smugglers, and only my pressing need to escape from Brange as fast as I could compelled me to travel that way.

"As I skirted the lake, I saw a truly astonishing sight. The flank of the Rock had opened, and from within came an amazing tide of gold. It covered the shores of the lake in the same way that the washer women cover the fields with their laundry in summer.

All that gold quieted my fears of the place. I tied my donkey to a tree and went to take a closer look. There were coins, ingots, gold bars, jewels of all shapes and styles, crowns of such prize as to make Kings pale, chiseled plaques, precious statues and much, much more. That treasure made mine seem as small and ridiculous as a child's. My eyes could not take it all in. My mind burned with fever. My head reeled. I knew one thing and one thing only, I wanted some of that gold to be mine!

"I ran to get sacks from my donkey. Then, I gathered as much gold as my hands could grasp and stuffed my bags full of it. After they were brimming over, I began to retrace my steps. But my eyes were caught by something shining on the ground. It was a beautiful pin, entirely made of gold. I could not resist its lure and took it, pinning it to my jacket, before setting off as fast as I could.

"As dawn neared, a low, rumbling sound shook the mountain. The gold began to be pulled back inside the Rock, like a carpet being rolled back. I watched this spectacle from afar in wonderment. Suddenly, I felt myself being pulled forward, torn from the peak where I stood and propelled so brutally that my feet stumbled upon the ground. It was the gold pin! It dragged me, cursing, screaming and begging for mercy, until I was inside that damned Rock. There, it threw me to the ground, which was nothing but a mountain of cold metal. Behind me, I felt the huge rocky gates close. I neither heard nor saw them do it, no more than I had heard them open, but I felt the weight, the icy, heavy weight of the musty air, falling upon my shoulders like a leaden shroud; a sinister reminder that I was now inside a tomb, a place of eternal death.

"I looked around and saw that I was in an impossibly vast hall, housing more treasures than my mind could encompass. There were columns of ruby and pillars of sapphire, and strange entities of diamond appeared to float through the air. No one paid any attention to me, until I heard her laugh, a thin, high-pitched laugh that I shall never forget, and which still rings in my head as I tell you this.

"Suddenly, *she* was before me, proudly sitting on a diamond throne. She looked like a beautiful woman, but appeared to be made of the deepest shades of burnished gold that I had ever seen. She was incredible to behold. My father had once seen her in Gridbhan, near the smoldering ruins of Marek's Tower, in Zekar. I knew her to be Seramize, the Keeper of the World's Treasures.

"According to the ancient covenant she made with the Keepers, she must expose her gold to the purifying rays of our twin moons every month, during Mandrake Night, or else lose her trust. But she is rumored to be the most jealous of guardians. A million times better to be roasted in the Deepest Pit than to be caught stealing from Seramize.

" 'You have violated my secrets, Woodsman,' she said. 'Intruded upon the Presence and tried to steal my treasure. As punishment, you shall remain here, my prisoner for all eternity.'

"I begged for mercy, until she seemed to relent. I now wonder if she did not have this encounter in mind when she said: 'Very well. You will stay here until the next Mandrake Night. Then, I shall allow you to leave. If you can bring me as much gold as you can carry before dawn, then, perhaps I will release you.'

"I spent horrible weeks in Seramize's Halls, chained to the damp metal, with no light, no food, no company, yet somehow remaining alive. After what felt like an eternity, the cave again opened. The gold moved beneath me like the sea. The voice of Seramize reminded me I had until dawn to bring her the gold, or her pin would drag me back to the Rock.

"I needed only an hour to bring the King's ransom to the Halls. Seramize looked at the four bags and, seemingly surprised that a poor Woodsman could gather so much wealth in so short a time, she asked if the gold was mine. I tried to tell her it was, but my mouth betrayed me. In the end, I had no choice but to tell the truth. Then, she said, 'I order you to remain prisoner here until the next Mandrake Night, then I shall allow you to alternate between spending a month free outside, and a month imprisoned inside my Halls, until your victim pardons you.'

"Last night was the second Mandrake Night, so faithful to her word, she released me and I decided to return here. Since she had kept the ransom, I had no place else to go. I thought the King would never pardon me, and I would be lucky to escape with my life. Frankly, I have resigned myself to spending half of the rest of it underground."

"I believe your story," said Gullivar. "I think the King will pardon you if I ask him to. But I want to return his ransom to him. Give me that gold pin."

"What if it drags you into Seramize's Halls?"

"That is a risk I am prepared to take," said Gullivar.

Then, the wanderer flew back to the Courts of Savaria to tell King Guillem his tale. The King was fascinated by the Woodsman's story, and willingly granted his royal pardon. He affixed his seal to the bottom of a vellum, and dispatched a messenger to deliver it to the Woodsman.

Meanwhile, Gullivar had the gold pin examined by several of the King's magicians, but they were not true Enchanters of Seth, and none saw anything more extraordinary than a mere pin. Recovering the King's ransom had become a personal challenge to the wanderer. King Guillem, who was a wise man, tried to discourage him and change his mind, for he was wary of having any kind of contact with such an entity as Seramize, but Gullivar would not listen.

Finally, as the next Mandrake Night approached, the wanderer decided to launch an expedition to the Rock of Despair, and break into Seramize's Halls. This time, he found no volunteers to accompany him, and the King did not have the heart to order one of his men on a mission where he might lose his immortal soul to recover four bags of gold.

Thus did Gullivar Jones flew to Direwood. There, he returned to the Woodsman's house to obtain directions to the Rock. When he saw his old apprentice, the Woodsman smiled.

"After I received the King's pardon, Seramize came to me in a dream. She said I was now free, and that I had been right to give you the gold pin. She asked me to tell you that she does not keep gold that is not hers. If you still wish the return of the King's ransom, you must go to the Rock and enter her Halls. The four bags will be there, to the right of the entrance. You have her inviolable word that no harm will come to you."

Then the Woodsman added, "For myself, I'd rather go through a thousand deaths than again set foot inside that accursed mountain, but you are welcome to take her up on her offer."

"That is exactly what I intend to do," said the Earthman.

And the next day, without a backward glance, he flew deep inside the Nihan Mountains, towards the Rock of Despair.

Gullivar Jones finally reached the Rock of Despair towards the third hour of the evening. After storing his carpet under a bush, he walked to the lake known as the Pool of Tears to take a closer look at the place. If the gargantuan faces of the Fallen Ones, sculpted on the rock, noticed him, they kept their own counsel, for the wanderer was allowed to proceed unhindered. By his reckoning, he had yet another hour before the Mandrake ate the second moon.

Much to his surprise, Gullivar found he was not alone on the lake's shore. There was also a Nihani, one of the strangelings who lived in those mountains. By the looks of his crest, and the color of his hue, Gullivar saw he was one of the Old Ones. The Nihani leaned heavily on a staff to help himself cross the uneven terrain. Gullivar approached him and saluted him.

"What are you doing here, O Most Blessed of the Red Mother," he said, using the honorific title he had heard employed by the Nihani tribes of the Burning Plains to the south. "Do you need my assistance?"

"Thank you, O Wanderer from the Blue Star," said the Old One, who saw the flame burning within Gullivar Jones' breast and recognized his otherworldly origin. "I am called Labioth Elaquanta. I am 299 years old by your reckoning, and I have come here unassisted every year for this Mandrake Night for the last 228 years."

"Why?" inquired Gullivar.

"In those days, I was a proud, young warrior of my brood, but poor. As is the custom of my people, I was caring for my son, Tath Labioth, then a mere infant. One night, while returning from the ripening, I lost my way in these mountains and found myself on these very shores. I saw the rock yonder open, and the gold disgorge from within the mountain. I lost my head and ran. Putting my child on the ground, I grabbed as much gold as I could carry and ran back to deposit it safely on this hill. I made 12 such trips, while keeping a careful eye on the second moon, for I knew of Seramize, and realized the rock would soon close. My greed made me believe there was time enough for a thirteenth trip. I took up a handful of gold, but I had miscalculated. When I returned, the gold had returned to the mountain, taking my child back with it."

Tears ran along the old Nihani's cheeks. Gullivar puts his hand on the aged shoulders, but remained wordless with compassion. Labioth Elaquanta continued.

"First, I threw the accursed gold back into the pool. Then, I begged Seramize, and struck the rock until my fists were bloody, but it remained closed. Then, I gathered several men of my tribe, as well as a Wise One, who knew the secrets of the powders that burn. Together, we launched an attack against the rock from these very shores. But Seramize summoned a lake monster that soundly defeated us and drove us away.

"Finally, as a last resort, I returned on the next Mandrake Night and again humbly begged Seramize to return my son to me.

" 'You are but a poor Nihani,' she said. 'Someday, I may give your child back, but only when I think you have done penance enough, and if you have not stopped loving him. Come on the same night each year and bring with you a new sarlasse, the ritual shirt worn by the young ones of your tribe, deposit it by the rock, then leave. Return the next morning and if I am satisfied, your child will be returned to you.'

"Ever since, for 227 years, I have come, from far-away battles, from the snows of Mount Hel; I have trekked to this rock to do Seramize's bidding. I have outlived all my companions, gone on beyond the time allotted to my people by the gods; somehow, I have found the strength to continue to carry out Seramize's orders.

"So, wanderer, let my tale be of warning to you. If it is wealth that you seek, go elsewhere. Steal not from Seramize, for she is a vengeful lady."

While talking, they had reached the Rock of De-spair. There, on its mossy ground, the old Nihani laid the ritual sarlasse, so clean that it sparkled whitely, resembling a freshly bloomed flower. Then, with weary steps, Labioth Elaquanta disappeared into the darkness.

The Earthman waited alone until, finally, the Man-drake began swallowing the second moon. Suddenly, the rock opened, and from the Halls of Seramize came the light of an impossible dawn. The cavern was deserted. Neither Seramize nor her gem-like servants were any-where to be seen, from the mountains of gold, which moved like the dunes near the sea to the mounds of precious stones.

Gullivar entered the mountain. To his right, near the opening, as had been promised, were the four bags that comprised King Guillem's ransom. Above them, hanging on the wall, was a strange staff of precious wood, ivory and gold, with a glowing gemstone for handle.

Gullivar took the first bag and, feeling its weight, was in retrospect amazed by the strength of the Woods-man, who had carried all four. He took two of the bags and hurried outside. As he turned around, he heard a voice:

"There is no need for haste. For he who reclaims what is his, time shall not be counted. The rock will remain open until you have taken the last bag."

The voice was that of a man and was somehow tinged with sorrow. Gullivar looked around but saw no one. He deposited the two bags outside, then returned to take the other two.

"Who spoke?" he asked upon re-entering the Halls.

"I did."

The voice issued from the Staff.

"Who are you?

"It matters not. I am but a servant of Seramize. Work in peace and do not concern yourself."

As Gullivar prepared to lift the two remaining bags, he suddenly noticed that there were again four bags in front of him. It seemed as if the first two bags had magically returned. He quickly walked outside to check, but the two bags he had previously taken were still where he had left them, sitting on the mossy ground. So he returned to the cavern and, this time, took only one bag. He went outside and carefully deposited it alongside the others.

He was not overly surprised to discover, upon his return, that there were again four bags, not three, waiting for him inside. Ignoring the new bags, he calmly took the fourth bag and deposited it outside, against the other three. As he was doing this, a cold sweat began to flow over his brow. His heart beat loudly. Finally, he sat down on the grass and watched the Pool of Tears, which shone softly in the night.

He remained there beyond the boundaries of the Mandrake Hour, but the Halls stubbornly remained

221

open. Then, the passion that devoured him proved too strong. He re-entered the Halls and stationing himself firmly before the four, mysterious bags of gold that seemed to beckon to him, said:

"May I ask a question?"

"Ask, but I cannot promise I will answer you," said the Staff.

"Where is Seramize?"

"Is that the only reason you came back?"

"What other reason could I have? My task here is done."

"What about these four bags of gold which await you?"

"I took the bags which belonged to the King. I do not need any more."

"What about the other jewels and gold worthy of a king?"

"I am not a king."

"Yet, you are the first in many years to enter these Halls with the soul of a king rather than that of a thief. It is in my power to grant you a prize. Ask what you desire and it shall be yours."

"I would like to see Seramize."

"The Keeper is the Guardian of all of the World's Treasures. She has many such Halls, which she visits in turn. Tonight, she trusted you, since she is elsewhere."

"I want no other prize."

"Would you refuse a gift more precious than gold: that of a human life?" asked the Staff.

"If I can return life and happiness to a wretched soul, I accept," said Gullivar.

"Then, I shall grant you the power to free anyone from among the thousands of lost souls who have tried to steal from these Halls."

As the Staff became silent, the echo of his voice reverberated through the Halls. After it had died away, the mysterious golden light dimmed until Gullivar was plunged into total darkness. The great stone gates closed with a silent burst of cold air that made the young wanderer feel as if a shroud had just been draped across his shoulders.

Then, from everywhere in the darkness, voices began to be heard. Each told a painful story and implored Gullivar's mercy.

"My father was ruined and his creditors threatened to have him arrested. I saw all this gold and was tempted, but I only wanted to help him."

"My lover was beautiful. I would have sold my soul for one of her smiles. But I was too poor for her. I had hoped to keep her with some of this gold."

"I toiled hard since I was a boy, and saved barely enough to buy my freedom, when a thief robbed me. I was ready to kill myself when I saw the Rock open. I thought the gods had answered my prayers."

There were hundreds, thousands, each calling out at the same time, yet Gullivar heard each story. The wanderer was alternately seized with pity or contempt at hearing these stories. In the end, the Halls grew silent. Then, the Earthman raised his voice and said, "You were all weak, but guilty. Yet, there is one whom I have not heard and who was truly blameless. Tath Labioth, the child of Labioth Elaquanta the Nihani, who was abandoned here by his father 228 years ago."

"I am he," said a voice, which Gullivar recognized as the voice of the Staff.

"Why did you not beg for mercy like all the others?"

"Why should I? My father must be dead by now, and I am all alone. I do not desire to see the world where he suffered so much, and where no memories await me."

"You are not alone. Your father is still alive, and I saw him this very night. I choose you to come with me."

"So be it. Hold out your hand."

Gullivar did as he was ordered, and felt another hand grab his. Then, the golden light returned and he saw that the Staff was gone and he now held the hand of a young Nihani.

"Were you expecting a child after so many years?" asked Tath Labioth.

Gullivar remembered the small sarlasse brought religiously by Labioth Elaquanta year after year, but said nothing. The gates opened and they went outside. They sat on the grass by the Pool of Tears while the Rock of Everlasting Despair closed silently behind them. The night was almost over.

"I am disappointed to have not met Seramize," said Gullivar.

"In truth, I did not know where she was tonight, but I do know she will be at the Fountains of Gade in time for the next equinox."

"Thank you," said Gullivar.

Dawn came and with it, the tall silhouette of Labioth Elaquanta. Gullivar signaled to the old Nihani.

As soon as he saw Tath, the Old One ran and embraced his son.

"Blessed be this warrior from the Blue Star who has freed you," Labioth Elaquanta said. "My life is spent now, and I will soon go to rest with the Red Mother, but I will have tasted the pleasure of watching my son one last time. I have only one regret: that I did not see you grow and partake with you of the many rites of crossing."

Labioth Elaquanta picked up the sarlasse, which he had brought the night before and was about to discard it when Tath stopped him.

"No, Father. We must respect Seramize's commands. Give me the sarlasse."

As the young Nihani slipped the shirt over his head, there was a golden flash and, for a minute, both elves were bathed in light. As the light vanished, Gullivar saw before him the young Nihani that Labioth Elaquanta had again become, playing with an infant, love in his eyes, whispering the words of the Keeper's Tongue.

Gullivar then understood the power of Seramize's magic and went away silently, looking forward to the time of the equinox when he would face the Keeper of the World's Treasures at the Fountains of Gade.

So, it came to pass that, after retrieving the four bags of gold that had been King Guillem's ransom from the Rock of Despair, Gullivar returned to the Courts of Savaria.

He arrived during the trial of the treacherous Barons who had supported Massoch's rebellion. The wanderer was granted immediate audience with the King, who was much impressed by Gullivar's story of how he had recovered the stolen gold.

"We owe you our life, and our daughter's life," said the King. "You may ask your heart's desire for a prize."

But Gullivar again declined the King's offer of wealth and titles.

"Do you not wish for Princess Aelia' hand? I rejected five suitors while you were away; and I know she looks upon you favorably."

"Sire, I am but a wanderer, from a land so far away in the South that it does not even figure on your maps," said Gullivar. "The Princess Aelia is fair, and to be granted her hand would be a great honor indeed, but I am already betrothed to another. Perhaps it is better that I advance my departure and leave on the morrow."

The King shook his head sadly and sighed. His pride forbade him from pleading his daughter's cause further. He handed the Earthman a purse filled with gold, and bade him farewell.

"Since that is your wish, of course, you may go, but you will always be welcome in my Kingdom."

The next day, Gullivar Jones left the Kingdom of Savaria and flew south towards the place known as the Fountains of Gade, where the Nihani Tath Elaquanti, who had once been Seramize's slave, had told the wanderer he might meet the Keeper of the World's Treasures.

Gullivar crossed the mighty river Arlas, then the vast forest of Direwood. There, by questioning the Wild Folk, he learned the story of the Fountains of Gade. It was there that Bal-Mani the Conqueror had buried all the treasures he had gathered during his sacking of Galehault. They lay within a secret valley in the Yamur Mountains, in the land of Samar, guarded by the statues of Bal-Mani's nine warlords. At the center of that valley, the Conqueror had built nine great fountains, tapping the waters of a magic source that flowed below, and which caused men who drank from it to lose their minds and their souls. The Fountains' waters now formed a moat surrounding the valley, ensuring that few men were brave enough to enter it.

Yet, because the Fountains of Gade were rumored to be one of Seramize's abodes, foolish mortals from time to time sought to invade their sanctuary. The last one to do so, Jihr the Gifted, had since been known as Jihr the Mad.

Gullivar finally arrived in Samar, and made his way to the town of Sarlune, the village nearest the valley of the Fountains of Gade. As he entered the town, he saw a crowd gesticulating and shouting outside an inn. He asked the innkeeper what was happening.

"Alas, wanderer, a traveler who owed me for a fortnight suddenly passed away. As he had incurred debts while in this town, his creditors are fighting over his equipment, which isn't worth three copper coins. What am I to do? I am not rich enough to pay for a funeral for a stranger who would have been better advised to go and die someplace else!"

Gullivar gave the innkeeper King Guillem's purse.

"Pay this poor soul's debts and use the rest to give him a proper burial."

Gullivar then found a hospitable man who would let him spend the night in his stable, for his gesture had cost him all the money King Guillem had given him. During the night, he had a dream in which a wraith appeared to him.

"I am the soul of the man whose burial you paid," said the ghost. "You freed me, and I would repay your kindness. Go at once to the river Orande that springs from the Fountains and hide among the laurel bushes by its edge. At dawn, three deer will come. They will drop their skins and turn into wintiis. Take the fur from one of them and do not return it until she promises to admit you to Seramize's Hall."

Then, the wraith vanished and Gullivar awoke. He decided to follow the ghost's advice and traveled at once to the river. There, he hid among the bushes and fell asleep.

When he awoke, dawn had turned the river purple. Three deer came out of the neighboring woods and stepped so near Gullivar's hiding place that he could almost feel the warmth of their breath. As the wraith had foretold, they dropped their beautiful coats of fur and turned into three young wintiis, who entered the water, swam, frolicked and began to play amongst themselves.

Gullivar stepped from his hiding place and seized one of the fur coats. The three wintiis saw him and rushed back to shore. Two slipped on their fur coats, turned back into deer and ran away. But the third had no such choice.

"Please, My Lord," she begged, "give me back my coat so I can return to Seramize, else she will punish me."

"I shall give it back to you only if you promise to let me inside her Halls."

"I cannot do that."

"Then, I shall keep your coat," said Gullivar.

"Seramize made us swore we would never betray her."

"Simply allow me to follow you. If you do this, I shall give you back your coat, and you will not have broken your word."

The wintii considered Gullivar's offer for a while, then agreed. Gullivar surrendered the coat, and the sprite turned back into a deer. Faithful to her word, the wintii walked so slowly that Gullivar had no difficulty following her across the hidden paths that led past the Fountains of Gade and into Seramize's Hall.

The sight that greeted Gullivar was not unlike that which he had seen inside the Rock of Despair. Seramize's treasures spread as far as mortal eye could see. The Keeper of the World's Treasures sat upon her throne of diamond. She looked like a woman made of the most precious gold. She was dressed in the finest silks, and held the great sword, Forever, in her hand. Her face was covered by a mask of ruby, behind which burned the flames of timeless battles.

"How did you come here, Man of Earth?" Seramize asked Gullivar, obviously aware of his origins.

"I walked."

"I thought our business had ended at the Rock of Despair. The passion with which you seek me is flattering. Tell me, why you have pursued me so far?"

"I am here to ask the One Gift from you."

Seramize then looked at Gullivar with the Sight.

"I see. You seek that which was stolen from the Golden Race. The Blue Shard. Yet, I do not traffic in souls, not even the souls of the Keepers. I can, however, intercede with them to grant you your request, but as ever, there is a price."

"Whatever it may be, I shall pay it gladly."

"Do not be so rash to speak, warrior. I will restore what was stolen from your adopted people if you kiss me three times. But the balance must be preserved. Each time, you will see the face of one of your deepest fears. By kissing it, you will be consigning its soul to the fiery pits of damnation."

"I understand."

"Be ready then."

Seramize stepped from her throne. Gullivar bent forward to kiss her as she slowly removed her ruby mask. Beneath it was the horrible face of Baron Massoch, his decomposing flesh bloated by putrefaction, his tongue dripping with black ichor, his eyes filled with maggots. Gullivar overcame his disgust and kissed the abominable thing on its foul-smelling lips.

Knowing that he had to perform the act again, the wanderer inhaled deeply. Then, as he bent a second time, he saw that Seramize's head had become that of the Black Beast itself. Its three, evil eyes glinted as tongues of flames came from its snake-encrusted mouth. It hissed with such venom and rage that even the bravest of men would have fainted at its sight. Gullivar's legs barely carried him and sheer horror filled his heart, for he knew that the Beast was no mortal foe and would someday return from whatever pit he was consigning it to by his kiss. It would never rest until it exacted from Gullivar this same suffering. At the very moment that Gullivar kissed the Beast on its fiery lips, he glimpsed a sight of the Pit and wished for death.

Only one kiss remained. Gullivar wondered what last horror from his past Seramize would conjure. All his thoughts concentrated on one single, vertiginous goal: to hold firm.

He reached down for the third, fateful kiss.

A beautiful, blonde-haired girl now stood before him. He recognized her at once. She was Princess Aelia. The fresh smell of her youth rose towards the Earthman, lulling him towards the promise of an easy kiss. "One of my deepest fears," thought Gullivar. He smiled at the Aelia-who-was-not, a bleak smile that she would never see, and whose cost she would never know.

He now could gain what Princess Heru and her people needed most; the key to the survival of the Golden Race. He could at last fulfill his mission, return to Nûr victorious and celebrated as the greatest warrior of Mars. All he had to do was consign a sweet 16-year-old princess to Hell.

He did not give her the third kiss. And suddenly it was over. Seramize again stood before him, her ruby mask upon her face, resplendent beneath the golden lights of the Fountains of Gade.

"Fool," she said softly. Then, she turned around and began to walk away. "You shall never see me again, Gullivar Jones of Earth. But I will shape a statue of the purest gold in your likeness; its lifeless image will forever remind me of your virtue."

Seramize's voice died away. The Fountains of Gade had become silent and deserted. A cold wind rose from the North, and in the distance, a basilisk howled.

Gullivar shrugged. The season of mists was over, and it was time for him to continue on his journey south towards Nûr. He pulled out his flute and began to play as his magic carpet carried him away through the night.

The Searing Glory Which Hath Shone

Outside the city, a long caravan of green and red-garbed pilgrims had just crossed the Desert of Tears on the sole trail leading through it and had arrived in sight of Holy Seth. They marveled at the huge, ancient, city, its odd jumble of towers and spires, mismatched levels and crooked temples, half-buried in the Arcane Mountains. Beams of intermittent light, almost like a signal, acted like calls to the faithful.

Riding in the caravan, disguised as pilgrims, were Montressor, Edgar Allan Poe and Gullivar Jones. Discovering the city for the first time, Poe gasped; he had never seen its like.

Looking at the light, Montressor chewed his fingernails. "I think we're just in time. This is Seth, the City of Enchanters, which Rodrik-Usher has turned into his personal fortress. Ligeia is within."

Poe looked at the imposing crowds, the blue-garbed soldiers manning the walls, and then turned towards Gullivar. "You are a fine warrior, Mr. Jones, but I do not believe that even you can fight your way through an army that size."

"We may not need to. I still have a few tricks up my sleeve," said Montressor.

Outside the gates of Seth, the line of green-robed pilgrims formed a pulsing mass of humanity waiting to be allowed to enter the holy city. Montressor pulled a covered basket out from under his cloak.

Two azure-clad guards stood at the gate's checkpoint. They examined the offerings brought by each pilgrim. These were a grim assortment of grisly trophies meant to cater to the exotic tastes of the evil Enchanter: shrunken heads, pickled hands and other unsavory ornaments.

When Montressor's turn came, he uncovered his basket. Inside were a pile of stuffed dolls: a Gullivar Jones doll, a Poe doll, several muru bird dolls, plus a few more dolls that came from Earth.

"Rogan, look," said the first guard. "This one brings children's toys." Laughing, he reached his hand into the basket and pulled out the Poe doll, twisting its head.

"They look so realistic too," the guard continued mockingly. "Rodrik-Usher will surely be pleased."

Nervously, Montressor held out his hand to try to take the doll back.

"Leave him alone, Gornak," said the other guard. "Or we'll never be finished in time for the ceremony."

Laughing contemptuously, the first guard threw the doll back into the basket and gestured to Montressor to go through.

Rogan's reference to the "ceremony" had not passed by Montressor unnoticed. The portly Enchanter rushed into the city. The normally uncrowded streets were for once filled with pilgrims, acolytes and soldiers. Montressor elbowed his way past several groups of visitors seeking accommodation. Knowing the city intimately, the Enchanter quickly moved through a maze of back alleys and half-hidden shortcuts that enabled him to cross the city without delay.

His destination was obvious: the grey tower that stood at the center of Seth, which Rodrik-Usher had claimed as his. Montressor was wise enough to avoid the front entrance, and knowledgeable enough to remember a rarely used underground passageway that his friend Prospero had shown him at a time when portions of the great library had been housed inside the metal edifice.

As Montressor emerged from the passageway into the underground level of the tower, he noted with surprise that the metal corridors were now sparklingly shiny and pristinely clean. The Enchanter remembered that, in his day, the metal tower, which was really the top part of a vast, buried structure, was mostly left to itself. Ancient tapestries hung on its walls, covering the cold metal; cobwebs filled its corners and dust gathered everywhere. All that had changed under Rodrik-Usher's exacting control and Montressor now felt that he had entered a wholly different world.

The Enchanter easily remembered the way through the corridors and pathways of the buried structure. Suddenly, his luck ran out. As he turned a corner, he bumped into an elderly man wearing the blue and yellow robes of an Enchanter. As they saw each other, the old man's face registered the shock of recognition.

"Montressor?" he said.

"Master Bargel?"

"Help! Montressor! The heretic has returned!" screamed the old man.

Montressor cursed and began to run. A group of guards immediately appeared responding to Bargel's call, but too late. Montressor has already managed to drop through a hatch to another level below.

The Enchanter ran through the maze of corridors as fast as he could go. He knew the direction he needed and was able, therefore, to gain a bit of distance on his pursuers. With the alert given, these grew in number. Unused to so much exercise, he was quickly out of breath.

At one point, judging that he had put enough distance between himself and the guards, Montressor pulled the Poe and Gullivar Jones dolls from the basket and threw them to the ground, where they exploded in a puff of smoke.

When it had cleared, a full-size Poe and Gullivar Jones were standing there, complete with swords. They did not seem the worse for their transformation, except for the writer who rubbed his neck, as if in pain.

Montressor then took another toy from the basket and threw that to the ground as well. This, too, came to life, turning into a beast that lumbered after the guards, squeaking with every step it took. Poe thought its effect was as funny as it was menacing. Yet, Rodrik-Usher's Guards, who had never seen such a creature before, were awe-struck and ran off in terror.

Montressor signaled to the others to hurry. With the Enchanter leading the way, the four of them ran through the corridors.

Meanwhile, Rodrik-Usher stood alone in the doorway of the Place of Silence, head down, in silent meditation.

A low melody filled the air, originating from an unknown source. It barely hid the thumping sound of the alien heartbeat.

The evil Enchanter raised his arms.

At his command, the walls slowly pulled up, like a huge stage curtain, incredibly making the room much larger. The new space was a huge amphitheater where seven men, cloaked from head to toe in blue and yellow robes stood. It was their chanting that filled the room.

Rodrik-Usher entered the vast space. Inside, floating at the height where the ceiling had been before, just above the area delineated by the black line mosaic, was a massively huge blue crystal, shaped like a giant egg, pulsating with raw energy, in rhythm to the heartbeat sound.

He stopped a few feet away from the black line.

"Where is Bargel?" he asked.

The singing stopped. One of the Elders shrugged, testifying to his ignorance. Rodrik-Usher frowned, but continued, "Bring Ligeia."

Escorted by two guards, the young woman, now dressed in a sacrificial outfit, her face still a total blank, was brought into the room.

Montressor, Gullivar and Poe arrived just behind her, unnoticed by the guards. They stopped outside the room, frozen by the prodigious sight. The Enchanter focused on the massive stone.

"By the Horns of Seramize!" he swore. "This is bad. Far worse than I thought."

"What is that object?" asked Poe.

"The Blue Crystal of Seth."

"What does it do?"

"It was left behind by the Keepers. No one ever truly understood what it was, but it is very, very dangerous. It is from it that we derive all our powers; it is the very essence of magic, and more. It mustn't be tampered with. Why do you think I came back?"

"I don't understand."

"Think of it," said Montressor, growing slightly irritated, "as a living barrel of gunpowder, the size of Baltimore."

Inside the Place of Silence, Rodrik-Usher stopped the chanting with an imperious gesture. He then put his hand on Ligeia's shoulder and propelled her forward towards the black line, just below the Crystal.

"The time has come for you to facilitate my ascension to godhood, Ligeia. Go forward."

The Enchantress began to walk mechanically towards the black line.

"What is he doing to Ligeia?" asked Poe, transfixed by the sight.

But Montressor remained silent. All his energy was now solely focused on his ward. "I didn't think he could break down her barriers," he muttered to himself, chewing on his fingernails nervously.

"I said, what is he going to do to her?" repeated Poe.

"Feed her to the Crystal," said the Enchanter at last. Somewhat unnecessarily, he added, "We have to stop him."

Poe suspected that he did not mean that it was just to save Ligeia's life, but that there was something far greater at stake.

Gullivar rushed forward, sword raised, screaming out a chilling battle cry that reverberated through the room. Poe followed him.

Immediately, several guards ran to confront the intruders.

Rodrik-Usher turned to see what the source of the disturbance was; his face clouded in fury as he saw the invaders.

"Kill them!" he shouted. He raised his hands (yet another set) to smite them down, but before he could do it, several guards were blasted by a golden bolt of magic, and turned into stuffed dolls.

The remaining guards parted to let Montressor through.

"I've got to, er, hand it to you, Rodrik-Usher," said the Enchanter, wiggling his hands.

Rodrik-Usher's normally pallid cheeks dotted with dark purple spots. Rage filled his eyes.

"Montressor!"

"So that's your replacement Nine," said the Enchanter, pointing at the seven robed Elders who stood there in muted impotence. "Not much to speak of. In my opinion, we wouldn't even have considered them for jobs in the scullery. Ah well, falling standards and all that. By the way, I ran across old Bargel earlier. I'm surprised you didn't just train a monkey. He would have been cheaper and more attractive and just as competent."

"How dare you challenge me here?" replied the evil Enchanter. "Look at yourself. You're old, you're fat. The Other World has made you weak."

He raised his arms and shot a bolt of mystical energy at Montressor, who parried it with relative ease.

"I may have been on Earth a tad too long, but I can still beat you without a problem."

The two Enchanters began to fight a magical duel, each of them deflecting the other's bolts, which ricocheted and hit Rodrik-Usher's own Elders, who did nothing to avoid them or defend themselves. Every time one of Rodrik-Usher's deflected bolts struck an Elder, the man turned to stone and crumbled. Every time one of Montressor's bolts struck, they turned into a small, stuffed doll. Soon, only one Elder remained standing.

Meanwhile, Poe and Gullivar held their own against the remaining guards who had not been scared away, enabling the faster and deadlier warrior of Nûr to make his way to the front of the room, where Ligeia stood.

With Rodrik-Usher's attention elsewhere, the young woman had stopped walking and just stood there, fixed in her trance-like state.

Gullivar reached the Enchantress and tried to shake her out of her trance, but Ligeia did not move and remained catatonic.

Meanwhile, the two Enchanters had begun to strain their powers beyond natural limits. Soon, an observer would have judged that Rodrik-Usher's earlier jibe was not entirely incorrect: Montressor's life on Earth had indeed taken its toll. The small Enchanter was sweating heavily and was obviously getting tired.

"So, Fat One, where is your bravado now?" gloated Rodrik-Usher.

"It's not over yet," replied Montressor.

But in the end, Montressor could no longer divert all of Rodrik-Usher's magic. A bolt struck the portly Enchanter. He screamed, turned into stone and crumbled.

With Montressor gone, Rodrik-Usher turned towards Ligeia and saw Gullivar. He raised his hands to blast him, but stopped in mid-air. It had just occurred to him that he might hit the girl. Instead, he stepped forward and addressed the warrior.

"Gullivar Jones! Look!"

From the folds of his robe, Rodrik-Usher pulled out something shiny and golden. Poe could not focus his eyes on exactly what it was the evil Enchanter held in his hand. However, the effect on Gullivar was immediate and powerful. The sight of Rodrik-Usher's possession transfixed the warrior.

"Yes, it is the soul of Princess Heru. It is yours if you let Ligeia go. I will make her a new body to house it. And with her at your side, you can redeem the honor of her clan and build a new life together. It is all you have ever wanted, is it not?"

Gullivar's face turned into a battlefield of conflicting emotions. His longing for Heru was so apparent that it was painful to behold, yet so was his sense of duty. He remained torn for a brief moment but, in the end, there was no real choice but to stand by Ligeia.

"I do not trust you, Enchanter."

"Very well. Then, perhaps you will trust one of Heru's own blood?"

Rodrik-Usher beckoned to the remaining Elder. The man slowly stepped forward and let his cloak drop. Underneath was Melnach, of the Clan of Nûr, long dead, yet still alive, held together by the magic of Rodrik-Usher.

Gullivar remembered gently cradling the body of the dying man in his arms; his village still filled with the smell of freshly spilled blood and smoke. How Rodrik-Usher had managed to secure and reanimate the corpse was truly beyond his understanding, but he did not doubt for an instant that it was indeed the body of Melnach which stood before him.

"Elder," he whispered softly.

"Do not doom our Clan, Gullivar Jones," said Melnach in a slow, dead voice. "Do not fail Heru, your betrothed. She has a second chance at life. Together, you can rebuild and Nûr may live again. How can you prefer to stand at an Otherworlder's side? Have you no honor left?" Melnach extended his hand towards Gullivar and ordered, "Obey Rodrik-Usher!"

Slowly, reluctantly, Gullivar stepped forward, away from Ligeia. But Poe had watched the scene from afar, and suddenly shouted, "Mr. Jones! Gullivar! My brother! No!"

Poe's words jolted the warrior, who suddenly stopped. He took another look at Melnach and what he now saw was that, inside its shell, was just another creature, like the Red Death. The soul of Heru which Rodrik-Usher dangled before him was but an illusion, a travesty of life, form without spirit; his Princess' real soul had long since departed.

Seeing that his illusion has been shattered, Rodrik-Usher cursed and issued a brief order. The Melnach zombie pulled out a scimitar and raised it, attempting to strike Gullivar. But the warrior was faster, and he dealt the creature a mortal blow.

"Begone, foul thing!" shouted Gullivar, as his blade pierced the monster to reemerge black and soiled on the other side.

The Melnach-thing collapsed on the floor, its body turned to rot and foul-smelling ichor.

Gullivar rushed back towards Ligeia, but Rodrik-Usher was faster. Just as the warrior was about to reach the young woman, the evil Enchanter hit him with a magic bolt.

Gullivar, too, turned to stone, shattering into a thousand pieces!

Poe screamed, "Ligeia!" With amazing skill, he battled past the last guard and reached the young woman.

"Ligeia! It's Mr. Poe! Edgar! Please wake up! You must wake up! Please!" he implored.

Her companion's voice seemed to penetrate the young woman's trance. As if awakening from a long, profound sleep, she opened her eyes.

At first, these looked normal, but almost immediately, they turned violently purple.

Rodrik-Usher, seeing that Ligeia was now free of his spell, took another step forward and concentrated hard on her, as he tried to reassert his control.

"You will obey me. You are mine," he uttered, teeth clenched, brow perspiring.

With a gesture, Rodrik-Usher summoned up the shimmering image of the Nekrosian to frighten the Enchantress into submission.

For a second, Ligeia's face did show naked, brutal, irrepressible fear; but quickly, she frowned, shook her head, and her eyes blinked rapidly.

"No... I... am... *not!*" she strained.

And the image of the Nekrosian was blasted apart, like a reflection in water shattered by a thrown rock.

Rodrik-Usher gritted his teeth in anger. The evil Enchanter now threw all his power into the battle. He exerted his mighty resources. The air shimmered around him, as wave upon wave of power radiated forth.

Ligeia was forced, against her will, to take a step forward, a step towards the fateful black line that separated her from the Blue Crystal.

Poe, sensing that crossing that line meant death, or worse, tried to grab her to stop her, but more guards rushed into the room and held him at bay.

Rodrik-Usher strained to his utmost. "You... have... lost... Ligeia," he whispered. Veins bulged on his forehead. His hands were disintegrating on his wrists, leaving only bleached bones and foul-smelling residues of flesh.

But Ligeia, too, was reaching deep within herself, tapping a mystic heritage that stretched back to the days when a small girl had played with fragile silvery things and dipped her hand into a cup of glittering, liquid diamonds. Her eyes now glowed a bright, burning blue.

And this time, it was Rodrik-Usher who was forced to take a step forward towards the black line.

The Enchanter's face reflected his incredulity as he saw his body would no longer obey his will. "No! You cannot..." he exclaimed.

The duel of wills continued for a seemingly endless time, in total silence, each opponent reluctantly forced by the other to take one more step forward in this deadly, macabre parody of a children's game, until they were both within a single step of the fateful black line.

Almost directly above them, the gigantic Blue Crystal loomed, larger and more powerful than ever, its heartbeat increasing as Rodrik-Usher and Ligeia got closer.

Beads of sweat rolled down Rodrik-Usher's and Ligeia's faces. Their limbs had become rigid and their muscles were knotted with tension. The very air crackled around them.

There was room for only one, final step.

It looked like Rodrik-Usher would win after all, when Ligeia suddenly kicked one of his mangled hands, then shoved him hard into the square area on the other side of the black line.

Rodrik-Usher's body was pulled upwards to the Blue Crystal, where it was absorbed, except for the remains of the hands, which fell back to the floor.

There was a violent flash, and the evil Enchanter's body, now a charred husk, was spit out by the Crystal, dropping like a mangled scarecrow onto the floor below.

At the sight of their master's fate, the guards fled in panic. Poe, now freed, ran towards Ligeia and embraced her, their happiness all too obvious on their smiling faces.

"Where is Montressor? And Mr. Jones?" asked the Enchantress after the writer had let her go.

"I am so sorry. They tried to save you, but Rodrik-Usher was stronger," said Poe.

"No! It cannot be! Where are they?"

Poe took her over to the shattered bits of stone that had been her mentor and the warrior of Nûr. The two of them stood looking at the rubble broken-heartedly, their arms around each other. Then Ligeia started to cry.

Behind them, the charred husk of Rodrik-Usher began to rise. He slowly lifted his black, seared arm to release a bolt of magic, then seemed to realize he no longer had hands, only stumps. The Enchanter crawled forward and managed to reattach one of the skeletal remains of the fallen hands to his right arm. Again, he prepared to strike...

But Ligeia, preternaturally aware of what was happening, turned and saw him. With nothing more than a blink of her eyes, she signaled to the Crystal.

The Stone emitted a brief flash of energy, and dropped right on top of Rodrik-Usher, crushing the evil Enchanter forever.

"Fool!" said Ligeia. And that was the epitaph of Rodrik-Usher of Mazan, Rodrik-Usher the Damned, who had aspired to become a god.

Ligeia walked over to the Crystal, and much to Poe's horror, put her hands directly on its surface. A few seconds passed. The Crystal's color progressively drained away–until it became a pure, shining white.

Ligeia turned back towards Poe to explain what happened.

"He was injured, but I made him well again."

Suddenly, two bolts shot out from the Crystal, hitting Montressor and Gullivar. Like a movie played backwards, the stone fragments were reassembled and the two men were miraculously restored to life.

Montressor rubbed his arms as if to restore its circulation. Ligeia ran to him and hugged her mentor. Then, she thanked the Crystal, which pulsed a soft series of white and blue flashes of light in acknowledgment.

Then, it was the turn of the Malachites and of all the people who Rodrik-Usher had "fed" to the Crystal to be released. They came out in an almost unending stream, all showing their amazement at being alive again, and expressing their undying thanks to Ligeia. Some bowed and even kissed her feet, making the Enchantress uncomfortable, but she bore it with grace and dignity.

After that, the Crystal started to glow an ever brighter and brighter white, then again levitated upward.

It burned a hole through the ceiling of the metal construction that had once been a mighty ship, and flew upwards into the Heavens.

There was a brief flash of light in the Northern sky. The Crystal was gone.

"It has returned home," said Ligeia.

"Home?" asked Poe.

"It was a child," she said. "No, not a child, more like an egg, which had been left behind by the Keepers. A long, long time ago. Now, it is finally free to go home. I released it."

Off to the side, Montressor was chewing his lips. Poe noticed this and asked, "You don't seem happy, Mr. Montressor?"

"No. Yes. I'm glad it ended the way it did, of course. Rodrik-Usher got his due. The world is saved. And no one ought to object to a child being freed from bondage, of course..." But one could tell that the Enchanter was still worried.

Turning towards Ligeia, he asked, "What *exactly* did you do to release him?"

"It's quite complicated to explain," she replied.

"Try. It's very important," said Montressor with intent eagerness.

Ligeia opened her mouth, but no sound issued from it. Instead, she grew faint and transparent, and vanished like a wisp of smoke in the wind. Her face reflected no fear, no pain, no surprise. In fact, Poe thought he saw a longing in her eyes, as if she was welcoming her transformation.

The writer screamed her name, moving his arm through the empty air where Ligeia had stood only seconds before.

"Montressor! Grandfather! Is there anything you can do?"

For the first time, Poe saw the Enchanter look defeated. He was no longer the jolly, rubicund, confident man the writer had known, but a pale shadow of that former self.

"I'm afraid not, young sir," he finally said, forlornly. "I have spent several lifetimes studying the Keepers and when Ligeia said she had *released* the Crystal, I feared the worst. The reason that child was matterbound on this plane, and didn't leave when his race did, at the dawn of this world, is because he lacked something... You might call it a *soul*..."

"Do you mean to say that that thing stole Ligeia's soul?"

"Oh no! The Keepers are not evil. They would never dream of doing such a thing. I would guess that that Crystal could have stolen a soul at any time, if that was all it needed. No, Ligeia freely surrendered herself. She became part of it, she completed it. For all I know, maybe she was always part of it. Perhaps that was the reason she was born–her *raison d'être*, as the French might say."

Poe was heart-broken. Only three months ago, when he had returned to Richmond, he had discovered that his childhood sweetheart, Elmira Royster, had become engaged to someone else because her parents did not approve of him. And now, Ligeia, too, had been wrested away from him by an unspeakable fate.

"That is not the worst of it," Montressor continued. "I told you that the Blue Crystal was the essence of our magic. It was the power we drew from to maintain the vast barriers that have long protected this world from the ravages of space. Mars will grow dry and desert-like. Our oceans will evaporate. Our air will dissipate. Our world will die. We knew that this was its fate, of course, and we postponed it for as long as we could, but it is over now. We never learned how it would come to pass... Now we know."

"How long do we have?" asked Gullivar.

"A millennium or so, I gather."

"Such things no longer matter to me," said Poe. "I want only to return to my own world, my own time."

"I will take you back, then return here, for there is much now to be done. Rodrik-Usher left festering sores behind, which must be healed. Then the time will come to think of the great migration..."

Gullivar Jones walked over to stand by Poe.

"Today, I rediscovered that it was more honorable to stand by a living brother than to die for a dead cause. I wish you well, brother."

"I, too, Mr. Jones. Perhaps our paths will cross again, tho I doubt it."

The Enchanter and Poe left the Place of Silence. Behind them, the Elder Charadine, addressing a gathered crowd of pilgrims, began in his most declamatory voice, "Hear the Lore of Edgar Allan Poe the Otherworlder..."

Epilogue

True to his word, Montressor returned Edgar Allan Poe to Baltimore at the end of April 1827. On May 26, still heart-broken over the loss of Ligeia, the writer enlisted in the United States Army under the name "Edgar A. Perry." He was to remain a soldier until April 15, 1829, and was promoted to the rank of Sergeant-Major of the Regiment of Artillery.

As Montressor had promised, Poe's first book, *Tamerlane and Other Poems*, was published in Boston, by Calvin F. S. Thomas, soon after his return. The thin pamphlet sold perhaps 50 copies, many distributed free for reviews. However, his second book, *Al Aaraaf, Tamerlane and Minor Poems*, was published in December 1829 in Baltimore by Hatch and Dunning, to a much better reception.

In 1838, after a stint in New York, Poe and his young wife, Virginia, moved to Philadelphia, where the by-then-established author met, in short order, Arthur Gordon Pym of Nantucket and C. August Dupin of Paris, who led him to write some of his most celebrated works.

History records that Edgar Allan Poe died at the Washington College Hospital in Baltimore, early on the morning of October 7, 1849, after having been found, four days earlier, wandering, delirious, in the streets. The writer was never coherent long enough to explain how he came to be in his dire condition, and, oddly, was wearing clothes that were not his own.

Some claimed that he had died from alcoholism, a disease he had developed during his wife's long illness, or from some other kind of disease. Those who do so are the pragmatists, the men of science.

Others believe that Poe was the inadvertent victim of one of the thuggish political gangs which roamed Baltimore at the time. Those who believe this are the mystery lovers, who seek to solve the unsolvable crime. Certainly, Monsieur Dupin would have concurred with them.

Others note that the Scrolls of Rhiannon mention that the serpent folk of Caer Dhu were once defeated across the Sarkean Sea by a blue-garbed wizard and an Otherworlder whose description resembles Poe. They remember that in the writer's veins flowed the blood of Montressor, and they wonder if the Great Enchanter of Seth did not summon his grandson for one last battle by his side, leaving a magical simulacrum in his place. Those who spin such yarns are the romantics and the adventurers, easily dismissed.

Finally, a few witnesses saw a blue star shine briefly, then vanish, in the firmament of Baltimore soon before 5 a.m. on the day of his death. They believe that the Goddess Ligeia did not forget her greatest love and that, in his direst hour, she returned to elevate him with her into the Heavens. Those who cling to this version are the spiritualists and the theosophists, and they are no more credible than the romantics.

Yet, Edgar Allan Poe was all those things: a man of science, a lover of mysteries, a romantic and a spiritualist. It is therefore fitting that his final fate embraced all four destinies.

For we must end on the road to that mystery where courage, death, and the dream of love give promise of sleep.

Norman Mailer. *The Armies of Night.*

Acknowledgements

Roy Thomas introduced me to Gullivar Jones. The year was 1973 and Marvel Comics was using its old anthology titles to test new series ideas. That's how *Gullivar Jones, Warrior of Mars*, made his first appearance in issue #16 of the old *Creatures on the Loose* comic, formerly *Tower of Shadows*, that had already featured a beautiful *King Kull* story by Berni Wrightson. The new *Gullivar Jones* feature was a loose adaptation of the Edwin Arnold story, scripted by Thomas and beautifully drawn by Gil Kane, at the top of his form. I was in high school then, and had read John Carter, but had never heard of Edwin Arnold's hero. Personally, I believe that, if Edgar Rice Burroughs was influenced for *A Princess of Mars* (1912), that inspiration is more likely to have been Gustavus W. Pope's *Journey to Mars* (1894), rather than Arnold's somewhat clumsy, rebellious and anarchistic hero.

In any event, Thomas and Kane worked their magic, and I immediately became a fan of Gullivar Jones. After the first three issues, George Alec Effinger and Gray Morrow continued the series in a moodier but equally successful tone. I still have a school notebook with a rather appalling pen and ink drawing I did of Gullivar Jones, intending to continue his adventures, using some materials drawn from the local Provençal legends from my home region of France. That's when I learned I couldn't draw, but I could write. Between one

253

thing and another, it's taken me nearly 35 years to return to Mars, but I couldn't be happier!

Jean-Marc Lofficier

I was just a girl, but the memory of it still haunts me. We had convinced my mother to let us see Roger Corman's filmed version of *The Fall of the House of Usher*. In retrospect, perhaps that was a mistake, because for several years, I would not leave my bedroom alone at night, to cross the spooky expanse of the darkened living room and dining room to get a glass of milk. There were shadows and noises and imaginary creatures all waiting to grab me and lock me alone inside a coffin, where my fingers would turn to bloody stumps as I clawed my way free.

On the other hand, perhaps it was a good idea, as those dark imaginings have blossomed over the years into words and pictures that flow onto paper, harming no one, not even me.

Randy Lofficier

Sources

With Many Cares & Toils Oppres'd... From Poe's earliest surviving poem, never published during his lifetime (1824).

Of a Wild Lake with Black Rock Bound... From *The Lake* (1827).

Kind Solace in a Dying Hour... From *Tamerlane* (1827).

'Mid Dark Thoughts of the Grey Tombstone... From *Spirits of the Dead* (1829).

The Melancholy Waters Lie... From *The Doomed City* (1831)

Dim Vales and Shadowy Floods... From *Fairy Land* (1829).

The Searing Glory Which Hath Shone... From *Tamerlane* (1827).

BLACK COAT PRESS
www.blackcoatpress.com

FICTION

Jean-Marc & Randy Lofficier (eds.). *Tales of the Shadowmen 1: The Modern Babylon*
Jean-Marc & Randy Lofficier (eds.). *Tales of the Shadowmen 2: Gentlemen of the Night*
Jean-Marc & Randy Lofficier (eds.). *Tales of the Shadowmen 3: Danse Macabre*
Xavier Mauméjean. *The League of Heroes*
Frank J. Morlock. *Sherlock Holmes: The Grand Horizontals*
Marie Nizet. *Captain Vampire*
Charles Nodier, Antoine Beraud & Jean Toussaint Merle. *Frankenstein*
Charles Nodier. *Lord Ruthven the Vampire*
John William Polidori. *Lord Ruthven the Vampire*
P.-A. Ponson du Terrail. *The Vampire and the Devil's Son*
Eugène Scribe. *Lord Ruthven the Vampire*
Brian Stableford. *The New Faust at the Tragicomique*
Brian Stableford. *The Stones of Camelot*
Brian Stableford. *The Wayward Muse*
Brian Stableford (ed.). *News from the Moon*
Villiers de l'Isle-Adam. *The Scaffold and Other Cruel Tales*
Villiers de l'Isle-Adam. *The Vampire Soul and Other Sardonic Tales*
Philippe Ward. *Artahe: The Legacy of Jules de Grandin*
David White. *Fantômas in America*

NON FICTION
Steephen R. Bissette. *Blur (Vol. 1)*
Stephen R. Bissette (ed.). *Green Mountain Cinema: Green Mountain Boys*
Jean-Marc & Randy Lofficier. *Shadowmen: Heroes and Villains of French Pulp Fiction*
Jean-Marc & Randy Lofficier. *Shadowmen 2: Heroes and Villains of French Comics*
Randy Lofficier. *Over Here: An American Expat in the South of France*